THE TALES FROM

VEYNEKAN

THE FLAMING QUEEN

F. J. THORNBURG

ISBN 9798770890495

A THANK YOU NOTE

Thank you to Joriel Rehbein-Verhoeven, Hal Rosenthal, and my family for all the time put into helping me edit, catch typos, giving story feedback, and much more. Thank you to everyone who had stuck around after I decided to turn the series into novels and waited so patiently. It's been a long journey and learning experience.

The Dominating Beasts of Veynekan

Gryphon

Large winged-felines native to the northern mountains along the ocean's shores, coming in many different coat colors such as: white, brown, black, gray, orange, or dun. As well as being commonly striped, piebald, tortoiseshell, or pointed. Strong-fliers with unrivaled eyesight. Their main prey are fish and seals. 3-4 ft at the shoulder.

HIPPOGRYPH

Equines with the same coat colors as horses, yet they are sometimes striped on their body. Wings are often striped, laced, or have layered feather colors. They live in small-to-large herds in the northern mountains. Their manes never grow long. They are the only strictly-carnivorous equines, feeding off of varied prey. 15-18 hands at the withers.

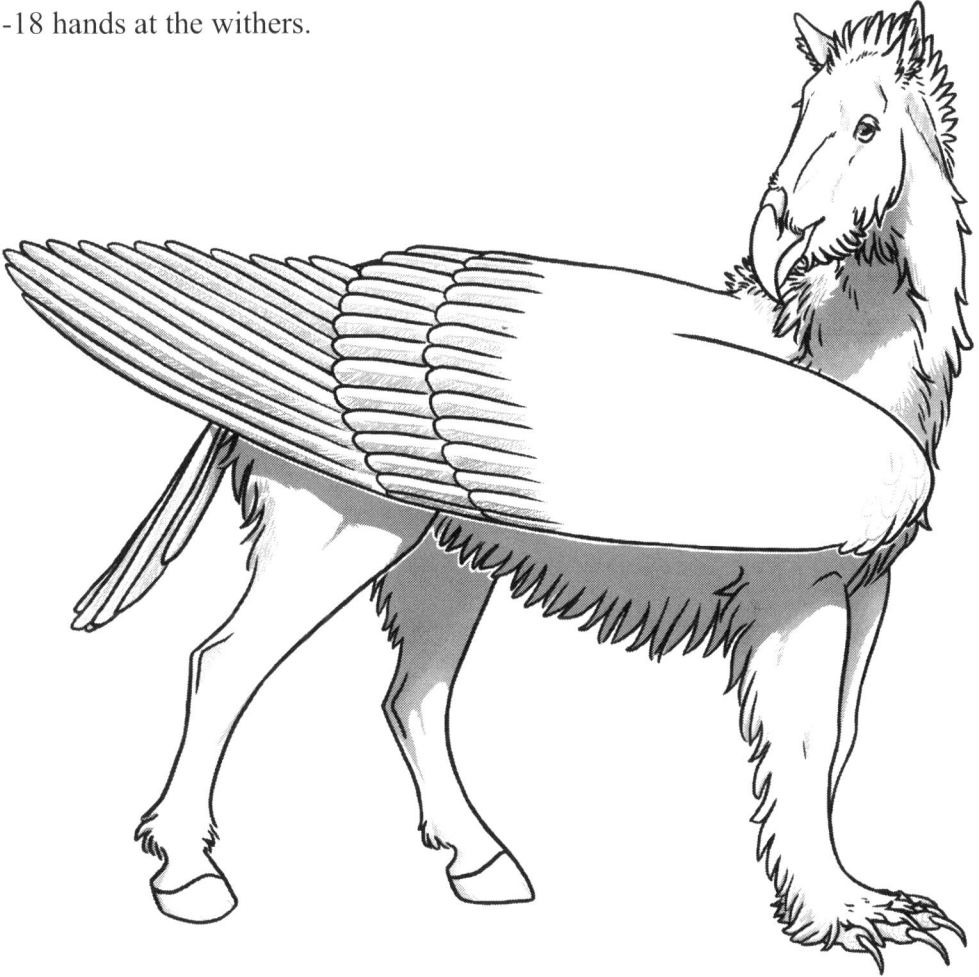

Unicorn

The smallest Veynekian equines. They could have all coat color possibilities as horses, sometimes with stripes on their withers or legs. They possessed magic within their forehorns, there were three different horn types a unicorn could grow depending on when they were born. The last unicorn sighting was over five centuries ago. Were 12-14 hands at the withers.

PEGASUS

Flying equines who choose to have no set territory, herds are frequently migrating with the change of the season. Their manes do not grow long. Able to have the same coat colors as horses but are often shades of brown and chestnut. Wing spurs are used to spar with other pegasi and self-defense. Live in small-to-large herds. 14-16 hands at the withers.

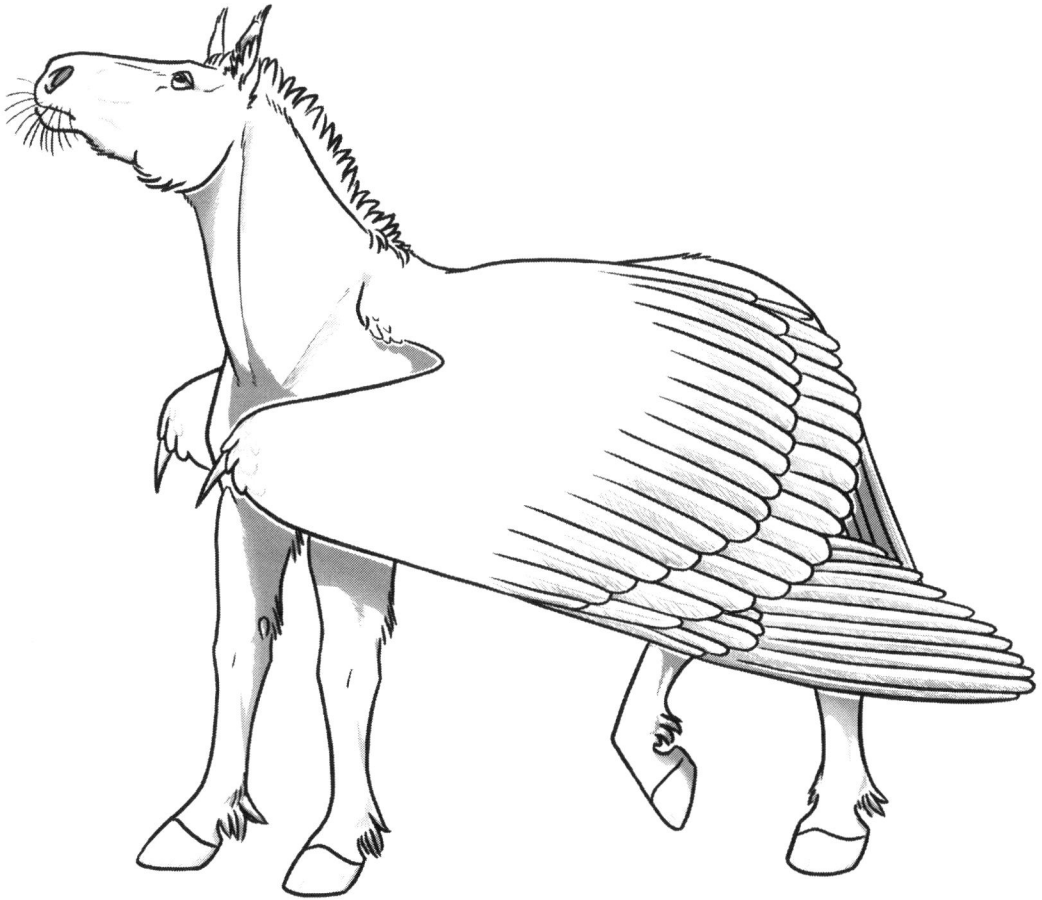

FOREST DRAGON

Large reptiles with green or brown scales, sometimes dappled or brindle, and narrow wings. They are long-legged and capable of bounding through the woods despite their size. They are omnivores, eating forest creatures, fruit, tree nuts, and some types of leaves. 6-9 ft at the shoulder. Medium-sized fire crop.

VOLCANIC DRAGON

The largest dragons on Veynekan, very powerful legs and claws built for digging out stone. They can have red, orange, gold, black, or pink scales, sometimes dappled, striped, or pointed. They can withstand high temperatures and have lungs resistant to smoke. Omnivores who eat leaves and fruit from time to time. 6-10 ft at the shoulder. Large fire crop.

CLOUD DRAGON

Lithe dragons with a coat of feathers, their patterns can be piebald, spotted, dappled, brindle, or pointed with varying marking size and colors. Their tails are a coil of muscle, which they use to hang onto cliffs and trees. They are carnivorous. 3-5 ft at the shoulder. Small fire crops.

WYVERN

Non-fire breathing dragons who often live in caves. Their scales can be, blues, grays, or white, they are uncommonly marked besides having a pale underbelly. Venom glands rest beside their molars, while not lethal, the venom is numbing and can be temporarily paralyzing. Wyverns have learned how to properly manage their venom doses for use as pain relief as well. 5-8 ft at the shoulder.

GRYHON ISLES

REDWOOD MOUNTAINS

FRITZ

ITTO

TAVIYA

SETIIR

FOREST PALACE

EIAH

THE GREAT GASH

HETTICIK

CLOUD PALACE

RUINS

VOLCANIC PALACE

STONE FANGS

UNICORN CITADEL
RUINS

FALGOR

PROLOGUE

1735 years ago

The sun was beginning to fall behind the mountains. Great shadows crept over the valley, covering it in darkness. Stripes of golden light peered through the peaks, shining on SearClaw, the city that sat at the base. Its castle in the center faced the sunset, shining like amber where the dying light touched. Its towers stretched up towards the sky where the pointed roofs raked the clouds. Viridian banners flapped in the wind, each one sharing the same design: a golden gryphon with four outstretched wings, symmetrical deep-blue flames roaring on each side of it, and several pairs of talons reaching up beneath the gryphon's paws.

Eight wide steps led up to a massive doorway whose steel hinges matched the ivory-colored walls of the castle. A balcony jutted out above the doors, surrounding the perimeter of the castle. The marble columns supporting it had hundreds of the dominating beasts carved into them. Gryphons, dragons, hippogryphs, wyverns, and pegasi soaring, with unicorns in midair bounding between it all. The city was formed in a circular shape. The pathways were a series of rings, getting smaller and smaller as they approached the castle, which connected through lines of stone like a web. The buildings were very diverse in shape and size with some built for dragons, some tall structures with craggy entrances designed for nesting beasts. Gryphons roosted, and wyverns watched from within.

Tons of beasts crowded the streets, talking and laughing together. Hatchlings and equine foals ran beneath the taller beasts, playfully chasing each other. Overhead, dragons and wyverns glided on the winds in the lavender sky. The beasts brimmed with excitement, but they seemed to be patiently waiting for someone. Around the castle was a garden filled with hundreds of plants, and many beasts who preferred to stay out of the crowds gathered in it. Equines rolled in the tall grass patches, nickering. Within the yard, three dragons sat on a large, flat stone no taller than a unicorn's withers. One of the dragons was a black, striped volcanic dragon, Queen Geshiya. Her body was lined with scars, the gold horns atop her head curved upward. Half of her top left horn was missing, but it was a wound from ages ago. Her olive eyes were locked on the sky.

To her right was a green and brown brindle forest dragon—Queen Iiku, who was much younger than Geshiya. A long scar ran down her spine. Her body language was impatient. The dragon to Geshiya's left was Queen Pivikeli. A white and blue piebald cloud dragon, she was coiled up and preening. A rather large spot on the platform was still empty.

Geshiya took a deep breath while she watched the sky grow darker as wispy clouds lazily floated along. Today was the fortieth anniversary of the defeat of Ru, a dragon tyrant, and the end of the war. During the summer of every four-season, the dragon queens and the queen of SearClaw, Hoyhenet, would hold a celebration here. Hoyhenet was usually the first to the stage, but no one had seen her all day.

Iiku swayed side to side boredly. She looked over at Geshiya and drew her attention away from above. "When did either of you last speak to Hoyhenet?"

Geshiya blinked. "A couple of days ago. I was here first, surprisingly, but there's been no sign of her."

Both dragons turned to Pivikeli, her pale eyes met Iiku's. "I don't get to speak to her as often as you two might, as I'm across the continent."

It was unlike Hoyhenet to be late for *anything,* especially a festival held in her own city. Iiku shuffled her claws. Geshiya's gaze drifted down towards the crowd and was now scanning the flock of beasts. She narrowed her eyes and slapped her spiny tail tip against the floor lightly. The rattle made Pivikeli flinch.

"There aren't any of her gryphons tonight," Geshiya whispered to them.

Pivikeli lifted her head, her crest raised. "Then something's obviously wrong. We should go look."

Pivikeli was uncoiling herself and Iiku sat up, but Geshiya put her wings out to stop both of them.

"I'll go with my guards. Stay here in case she shows up," she told them calmly.

The younger queens nodded and laid back down. Geshiya leaped to the ground. "Follow me! We're going to look for Queen Hoyhenet!" she called her dragons. Eight volcanic dragons in armor cantered over to her, the metal clanging with each stride.

"Your Majesty, do you know why she's not shown up yet?" a crimson-scaled guard asked.

Geshiya couldn't think of a reason. Was she mad at her or the other Queens? The worst-case scenario was that she was in danger, but that was unrealistic. A magicless beast had almost no chance against her. "Afraid not. I just hope everything's all right," she sighed.

Geshiya and her guards made their way into Hoyhenet's castle. It fell unsettlingly silent. Geshiya sniffed and listened carefully. Not a single talon could be heard clinking against the floor. Any scent was faint and half a day old or more. She'd never seen the main hall so empty.

"Hoyhenet!" Geshiya called, her voice echoing.

Nothing. Only her guards could be heard stirring. They inched in, their steps slow and quiet. Geshiya perked her ears up, searching for any noise.

"Two of you stay with me, the rest of you check this floor. I'm going to the throne room," she ordered.

Six guards nodded and headed into the rooms in pairs. The remaining trio carefully trod down the hall. At the end stood two great doors. Slowly, the guards went up to it and pushed it out of their way, opening up to Hoyhenet's throne weaved from a sturdy shrub planted in the floor with tightly knotted branches. Geshiya padded down the trail of stones embedded in the floor. It was empty, only filled with old feathers. She could feel the pounding of her heart grow stronger but she fought back.

"Follow me to her chamber," she called her guards over.

They left the throne room and headed for the stairway. The queen hastily ascended the stairs and into the gryphon's nesting room, her guards struggled to keep up with her without breaking into a trot. She accidentally scratched the floor when she turned the corner. Her heart sank when she saw the door was dangling off one of its hinges and battered with claw marks… Maybe even slightly burnt? She slammed the door open, it splintered as it flung into the wall beside it.

"Hoyhenet!" she yelled.

The room was empty and in much worse shape than the door. Feathers and sticks from Hoyhenet's nest were scattered all over the floor like they'd been ripped out. Papers of tomes and scrolls laid shredded, claw marks covered the walls, the perch that was once by the window was now smoldering its side. The window was broken in a rather large shape, bigger than a dragon.

Geshiya scrambled back out of the room in alarm, pulling on one of the guards' wings. "We have to get back to Queen Iiku and Pivikeli now!"

The two turned to follow her as quickly as they could. Geshiya recklessly galloped back down the stairs, calling the other guards back. None had any luck finding Hoyhenet or anyone else. The group dashed through the castle.

Both Pivikili and Iiku worried. The stars began to shine through the twilight and she still hadn't shown up. The beasts didn't seem to notice, though, they were all too wrapped up in each other's company as if nothing was wrong. Pivikeli wished she could be that relaxed right now. Her head was filling with fears, *What if something horrible happened? Did someone capture her? Kill her...? But Hoyhenet can see the future, surely she'd know if one were to come. But where is she?*

Pivikeli was snapped out of her thoughts and jerked in surprise when Iiku's tail patted her side.

"It'll be okay. Maybe Geshiya's speaking to her right now," Iiku said softly.

Pivikeli's friends could always tell when she'd get nervous like that. She did appreciate them taking her out of it. Something glinting in the sky caught Iiku's attention, Pivikeli stared up at it too. It was like a massive star, and Iiku swore it was getting closer. The two shifted uneasily. Iiku reared, spread out her wings, and bellowed her great roar. The muddled together voices fell silent as the Forest Queen began to speak.

"Beasts of Veynekan! There is an unknown light in the sky, and it looks to be coming this way. For now, get inside somewhere safe, even the castle," Iiku announced.

The beasts looked up above in confusion. They parted from the streets, and into the buildings. Pivikeli's feathers were bristling. Iiku's sight was fixed on the glowing shape, it was definitely getting closer. Everyone at the castle doors suddenly gasped and yowled as Queen Geshiya flew out, crashing into several others. Pivikeli whipped around and before either of them could speak, the sky lit up completely white for a moment as the blinding sphere came hurtling at them.

"Move!" roared Iiku, pulling Pivikeli with her as she ducked behind the stage.

BOOOOM

Iiku was sent flying into the wall of the castle, sprayed with shards of marble. The wind had been knocked out of her and she struggled to regain her breath. Slowly, she opened her eyes. Her vision was blurry. Fuzzy blobs of orange danced and black shapes darted across her line of sight. Someone was tugging on her wing. She turned her head and could make out Geshiya's face just enough. She was yelling something but Iiku sat there dazed. Geshiya ran past her to Pivikeli. Blood gushed from the cloud dragon's mouth and shoulders, a large fragment of stone was lodged in the base of her wing.

"H-help, Geshiya!" she coughed.

"Don't move!" Geshiya cried. Iiku slowly pulled herself up, blinking.

An explosion had hit SearClaw, the garden was in flames, buildings were reduced to piles of rocks. Everyone was running through the carnage, panicked and shocked.

The dragons in the city gathered around the queens. "Are you okay?"

"What's happening?!"

"Queen Pivikeli!"

"What are we going to do?!"

Forest dragons crowded and called out to Iiku, who was still having trouble processing everything.

Geshiya quickly ordered them. "We need to get Queen Pivikeli out of here! You three volcanic dragons, gently carry her to Setiir, it's the nearest village. Be extremely careful but fast!"

The three softly took hold of Pivikeli in their large claws and flew out of SearClaw

"Iiku, can you hear me?" Geshiya asked, staring seriously into her emerald eyes.

"...Yes," she muttered.

"We need to get everyone out of here and rescue anyone who might be trapped! I don't know what's happening but I'm not waiting for an answer."

Iiku nodded slightly. Standing up, she still hadn't fully got a hold of herself yet. She limped alongside Geshiya and the band of dragons around them.

"Is anybody trapped or injured?! Call out to us, we'll come and help you!" Geshiya roared.

As Iiku recovered, the barrage of screams for help and the crackling flames became more audible to her. She didn't even notice until now that her left side was badly burned. Geshiya and two forest dragons were digging through a half-destroyed tower. Everything Iiku saw flashed white again without warning. Her heart lurched, but she couldn't speak out fast enough. Even if she had, nobody could've taken cover before they were hit.

BOOOM

Another explosion. A building was struck at its base and began toppling over. Blinded by the flash, Iiku couldn't escape its path. It smashed onto her, wrecking her spine. She couldn't speak or move, the weight forced the air out from her lungs. She didn't have the strength to push through the stones that buried her. The little specks of light from the fires disappeared into the darkness as her senses began to fade. She could only hope that everyone else would escape alive.

The blast sent Geshiya flying off her claws, her limbs splayed out to her sides. Her head pounded heavily, she fought to keep herself from blacking out. Her front legs felt like they were on fire, riddled with jagged shrapnel. Blood trickled down to her claws. She pulled herself up, her legs begging to collapse. She focused her vision and couldn't see anyone alive, not a single beast. The charred corpses of creatures covered the ground, left unrecognizable. Many had large portions of their flesh scorched completely off. The horrific sight made Geshiya's stomach churn, but she felt frozen in place, unable to look away.

Her breath was heavy. Above her loomed a great pillar, cracked and fallen. If it hadn't been for Hoyhenet's castle, it would have crushed her. Geshiya climbed atop a pile of rubble, looking on in terror at the destroyed city. Most of SearClaw was on fire now, countless buildings had fallen over or were completely demolished.

"Iiku! ...Anyone?!" Geshiya desperately called out. The crackling flames were all that answered. *Pivikeli! Pivikeli probably escaped!* She sprinted away and tried to spread her wings only to realize she'd been dragging them on the ground ever since the second explosion hit. She could barely lift them. Her scales felt like they had turned to ice. She couldn't escape. *No.* There was one way she could still get out of here, smoke wasn't as harmful to her as other beasts. She limped ahead into the streets, it was almost a straight shot out. Eventually, the pathways reached the edge. She kept an eye out for anyone else still living.

Suddenly, the flames leaped out in front of Geshiya, roaring and stretching far too high for her to jump over. The path was made of stone, yet the fire was able to burn on top of it and stirred as if it were sentient. Geshiya backed away slowly. The flames remained in one spot for a while then lunged for her again. She scrambled and spun around, cantering to the castle. She fled into it, slamming the doors behind her with a whack of her tail, even if it wouldn't do her any good. She thought she'd see someone in here but nobody managed to get inside the castle before they were struck. She bolted straight to the stairs, staggering and tripping up them. No matter how much farther she got from the ground, the heat rose with her. But it felt *too* hot, like the fire was right beneath her claws at all times.

Now near the top of the stairs, Geshiya was dragging herself, exhausted and wounded, but she couldn't give up. She pulled herself into the small room at the top of the highest tower. She lay there very still, she didn't want to move anymore. For all she knew, Iiku, Pivikeli, and Hoyhenet were all dead. Hundreds of beasts were killed in the explosions. She still received no answer for all this. A rumbling growing near awoke Geshiya from her light slumber. She didn't have the energy to stand, but she was alert, her ears pointing in different directions. The sound seemed to come from all around. It kept getting closer and closer until she felt it shaking in her lungs and the tower. It abruptly stopped. She held her breath.

A harsh amber light spilled into the room as massive cracks appeared in the roof and walls. The roof snapped like a twig as a giant pair of opaque, teal claws of magic tore it off. The walls crumbled down into the smoldering city, disintegrating into ash just moments after touching the flames that now transformed into a mystifying blue. Geshiya sat up and twisted around, her eyes lit up at what was behind her: a pure-white gryphon with four wings, a red crest, and fierce, icy eyes standing on a magical platform that matched the claws floating above.

"Hoyhenet! You're alive! Please help us!" Geshiya finally broke down and pleaded to the gryphon.

Where Hoyhenet had been was a mystery, but now was not the time to ask. Hoyhenet remained unnaturally still and glared imposingly at the Queen like a statue, the only movement from her was a blink. Geshiya's relief turned to confusion. Unease grew in her as they both kept silent, watching each other as the fire flickered around them. Hoyhenet's eyes were like icicles stabbing into Geshiya's scales, but at the same time, they held a burning hate. It was obvious that she was mad, but why point her anger at Geshiya?

"Hoyhenet?" Geshiya pushed herself to stand, looking the pale gryphon in the eyes.

She only narrowed her gaze, ignoring her again. The quietness felt so strong. Even the roar of the flames seemed to die down as if it wouldn't answer either.

Geshiya flattened her ears. "Answer me, Hoyhenet."

Hoyhenet's mane bristled. "None of you deserved help," her voice sounded like two beasts speaking at once, one was much weaker and mumbling.

Geshiya only understood her from the more aggressive voice. It shook Geshiya, as well as her words. It was unfamiliar and sounded nothing like her. Hoyhenet would never leave beasts to die horribly.

"What? Who are you?!" Geshiya growled.

"You know who I am."

Geshiya snorted at their vague answer, lashing her tail against the floor.

"You've met me before. I agreed to create this form *only* to fight the war, she agreed as well. But then she didn't let go of me," Hoyhenet flared out her wings, embers flew off the tips of her feathers. "The ashpit below us is Hoyhenet's fault."

"How and why is this Hoyhenet's fault?" Geshiya demanded an answer.

"It's her punishment. She used my magic and lied to me. If she kept to her word I would be free and Hoyhenet would be here now."

Geshiya blinked at the gryphon, then she realized who this was. *Astiriuh.* The Guardian Phoenix of Veynekan.

"Guardian Astiriuh… I'm sorry," Geshiya whispered, her anger turned into fear. She sank back to the floor and trembled before him. She didn't know what else to say.

"Hoyhenet knew what she was doing. She wanted to keep my power for herself. Her greed has caused this!" Astiriuh spread out all four of the gryphon's wings, gesturing to the fire.

"You're mad at Hoyhenet! Why did you take it out on all these innocent beasts?! *Everyone* here tonight was one of your subjects too!" Geshiya spat, surprising herself that she managed to speak with such volume at the Guardian.

Jets of fire shot from the corners of the gryphon's mouth, hackles raised. "You encouraged her to keep me trapped in this body! All of you adored when she would use *my* magic! I have heard Hoyhenet's thoughts for many seasons. She will do whatever for everyone to praise her, even if it meant keeping me bound."

How could that be the true Hoyhenet? Geshiya had known her for seasons and she was always a smart, selfless, and reasonable gryphon. None of the things Astiriuh said seemed like they could be real.

"But why couldn't you just separate yourselves? We thought you two just wanted to stay together," questioned Geshiya.

"Both beasts must mutually want to break the spell! And even though she's dead now I'm trapped in this form," he growled as if he expected her to know that.

The casual mention of Hoyhenet's death shocked Geshiya. "How...did she die?"

"I killed her. It was the only way I could take full control of this beast. You've distracted me long enough, I will destroy Hoyhenet's city and everyone who let her imprison me like this."

The gryphon raised its head, smoke streamed from Astiriuh's beak as he built up the fire in his crop. Geshiya felt like her heart stopped. There was truly no escape. Astiriuh unleashed a sea of blue flames. The magical claws slammed into the side of the tower Geshiya stood on and it toppled over, falling into the flames. She plummeted into the inferno, wailing a mournful roar. The wave of fire engulfed her as she descended, burning her scales as if the flames had grown limbs to drag her down.

The last of the buildings that stood, fell with Astiriuh's wrath. The gryphon dived and flew through the ruined, flaming city. He was unharmed by the fire, completely immune. Astiriuh blasted beams of flames at any structure that was even remotely still intact. But he always felt uncomfortable in this form, and Hoyhenet, a mundane beast, limited his magic abilities. He felt nothing but contempt for her. Astiriuh hovered in the air, glaring down at the burning vortex.

He was caught off guard by a falling pillar from behind, slamming into him and pulling him to the ground. Too exhausted from excessive use of his magic, he didn't have the energy to fight his way out from under it. He let himself collapse. The flames unlatched themselves from the walls and sank to the dirt, returning to a natural amber hue. All the dead beasts' bodies had been cremated, there was hardly any evidence that they were ever there.

SearClaw was gone. The dragon queens were gone, not even Queen Pivikeli could escape Astiriuh's attack. Hundreds were dead. Veynekan was shaken with the loss of four queens and the Guardian. No one present that night had survived. Without the help of unicorn magic, they would have never known what happened. Beasts across the continent dreaded the return of Astiriuh. Once their protector, now they only remembered him for his devastating onslaught.

CHAPTER 1

Above the rolling hills below, tall clouds cast blotchy shadows on the grass. The plateau went on for miles, mountains, and woods bordering the hazy edges. There were hardly any flat surfaces, the hills rose and fell unevenly. Narrow trees were sparsely scattered about and in clusters. Long grass swayed gently with the wind, swallows swooping just above it. Spring was in full bloom, the leaves had just grown back after the winter. A wide river ran through the dips between the hills, leading to Dragoneye Lake. The distant mountains seemed to stretch up endlessly towards the sky.

Soaring in and out of clouds was a dark figure, the beast high over the hills was a hippogryph, her coat was as black as a moonless night. Faint, long scars like cracks went across her ribs and flank. The cloud-height gusts blew harshly, ruffling her feathery neck. The wind caught beneath her broad wings carried her effortlessly. Her fiery eyes searched the meadow, even the slightest movement couldn't escape her view.

Within the long blades of grass, something glinting in the sunlight had caught her attention. Interested, she tilted her wings to descend. As she fluttered down and landed, the grasses were blown back from the beat of her wings. She folded her wings against her sides, sniffing and blinking. She lifted a front leg, slowly clawing away the stems that surrounded it. Her ears were perked forward. Once she freed the object enveloped in the tangled grass, she stretched her neck down, inspecting it closely. What she uncovered was round, smooth, and iridescent white. It was fairly large and splattered with peach-colored speckles. The hippogryph lowered her beak to touch it. It was somewhat soft, surprisingly, and not a hard stone as she had guessed. She flicked an ear back, realizing what it may be. Not a gem or stone, but possibly an egg. However, it was much too large for a gryphon or hippogryph, neither species would've made their home in the plains.

The mare's head quickly shot up, glancing around her, smelling near the egg and the breeze. There were no footprints, flattened grass, or even a trace of fresh scents lingering. The egg had been left alone for some time, and a snarled patch of grass was not nest-worthy. She decided to wait around and see if anyone would return. She wasn't in a big hurry, after all.

She cantered back and forth across the hills, the grass slapped against her legs as she bounded through the meadow. She searched for feathers, dry plants, and sticks, gathering them in her beak and a few between her talons. She brought them back to the egg to hastily make a nest. Though it was more like a bunch of stuff just piled around it, wanting to keep the egg warm but not get too much of her scent on it. The mare got up now and then to search for footprints or just anything that would suggest a dragon had been around recently. Still uncertain, she stuck around a while longer, pacing around but not straying too far from the egg. The wind carried no new scents, only the same plants, and nearby creatures. She flew up and twisted back around towards the makeshift nest. She could see movement in the grass ahead. Between the stems was the familiar sorrel and silver pelt of a coyote, stalking with its head low through the meadow. It was headed towards the egg.

Panic flared up in the hippogryph. Even if the egg was big, she didn't want it near it. Her ears flattened back, she thrust herself forwards. Diving swiftly, the canid heard the mare's whinny-like screech as its head popped up. She nipped at the coyote's scruff as she glided past. It yelped in alarm and scurried away to flee. The mare pulled up back into the sky, turning around in a semicircle, and flew back to land hard between the egg and sprinting coyote. She tossed her head, and began to relax her wings and feathers. She returned to the nest, thankful that it was untouched. For having found the supposedly abandoned egg not long ago, she had grown quite attached to it. She laid down in the grass but not too close, just in case the parent would fly over and see her. Now, she would wait. Thoughts of what she may do if no one came flooded her mind.

The sun had lowered just above the mountain ridge, the foothills veiled in the mountains' shade. No one returned to the nest. Shadows would soon creep across the tallest hills, too. The mare was lying on her side. She stretched her neck up, watching birds fly over, her gaze following them. She blinked and closed her eyes for a while. The cool breeze ran through her feathers. A lonely bird's call rang out over the grassland. The hippogryph pulled herself upright and shook the dust off of her coat. She turned to the egg. If she left it, it would die out here if it hadn't already. Remembering her encounter with the coyote, she worried a bigger predator could come along. She stared at the pale shell, and at that moment, made her decision. She would take the egg back to her herd. She stepped over to the nest and scooped it up with her talons. Bits of the nest fell off, but she got as good of a grip as she could. Opening her wings, she flew towards her homeland in the mountains.

The plains below turned into moss and shrub-covered foothills, creeks ran through the crevices. Ahead was a wall of mountains that curved up in a jagged slope, quickly becoming a steep cliff that would be impossible to climb. She rose with the curve of the mountain. The peaks held sheets of snow that spring's warmth could not melt. Once above the ridge, she was presented with a beautiful view: vast, icy mountains with tall, dense pine forests bathed in fleeting sunlight, stretching out farther than even a hippogryph could see. Eagles soared between them and split clouds with the summits. A river rushed between the crags, surrounded by trees and jagged rocks.

In a valley past the stream, was where the hippogryph herd settled. Grass poked out from the thin snow with a few conifers dotted here and there while thin layers of frost still hid in the shadows. A couple of stones larger than an equine rearing stood tall throughout the land. The dark hippogryph approached a cliff with much softer soil. A couple of unnatural caves were riddled along it, dug out by claws. She slowly sank to the ground, preparing to land. The curious herd looked up at her as she drew near. Some got up and cantered below her, whickering and tossing their heads. They were an average size herd, only a little less than two dozen members.

She flew under an overhanging cliff into one of the caves very near to the ground. Landing awkwardly on her hind legs, she gently set the egg down in a dent on the cave floor. Three large nests were against the back wall. She looked up and saw a figure in the shadows watching from her far left, but she quickly realized it was only her sister.

"Hello, Conifer," said the black hippogryph.

"Good evening, Obsidian," the smokey gray mare replied in a welcoming tone. There was a silver fleck below her left eye and a white mark on her forehead.

Obsidian stepped farther into the cave, folding her wings. Conifer shook her neck, little tufts flew off her. A scruffy colt covered in down was resting under her ruff. He had the same white mark on his forehead and a stripe beneath it down toward his beak.

"What have you got there?" Conifer asked, her ears perked forwards.

"An egg, probably."

Conifer stretched her neck out towards it. "Ooh. Where did you find it?"

"Just in the meadow, left alone, and stuck under plants… But would you mind warming it for me until I make it a nest?"

"Not at all!" Conifer whickered, she didn't hesitate to scoot the egg beneath her soft feathers against her chest, her foal peeped irritably when it bumped him.

"Thank you," Obsidian said. She turned around to exit the cave and was about to fly away when her sister's voice stopped her.

"Do you know what kind of egg it is?" she asked.

Obsidian returned her gaze to her. "I think it's a dragon."

Conifer's eyes widened in surprise.

Obsidian flew away to gather materials, the egg was too big to fit into her own nest with her. She heard the endless roar of the river as she approached, the water was rarely still. As she landed on the rocky shore, mist sprayed her feathers. She snapped flexible branches from stout pines with her beak, pulled moss and plants with her talons from the cliffs, and picked through her plumage for loose feathers to add. She brought it all back in several trips, and every time she went out for more, a few hippogryphs below would watch her soar over. It was unusual to see Obsidian so busy.

Obsidian flew back into the cave one last time, finishing the nest. She didn't have much experience building them, but she thought it turned out alright. All it needed to be was large enough. Obsidian pushed the nest over to hers on the other side of the cave. Conifer lifted her head to let Obsidian take the egg out from under her.

"Thank you," Obsidian said again. Conifer nodded, blinking slowly.

She set the egg in, stepped into her own nest, and laid down. She puffed up her neck feathers, covering up the egg.

"What kind of dragon do you think it is?" Conifer asked.

Obsidian thought for a moment. "I'm not sure. Normally a dragon's egg color indicates the scales but neither forest nor volcanic dragons can be white."

"What about cloud dragons or wyverns?"

"Neither lay eggs this shape and size. I don't think a cloud dragon would fly across the continent to leave an egg in the plains."

Conifer flicked her ears. "Probably not, but not knowing what it'll be is exciting."

Obsidian nodded and rested her head. Only now did she feel the wave of exhaustion wash over her, like her feathers turned to piles of sand. She let her wings lazily slip out to her sides, and closed her eyes. Neither of the mares spoke much for a while, Conifer kept her head up but was resting peacefully. They were simply just relaxing, each other's company was all they needed sometimes. Occasionally Conifer's colt would coo, but he mostly just slept. Obsidian's ear flicked towards the cave's entrance as hoofbeats approached. She opened her eyes and saw a young gray mare walking up to the cave. A white stripe went down her face and there was a scar on the back of her neck that created a gap in her mane. The filly's hazel eyes were narrowed as she prowled into the cave then raised her head and looked at Obsidian.

"Everyone's saying it looked like you were collecting nest materials," she said suspiciously.

Obsidian lifted her neck. "Avalanche, all I did was find an abandoned egg," she raised her chest to show her.

Avalanche's ears flattened when she saw it.

"That's a dragon!" she snorted.

"No, it's an egg," Conifer snickered.

"You know what I meant!" her head pointed towards her dam, then back to Obsidian. "Why would you bring a dragon egg here?!"

Obsidian took a deep breath. "You're acting like a dragon is the same as a boar. When's the last time dragons attacked us?"

Before Avalanche could speak, Obsidian continued. "Also, if they're raised among hippogryphs what would make them *want* to harm us?"

Avalanche flicked her tail and took a moment to reply. "Well, if someone gets burned, it's not my fault."

The filly turned and left, her neck bristled up. Obsidian looked to Conifer who had the same calm expression as usual.

"That filly is almost two four-seasons old and she still acts like this. Why do you let her snap at you like that?" Obsidian tried not to sound like she was insulting her.

"I think she's just being cautious. She'll grow out of it," yawned Conifer.

Obsidian sighed and lowered her head back down. She found that hard to believe, Avalanche seemed like she was trying to always be worked up about something.

The night sky's stars twinkled while small clouds unhurriedly rolled past the sliver of the moon. Both Obsidian and Conifer had fallen asleep by the time Avalanche later returned and plopped down into her nest in the middle.

Obsidian was awoken by Conifer and her colt, Komodo, exiting the cave. Komodo bounded away on his spindly legs. The sun had barely risen and the sky was still a deep blue. Obsidian didn't want to be awake yet, but she couldn't fall back asleep. Eventually, she became hungry though she worried about leaving the egg, even for a short while. Instead, she stayed in her nest, watching the sky slowly change color. She observed the herd from the cave as the hippogryphs galloped, soared, and brought back prey; just like any average day.

Obsidian had a sudden mood drop as the possibility of the egg being dead invaded her mind. What if this would all be for nothing?

CHAPTER 2

Several days had passed since Obsidian had found the egg and she rarely rose from her nest. Any time that she did, she'd briefly stretch her legs and wings though she hadn't left the valley, not even to hunt, too paranoid to leave the egg for more than a few moments. Hatching the egg was going to be a long and boring process. Obsidian was already growing tired of lying down all day, and she had no mate to switch places with for a while. Hippogryph eggs only took about two moon-cycles to hatch, but she had no idea how long it would take for any species of dragon.

Conifer, Komodo, and Avalanche were mostly out during the day among the herd. It was lonely in the shallow cave. Obsidian's eyes were closed but she was not asleep. Her ears pointed towards the entrance of the cave, listening to the soft raindrops pattering faintly on the grass. The sound of hoofsteps on the soggy ground came near. The rain drowned their scent but it became clear who it was once they were a few feet from the entrance. A friendly whicker came from Conifer as she carried a rabbit in her beak then set it down in front of Obsidian.

"Here. You haven't been eating much," she said.

"Oh, thank you," Obsidian hooked it with a talon and pulled it closer.

Conifer walked to her nest and laid down. "It's no problem at all," she shook her coat and began to preen her chest.

Obsidian tore apart the rabbit in strips. The two sat in silence as the rain outside dragged on. Obsidian finished quickly, feaking her beak against the stones to clean herself. Conifer let go of a long feather on her wing which whipped and realigned back with the rest before she turned her attention to Obsidian.

"Avalanche is with Komodo right now. If you want to go out for a while, I could warm the egg," offered Conifer.

Obsidian perked her ears towards her. "You don't have to do that, it's my responsibility."

"Mares and stallions take turns warming eggs all the time."

"I am aware but you don't have to set aside time for this."

"I know where my foals are and I don't have anywhere to be. I *insist* that you take a break."

Obsidian tapped the cave floor with her talons and drew in a breath. "Alright," she pulled herself away from her nest, and Conifer moved over into it, concealing the egg in her soft charcoal feathers.

"Go out for as long as you like," Conifer nickered.

Obsidian exited the cave feeling perturbed. She didn't have a reason to be so anxious about the egg but she was. It was with her sister who successfully hatched both her previous eggs, also safe and low to the ground. She hoped that she could find something or someone to take her mind off of it. The slippery grass and mud squished beneath her talons as she made her way to where the herd was gathered, huddled together out on the valley with their hindquarters facing the wind. Obsidian was greeted with a wave of whickering as they noticed their Lead Mare.

"It's good to see you out," a seal brown mare spoke.

A young chestnut hippogryph pushed out from the center. "How have you been, Obsidian?" they asked, "You haven't gotten up from your nest much."

"Same as usual, Chasm," she replied with a sigh.

Chasm blinked and nodded slowly.

The group's concerned faces met Obsidian's. They had hoped she might be feeling better after finding the egg.

"Is there anything we could do for you?" a molting silver filly wondered.

"I don't think so. Not right now. Sorry, Echo," Obsidian shook her head. She turned to an old friend, a palomino mare near the edge of the group. "Sunflower, how's the hunting been?"

She perked her ears towards Obsidian. "It's been fairly good now that winter's behind us."

"Glad to hear," Obsidian nickered, then continued walking past the equines.

They watched as she left them, the excitement in their eyes faded. She was immediately feeling bad about her abrupt leave and barely speaking, but she didn't have the energy to socialize at the moment.

She trod across the valley down to the river and stared at the foamy bubbles clinging to the stones, once-damp pine needles had glued themselves to the sides. Obsidian's head hung low, the tip of her beak hovering just above her talons. She took a breath and sighed. She wasn't hungry, she didn't need to hunt, and it was wet and muddy so she didn't feel like venturing around the mountains. The rain pelted her back, drenching her coat. Loneliness and boredom made it impossible to draw her mind away from her endless stream of anxious thoughts.

Sometimes she wondered if becoming leader was a poor decision, sometimes it felt like it may have been. None of this had gone the way she ever wanted. Every time she went into the valley, she hoped to see the golden coat of her former Herd Stallion, Cedar, upon the hills. But that could no longer be. They were without a Herd Stallion for a long time now, yet she knew if she said she wanted another one she'd be lying. She felt lost in her memories of the stallion she once loved.

She flapped her wings, hoping to fling those thoughts away, as black fluff and droplets scattered into the air. She plodded along the riverbank while low rumbles of thunder roared through the sky. The approaching beat of a gallop began overpowering the river. Obsidian raised her head and her heart fluttered for a moment. The same palomino she had spoken to a moment ago was running up toward her. Sunflower was Cedar's twin sister, the two were very similar in color but set apart by the gray stripe that ran down her tan beak.

"Obsidian!" Sunflower slowed to a trot and halted beside the dark mare and softly nickered. Obsidian returned the greeting but it was nearly inaudible.

"The one time you're up and about you still go off alone. Why don't we walk for a while, if you want to, that is," Sunflower offered.

"Sure," replied Obsidian, shaking her coat once more.

Sunflower took the lead and Obsidian slowly followed her.

"We just don't get to talk as much anymore. I heard you found a dragon or something's egg," commented Sunflower.

"I know. I'm sorry," Obsidian sighed. "But yes, I did."

"Do you know what kind?"

"No. It's all white with pink specks."

"Hmm. I hope it hatches. It'll be interesting to see what it is!"

Obsidian nodded. She had slowed her pace even more. Sunflower tilted her ears and glanced at her worriedly. Obsidian sped up, catching her body language.

"Where did you find it?" Sunflower quickly asked.

"Out in the meadow, near the lake. It was alone tangled in the grass. I worry that it's dead," she told her.

"If it's a dragon egg it's probably fine. If I remember correctly, the fire in a dragon's body develops early on, allowing them to survive without constant attention."

Sunflower brushed Obsidian's wing with hers. Obsidian seemed to be more at ease with this information, just a little though.

"How much do you know about dragons?" Sunflower asked again, knowing Obsidian would've fallen silent again there.

Obsidian thought for a moment. "Not...a whole lot. I've met quite a few but not young ones. The fledglings never come up this far."

"What do you plan on doing to raise it? Do you think it'll be fine in the winter?"

"I think I'll just treat it like a foal. If that doesn't go well then I'll search for advice. And I think winter will be fine, all three species experience snow. If it gets too cold, there's a whole herd of hippogryphs to huddle beside."

"For its sake, I hope it's a cloud dragon," Sunflower responded.

She found herself and Obsidian having to shout over the storm. The deep growl of thunder tore through the sky.

"Why don't we fly above the storm? We won't have to strain our voices so much," she suggested.

"Alright," Obsidian replied, stretching her wings, droplets falling from her feathers.

The mares broke into a canter, treading carefully on the slippery grass. They drifted away from each other a bit to avoid striking the other with their wings. Gusts pushed against them as they ascended and the rain pelted their bodies. Thankfully, it was not a lightning storm. Obsidian followed the tawny mare into the layer of dreary clouds and she closed her eyes as she sliced through the damp, airy mass.

Sunflower went up first, waiting for Obsidian. She bolted up next to her, flapping her wings fiercely, and slowed to the hover that Sunflower maintained. Obsidian blinked and squinted, getting used to the change from the gray skies to the blinding sun.

It was like a tundra above the sky, nothing but a sheet of clouds and mountain peaks that pierced above. Once Obsidian's eyes adjusted, she could see Sunflower clearly, who seemed to glow like the sun itself as her soggy feathers shone a beautiful bronze.

"That's much better," cooed Sunflower. "It's only been a few days but have you got any names in mind?"

"No. Not yet," Obsidian flapped closer. "I don't know whether or not I should name it like a hippogryph or whatever beast it is."

"That's up to you. If you decide to use hippogryph names, maybe something snowy?"

"I'll keep that in mind."

The pair flew laps around the mountains, eventually perching on top of a peak, watching as the storm below rolled through. Sunflower shook her mane and stretched her legs.

"I wish it wasn't so cloudy," she sighed. "I love the view of the mountain range from above."

Obsidian nodded. There was a moment of silence between them, accompanied by the faint howl of the wind.

"And it was just the other day we finally got a bit of the spring sun, too," Sunflower spoke again. "Now it's chilly again. Dandelion and I had taken Chasm along when it was warmer to test their strength for future hunting."

"How are they coming along?" inquired Obsidian.

"Pretty nice, they've still got some room to fill out as they get older though."

There was a pause again.

"Do you miss hunting, Obsidian?" asked Sunflower.

"...A part of me does," she answered.

"I understand."

Sunflower dropped down to lay in the small patch of exposed grass. "Well, I hope you don't mind that I've been organizing the hunting plans and digging trenches to keep the soon-to-be floods out."

Obsidian tilted her ears back.

"But that's a part of my role as Lead Mare, you shouldn't have to do that extra work," she said as she laid down beside her.

"I mean this in the nicest way possible when I say that you haven't been doing it enough. You hadn't started preparing for the snowmelt at all."

Obsidian looked at her talons. "I'm sorry."

"I promise you it's okay, I don't mind," Sunflower whickered, brushing the other mare's withers with the wrist of her wing. "Losing Cedar affected both of us."

Obsidian stared down the cliffside. Sunflower scooted closer.

"Just do things at your own pace and focus on that egg," she told her.

"I'll try," breathed Obsidian.

Sunflower nickered, then rolled onto her side into the snow next to her, letting herself slowly slide down the slope. Obsidian craned her neck to watch her. The mare stood up after a moment and shook snowflakes from her coat. She looked up at Obsidian then tossed her head playfully, beckoning to follow her as she trotted down the mountain. Obsidian rose to her feet and joined her, reaching flatter terrain a little way down. Sunflower got down again and rolled in the snow. Obsidian caught up, gave in, and allowed herself to lay down, covering her fur in it. The dusty snow felt nice between her feathers.

They had stayed up there for nearly half the day even after the storm had left. The mares descended back to the ground after a while. Folding their wings and shaking their necks, the mares whickered to each other.

"I feel...a bit better," Obsidian said to Sunflower as they walked down the slope, she was reminded how much she enjoyed the mare's company.

"I'm glad!" Sunflower whinnied.

Before Obsidian could walk away towards her cave Sunflower tugged on her tail feathers lightly. Obsidian turned her head back.

"I enjoy talking with you and miss you. If you ever want help with the hatchling, I'll be here for you," Sunflower nickered, her umber eyes bright.

Obsidian blinked, it was an unexpected offer. Warming eggs was a responsibility that could be shared between the herd but raising the hatchling itself was only ever done by parents. "Thank you, Sunflower."

The mares groomed each other's withers before parting. Obsidian returned to where Conifer was waiting for her and brushing through her coat once again. Conifer rose from her sister's nest. The two of them exchanged whickers. Conifer exited the cave and trotted away to search for her foals. Obsidian kneeled and gently laid down into her nest. She would think of possible names but she wanted to nap first.

Obsidian's wings still felt heavy. But she decided to get up and stretched over her nest. None of her relatives were in the cave. Straightening herself back up, ears flicking, she looked down at the pale egg. If she were going to give it a hippogryph name there were plenty of options.

Squall? Hail? Frostbite?

She liked the idea of the name Frostbite if it was a dragon, but she was still unsure if she wanted to give it a name like that. She couldn't remember the names of most dragons who passed through the mountains, giving her no ideas. The closest thing to a dragon's name that she could think of were the names of gryphons who did not live too far from her herd. Only a few came to mind, but one name in particular stuck out to her. *Ben.* Neither name was a definite choice, also, the egg's peach spots didn't exactly say 'cold' to her. She considered names for a while longer, but still only kept the two she liked in mind.

Remembering what Sunflower had told her about dragon eggs needing less attention than others, she rose from the nest and made herself get out of the cave for some time. She could see the herd around the valley. Komodo was bounding and bucking after Avalanche on his narrow, striped legs. His sister was trotting towards two young mares, Monarch, a painted chestnut, and Spruce, a seal brown, both about her age. She did not see Sunflower among the valley, perhaps she had joined a hunting party. She appreciated Sunflower staying on top of feeding the herd, but she still felt guilty that she was failing to do the basic duty of being Lead Mare. She wanted to sulk back to the cave but fought herself.

She browsed along the edges of the valley, nothing seemed out of the ordinary. Night had swiftly crept up, she gazed into the trees one last time before making her way to the nest. Ducking inside, she rested the palm of her front leg gently on the shell. As Sunflower had said, the egg's temperature didn't seem to have dropped in her absence. Still anxious, she got down in her nest and warmed it again.

The season grew warmer by the day and soon the deciduous trees were fully clad in emerald leaves. The herds' pelts had become sleek and glossy. Obsidian would sit in the sunshine out in the valley with the egg between her front legs. It was definitely alive and kept itself warm for the most part and was certainly taking longer than a hippogryph to hatch. The shell had also gone from leathery to hardened like a bird's egg, Obsidian wasn't sure what to think of it.

She watched Komodo, now a lanky colt, canter around Conifer. His silver down was nearly gone and the majority of his coat was a dark soot color like his dam's with the addition of pale flecks dotted all over his neck. His wings were already growing in and looked a little silly on his small body.

In the late summer, Obsidian began to worry again. Although nothing changed, the egg still had not hatched. Perhaps it was normal, but four moon-cycles seemed like an awfully long time for any beast to hatch. She kept a close eye on it for the days to come.

The warm breeze would flood into the cave occasionally. She watched the pines' long needles sway with the wind, tiny green pine cones growing at the tips of branches. The sky was filled with gentle pastel hues as the sun peered from behind the mountains in the quiet morning. Obsidian found herself lost in thought… until a faint scratching sound came from behind her. She pricked her ears at the noise and turned around. As the scratching continued, little outlines of cracks appeared on the shell. She hurried toward it, watching it closely. Obsidian leaned in as a pink spike pierced through. The creature drew its head back and shoved its snout against the shell. It split apart and a white dragon's head peeked through. It didn't hesitate but struggled to pull its limbs out from the egg and chirped. Obsidian lifted a talon and gently assisted the hatchling.

A dragon broke free and lay on its chest, it was white with light peach marks around its eyes and snout. Its eyes were wide and red. *An albino?* It was an unusual-looking dragon, Obsidian had not seen any like it before. It had similar proportions to a forest dragon but not quite the head shape, and there were three brow spikes on each side. Unlike hippogryphs, Obsidian couldn't yet determine the sex of the dragon hatchling. She would be able to figure it out through scent after it dried off a little.

Obsidian decided not to use the name Frostbite, as the dragon was pink and white. *Daybreak*, a new name came to mind. Again, it was a name for a hippogryph so she was still unsure. She liked the sound of it and it matched the creamy sky of this morning. The hatchling was getting up on its feet immediately, although very off-balanced.

Obsidian blinked. "You're probably hungry," she said to the hatchling.

It stared at her with vermillion eyes. She turned to go hunt for something small, the dragon's shoulders didn't even reach above her cannon bones. It started to climb out from the nest to follow her.

"No, stay here," Obsidian told it, nudging them back.

It didn't understand but remained still for a moment, then moved to follow her again. She wasn't sure if just leaving it alone was the best idea, she looked out from the cave's opening and saw her sister nearby. Glancing back at the dragon once more, then hurrying over to Conifer.

"What's got you in a rush?" Conifer asked.

"The egg hatched! It's a dragon, and I need someone to watch them while I hunt," panted Obsidian.

"Oh! Then let's go back quickly!"

The sisters cantered back to their cave. To Obsidian's relief, the hatchling had not left.

When Conifer saw the dragon she blinked and raised her ears. "How interesting. I've never seen one like it."

She began to walk towards it, whickering. It watched them at the opening of the cave.

"I'll be right back, I won't go after something big," Obsidian told her, then took off to the wooded area on the mountainside.

However, finding smaller prey could be difficult for an adult hippogryph. She landed on the soft, pine needle-covered ground and tread quietly, her ears darted in all directions. There was faint crunching not far away, Obsidian looked and saw a squirrel biting a pine cone. She approached it from the ground slowly, her head low, as if she was paying no attention to it. Once she was beneath it, she quickly reared up and snapped her beak around the squirrel, dying quickly from her strike. She landed back on all fours and opened her wings to return.

When Obsidian arrived at her cave she saw Komodo now in the cave as well. He watched the tiny dragon sniff his beak. Obsidian nickered a greeting when she entered.

"Welcome back. I think this dragon's male if you didn't already know," Conifer told her.

"Ah, I wasn't able to tell sooner," Obsidian answered.

"He looks a little strange," whickered Komodo, not with rude intent.

Obsidian set down the squirrel in front of the dragon. He turned away from the colt, blinked, and sniffed at it.

"You should probably shred it for him," Conifer suggested.

"Right," muttered Obsidian, shaking her neck out of slight embarrassment.

She laid down, bit the rodent, and pulled a stringy piece which she held out to him. He sniffed it again then took it from her.

"Does he have a name?" asked Conifer.

Obsidian thought for a moment. She liked Daybreak but, again, she didn't want to use a hippogryph name if she didn't have to. Since he resembled a forest dragon, though, perhaps she would decide on Ben. Forest dragons tended to have names with few syllables.

Obsidian paused from feeding the dragon for a moment. "I think I'll name him Ben."

CHAPTER 3

Later that day, Obsidian exited the cave with Ben who was already walking, though still stumbling. Komodo stuck around, curious about the little dragon. He bounded around the entrance with his ears raised. Obsidian stood on the grass, looking back at Ben who was at the edge of the cave, staring at the emerald valley. He swiped at the grass before deciding to step into it, his tail swaying side to side, not quite sure what to make of it. He lifted his snout and pushed through to Obsidian with high steps. Ben's nostrils flared, taking in the new scents around him. His warm eyes were wide and observant. He paused under Obsidian and scanned the area, his ears perked like Komodo's as he watched the herd.

"Can he make sounds?" Komodo asked, skidding to a halt beside Obsidian.

"He can, he was when he was hatching," she answered.

Ben hadn't made a sound since then, though. He was unusually quiet when compared to the barrage of peeping from a newly hatched hippogryph. Perhaps it was normal for a dragon. It wasn't long before the sight of Ben quickly attracted the herd, but they respectfully stayed out of Obsidian's space. They observed the tiny dragon with their heads low, ears forward. Ben stared back at them, his attention darting from one to another.

"What kind of dragon is he? What kind of dragons are there?" Komodo asked breathily as he lay down after bolting in laps around them.

"There are forest, volcanic, and cloud dragons on Veynekan, but I'm not sure what he is. He has similar characteristics to a forest dragon but he isn't quite the same," Obsidian explained.

"I think that's cool! What if he's not from Veynekan?" the foal sprung back up.

Obsidian gave a soft snort. "Perhaps. But he may be a hybrid."

Komodo froze mid-stride in his prance, his ears tilted. "What?"

"A beast whose parents aren't the same kind of beast. They might look very similar to one of them, or a mixture of both."

She lowered her beak to Ben who was gnawing on blades of grass before letting them go with a disgusted expression. Komodo blinked and looked down to where Ben was sitting.

"Whoa," he'd never considered the possibility of that before. "Can there be hybrid hippogryphs?"

Obsidian turned back to the colt. "I've never met one myself, so I don't know. We lay eggs though, so one couldn't have a foal with a pegasus or unicorn."

Komodo unpaused and continued to race in circles. Ben crawled out from under Obsidian, feeling adventurous as he inched farther out into the valley. He lifted his head and looked to his sides every few steps, watching the herd around him. Obsidian watched him move along, he'd crane his neck around to look back at her, too. Komodo rushed past him, the draft following him rustling the grass. It startled Ben when he came so close. He shook himself and then broke into what looked like a wobbly canter, trying to mimic the colt's gait. His legs were short so he wasn't going to get very far. Obsidian followed him at a walking pace.

Komodo slowed and spun around, watching the dragon come after him, he let out a high-pitched whinny of amusement. "He's trying to canter!"

The hatchling bounded up to the lanky foal. Komodo put his beak down to his snout and fanned his tail out excitedly. The sight of the two made Obsidian's heart feel soft. This is what she always wanted and waited so long for. She watched the boys hop and trot around the area in front of her. She thought that Ben would fit in nicely. Although, she would always need to be prepared for the possibility that he may one day want to leave. But, for now, she shouldn't worry about it and just enjoy her time with him.

Up in a cave high within the mountainside, the coat of Sunflower gleamed in the sun, standing at the edge of the entrance. She darted from the cavern, spreading her gold-tinged wings. She glided down towards Obsidian. Ben crouched into the grass and watched her shadow cross over him as she landed and trotted around to lose momentum. She and Obsidian greeted each other by touching their beaks.

Sunflower turned to face Ben. He was a little intimidated by the new mare.

"So, you're the mysterious little egg," she chirped, she lowered her head down to his level. "They're cute!"

Ben warily stalked towards her, mostly because he wanted to be back by Obsidian. He sniffed her beak, his ears twitched.

"His name is Ben," Obsidian told her. "We were discussing that he may be a hybrid a few moments ago."

"He certainly does look it," Sunflower agreed, keeping her eyes on him.

Komodo trotted back over, his wind-ruffled coat stuck out in all directions. "Can we show him around the valley?"

"I think he's too small to do that right now," Obsidian nickered. "He can explore at his own pace."

Komodo nodded and rushed off again, Ben watched him and left Obsidian's shadow to pursue him again while the mares followed behind. Komodo would slow his trot or start walking briefly for Ben to catch up. Occasionally, Ben would want to stop in his tracks to smell small bones or flowers sticking out from the grass. He noticed that Komodo had fluttered up onto one of the boulders, he immediately wanted to check it out. He gazed up at it, the rock was taller than Obsidian. Komodo's head peeked out from the top. Ben only managed to climb up a few inches before getting stuck and anxious. He looked around and squeaked at Obsidian.

"You gotta use your wings!" Komodo chirped, fanning his wings.

Ben looked up at the colt when he heard his voice.

Komodo flapped. "Your wings!"

"His wings are too small at this moment," said Obsidian.

She lowered her head to Ben's level to help him down, giving him a tiny nudge. He blinked at her, then climbed onto her neck instead, crawling to the space between her wings.

He sniffed at and pushed aside feathers, nestling into her dark plumage. Obsidian glanced back at him and Sunflower nickered at the sight.

"I think I'm going to take him back to my nest," Obsidian said.

"Is it all right if I join you?" asked Sunflower.

"Of course," Obsidian nickered.

Komodo raised his tail. "I'll come, too!" He sped off towards the cave.

The mares headed back much more slowly. Komodo had swiftly dashed into the shadowy entrance. When the pair entered, Komodo was already settled down in his dam's nest. Obsidian gently laid down, tensing her wings to keep Ben from slipping. She scooted to one side to make room for Sunflower.

"It's so strange to see a dragon canter like a hippogryph. His gait was cute but clumsy," Sunflower said, fluffing up her neck.

"He'll grow into it," cooed Obsidian.

Sunflower rested her head on Obsidian's shoulder. "It'll be interesting to see how he behaves as he grows in a herd."

"It will," Obsidian nodded, looking towards the cave's opening. She lowered her head.

She felt fine a moment ago, yet Obsidian's thoughts started to drag her down again. She was worried about the future once more, but she couldn't control the decisions Ben may make.

Sunflower flicked her ears. "What's wrong now? You always look away from conversations when you're thinking about something."

Obsidian wished Sunflower didn't know her body language so well sometimes. She exhaled. "He's not even a day old, but I'm worried he'll want to live with dragons someday."

Sunflower took a moment to respond. "Well, if he's raised here I don't think he would, but I can't predict the future."

"I know, you're probably right. You know how my brain works. It's not something I'd normally worry about since foals rarely leave," Obsidian raised her hackles and rested her head on the edge of the nest. "I hate my thoughts wandering so far ahead, I haven't felt truly at ease in so long. It's like a snowflake of a single troubling thought spiraling into an avalanche every day."

Sunflower groomed Obsidian's withers. "I'm sorry, I know," Sunflower relaxed her head next to hers. "It might not be easy for you to start, but I've always tried to live for the present and avoid worrying about every little thing the future may hold. Spend time with your herd and family while you can."

Obsidian closed her eyes and didn't reply, but Sunflower could tell the troubled mare was thinking. She shifted around to get more comfortable in the nest. Sunflower was thinking, too.

"Obsidian?" Sunflower tilted her head against the dark mare's softly. Her eyes opened.

"I feel like I should tell you that ever since we were fillies I've admired you. You always knew what to do, you kept your composure, and have always cared deeply about the herd. When you and Cedar became mates, I was happy that you were happy. Even though I knew I had to accept that I could never be with you. But I'd still be there for you, and I am," Sunflower spoke softly, lifting her head, her gaze met Obsidian's. "But, maybe I was wrong. If you're ready now, if you feel the same... I love you very much."

Both mares had lifted their heads. Obsidian stared back at Sunflower, awaiting her reply. Obsidian thought for a moment, asking herself how she really felt. It never crossed her mind much in recent times, but perhaps she did care for Sunflower. She felt a pang of guilt for a moment like she would be betraying Cedar. But he was gone. This wouldn't affect him and he wouldn't want her to be unhappy.

"I think… I'm ready," she began, raising her ears. "I don't think I realized it, but I feel that way too. Most personalities like yours would wear me down, but you never have."

Sunflower's face beamed, her eyes were soft.

"I'm so glad you feel the same. I know these last few four-seasons have been hard for you, and I want to help you in any way I can," She nickered, resting her head back down. Obsidian laid her head beside her.

About half a moon-cycle had passed since Ben had hatched and he had grown quickly. Obsidian had to expand her nest more to make room for him as he was easily catching up to the size of a days-old hippogryph foal. Sunflower had also moved into the cave.

Early one morning before the sun peered above the mountains, Obsidian was woken up by a rustling feeling under her neck feathers. Something slipped out from beneath her and she groggily opened her eyes. Ben woke up and was crawling out of her nest.

"Where are you going?" Obsidian whispered in a soft tone.

Ben looked back at her, making a small peep noise through his nostrils, and turned to the valley. He hopped into the dewy grass, after a couple of steps he paused and stared at Obsidian again, not feeling secure on his own. Obsidian rose from her nest and approached him, walking onto the cold grass. The indigo sky above loomed over the valley.

Ben shivered where he stood as he scanned the valley. Sleeping hippogryphs were piled up together, the others in caves. A few birds could be seen flying overhead. He was curious as to why everything looked so different at this time. He padded forward, checking behind him to make sure Obsidian was there.

Frightened insects fluttered up from the damp grass as he approached. The bugs surprised him at first, then he began hopping around, chasing moths that fled from him. He started flapping his wings and leaping around like an ecstatic foal. He cantered to where Obsidian stood and ran between her front legs, wrapping his tail around one.

Ben stopped for a moment to breathe. Some pines atop a hill caught his attention. He wanted to run up there, having become a little faster in the small span he lived. He left Obsidian's leg and bounded to the conifers. Obsidian followed but she didn't need to move faster than an energetic walk. Ben lept when he reached the top to clamp the long needles in his jaws. Loose, dried pine needles scattered down onto him. The low branch he grabbed was so flexible that when he landed, it didn't snap. He pulled back while biting on the limb. Obsidian came over to him and held onto the twig with a talon.

"If you pull that hard on it you'll go flying backward," she told him.

When Ben relaxed his grip a little, she snipped the stick with her beak, softly letting it go. Ben playfully chewed the piece, snorting when the needles poked him. He threw it and jumped to where it landed to try pouncing on it. He repeated this a few times, then Obsidian picked it up between her talons before Ben could leap. He lunged at the leg she carried it with, she lifted her leg, and he landed beneath her. She brushed its needles along his spine, the tickly feeling made Ben flip over onto his back and swipe with all his legs, his jaws open and ready to playfully chomp. Obsidian gently poked him with the pine needles on his chest and let him have the twig back. Ben grabbed at her fetlocks with his teeth and took the stick in his claws.

Crrck. The snap of a branch. Obsidian immediately became alert. Ben paused, noticing the sudden change in Obsidian's body language. From the shadows came a dark mare. Only Conifer. Obsidian softened her muscles.

"You frightened me," she whispered.

"Sorry," apologized Conifer. "I just wondered where you had gone."

"He just wanted to go out."

Feeling spooked by Conifer's unexpected appearance, Ben had forgotten about the twig, though a scent quickly caught his attention. He began following the trail curiously.

Conifer watched with her ears raised. "I wonder what he's picked up."

Ben pursued the scent in weaving lines, his snout to the ground. Obsidian sniffed the air herself. It was a faint smell, but once potent and earthy. The sisters observed him, Ben began climbing up a small slope digging his claws into the dirt to pull himself up. Obsidian nudged him up the mound with her wrist. Once Ben was up there, he sniffed for a moment then went off in the direction in which he picked up the scent again.

"What's got him so excited?" Obsidian wondered aloud.

"Maybe we'll see, he's stopped ahead," Conifer pointed out.

The hatchling paused and looked around before he faced Obsidian and a soft but confused-sounding trill rose from his throat. He returned to her, the scent was stronger now but didn't seem to go any farther. It was like the thick smell of mud but something seemed…unusual. Obsidian didn't have the flexible nostrils of a dragon and even she could tell. Unease spread throughout her body. Something wasn't right and she wasn't going to stay and find out what it was.

"I don't like this," Obsidian said with flattened ears. "I'm going back."

Obsidian lowered her neck for Ben to climb and he did without hesitation. She quickly got to a brisk pace. Conifer stayed beside her.

We were not alone there. I'm sure of it.

CHAPTER 4

Beneath the towering redwoods wandered a young elk, his steps light and quiet on the blanket of fallen pine needles. Branches shook as the breeze picked up. The rustling of trees drowned out most other noises. The elk spied a flying creature above for a moment. He paused, his ears darting in different directions. As the wind died, the woods fell silent, but the unnerved animal did not move. Then, a sudden force slammed into the elk's rib cage. He and his attacker skid across the ground, pine needles flying up around them. The two crashed into the base of a thick conifer, dazed and stunned, the elk was unable to fight back. A chestnut hippogryph had ferociously dived into it. She gathered herself and attacked once more, plunging her sharp beak into the elk's throat. He retaliated and kicked a hoof into the mare's shoulder. She was ripped away from her prey but not without tearing off some flesh. The elk scrambled to get off his side. The hippogryph came back at it, rearing and lunging with her talons outstretched.

Before either of them could make a move, another hippogryph plummeted from the sky landing atop the elk and wrecking his spine, finishing him off. Breathing hard, the two mares relaxed.

"Good work, Swallowtail," nickered the mare getting off their catch, she had a liver bay coat.

"Thank you! Thanks for taking him out, Char," Swallowtail practically sang to her. Nuzzling her mate's withers.

"Thanks, I love it when you get blood on my mane," Char said in a playfully sarcastic tone.

The two of them got a good grip on the elk and with their broad wings, they heaved themselves into the sky. Out of sight, two more mares awaited them. Sunflower and a bay mare named Coyote, who held a buck in her talons.

"Let's start heading back, I'll hunt on the way," nickered Sunflower.

The hippogryphs nodded and set out towards the herd. Sunflower scanned the mountain range below as they made their way back, hoping to spot an animal. The sun was just above the mountains' ridges though long shadows still shaded the woods.

Coyote inhaled, then sighed. "Better enjoy the sun while we can. Not even a few moon-cycles till it snows, we'll be lucky if we can get even a streak of sunlight down in the valley by then."

"Unfortunate," Char snorted. "Can't say I'm looking forward to the blizzards."

Winters in the Redwood Mountains could be rough, snow did come earlier there than the rest of Veynekan. Sunflower worried about how Ben may handle the weather, even with his fire.

"Just as long as it's not like the winter from three four-seasons ago," Swallowtail hoped. "I don't think that one'll ever be topped."

"I hope we never face one like that again," Sunflower shut her eyes tightly.

"Oh, right. I'm sorry," Swallowtail apologized, flicking her ears.

"It's alright. If we're faced with weather that treacherous, we won't let it happen again," said Sunflower, sounding as if she needed to reassure herself, too.

Opening her eyes, Sunflower noticed a doe grazing near an overhang. She signaled her group with her tail, they slowed and then scattered out of sight. Sunflower flew around stealthily for a better angle to strike from. She hovered while facing the tip of the overhang, the doe had her back to Sunflower with her snout in the grass. Sunflower dived, swiftly picking up speed. The doe noticed too late and the weight of the hippogryph came crashing into her, Sunflower's powerful grip around the doe's neck snapped it in a heartbeat. She and her catch slid across the grass, knocking into the wall of rocks beneath the overhang. Thankfully, it didn't hurt as much as it could've. Sunflower shook herself off, and got ahold of the doe, dragging her into the open. She took flight to rejoin her herdmates where only Swallowtail and Char were awaiting her.

She looked around. "Where's Coyote?" asked Sunflower.

"I saw her land after she went south. Not too far," Swallowtail informed her.

She nodded and soared in that direction. Sure enough, the bay mare was standing on a mound a few yards away. She had set down her buck and her head was low to the ground, inspecting something. Sunflower, being careful not to mangle her own deer, landed cautiously. Swallowtail and Char remained in the sky. Sunflower left her catch near Coyote's. In the patches of dirt, there were large footprints that seemed fresh.

"Another bear?" Sunflower questioned.

"Looks like it. We should tell Obsidian immediately," snorted Coyote.

"Are you sure it's a bear?!" Swallowtail shouted from above. "I'm a little far away, but bears don't have claw marks like that, do they?"

Sunflower took a second glance at the print. It was certainly large and five-toed, but no hind footprints matched a bear's.

"You might be right. Whatever it is, we probably don't want it on our territory," Sunflower spun around to retrieve her doe.

Coyote followed, the two reached the other half of the party and hurried back to the valley.

Three beasts traversed atop the mountain's ridge, Ben, Komodo, and Obsidian. Komodo marched with his ear tips pointed to the sky, watchful of the valleys surrounding them. Trotting up behind him was Ben who had grown much in his single moon of life. His shoulders were nearly level with the six moon-cycle old colt's elbows and while his wings had grown, he was not yet a strong flier. Obsidian followed behind. Gusts that blew over them ruffled Komodo's coat. Ben's nostrils flared, taking in the rush of scents. Obsidian caught up with them and stopped alongside Ben while they watched a cloud be split by a distant peak.

"No danger here!" Komodo proclaimed and started along the narrow path of the ridge again.

Ben scrambled after Komodo. Obsidian lingered a while longer before joining them.

"Will we see any danger?" Ben panted.

"Hopefully not," Obsidian answered first.

"You never know. We need to make sure the mountains are safe!" whinnied Komodo. "If a bunch of hippogryphs go hunting, somebody's gotta watch!"

Komodo bounded down the slope. Ben carefully made his way to the bottom, his legs weren't quite *that* strong yet.

"The worst thing we could come across would be a bear, but I think we've gotten the message across that we're not sharing territory enough times for now. But I admire your desire to protect the herd," Obsidian told the foal.

The soft expression and words of his aunt made him beam with joy and do a springy buck. Ben watched the colt frolic for a moment then looked at Obsidian.

"What if we do see something dangerous?" asked Ben.

"We'll go home and get others," Obsidian said calmly.

"But there's three of us!" Komodo whipped around.

"You still have some growing to do," she nickered.

Komodo continued in his bouncy canter, head held high.

Obsidian started after him, and Ben walked beside her. Not even four strides later, Komodo turned back to them.

"Maybe when I'm old enough I can be the Herd Stallion?" Komodo said, looking at Obsidian with hopeful eyes.

Obsidian chuckled. "We'll see."

Ben looked at Obsidian then Komodo, and back to Obsidian. "I heard someone talking about that, but I dunno what it means."

"The Herd Stallion alerts everyone of danger!" Komodo yipped.

"As Lead Mare, I make sure everyone's fed and kept together. The Herd Stallion does warn us of danger and usually fights alongside a Lead Mare in battles but he is never to organize a group of the herd to battle without my permission," explained Obsidian. "It is a position only earned through the herd's trust and mine."

"Do we have one right now?" asked Ben.

"No."

"Why?"

"We've been fine without one for a long time now."

Obsidian raised her head high. Ben lowered his neck. She didn't seem upset, but Ben felt like he said something Obsidian didn't like.

"Why is the top of the mountain always white?" he tried asking a different question, squinting at the shining peak.

Obsidian gazed at where he was pointed. "It's snow. It's very cold up there, so all the rain became solid."

"Can we see it?"

"Not right now, that's a very far flight for you. It'll snow in the valley soon enough, anyway."

What did she mean by that? It wasn't too cold at home. Komodo froze again, his attention fixated ahead of them. Four figures were flying towards the valley out from the clouds, all carrying something.

"Hey! They're back!" Komodo blurted.

Sunflower and her hunting party were approaching. Obsidian's body language changed at the sight.

She stretched her neck down to Ben "We can eat soon. You'll get to have bigger prey this time," she cooed.

Ben perked his ears, though he couldn't see Sunflower and the others that well, the sky was so glaring. Komodo rushed away, spreading his wings that he finally grew into, and took off. Home was just down the mountainside, but Ben didn't feel confident copying Komodo. He lifted his head to Obsidian, wanting her to pick him up, she opened her wings and grasped him gently in her talons. He felt safer in her claws and the wind rushing past never frightened him.

It was once awkward for Obsidian to land while holding Ben, now it was no different than descending normally. Komodo did not bother slowing down until he made contact with the grass. He leaped around, wings flailing, then turned around back to the herd. Sunflower and the other mares landed with a thud from their catches. They dragged them towards the crowd and the four were greeted with soft whickering and wither grooming. Obsidian released Ben and trod over to Sunflower.

"Welcome back. I see you were successful," Obsidian whickered.

"Thank you, we were," Sunflower replied. She straightened up her neck when she remembered the news. "Though, we did come across something while we were out. Some giant footprints. We thought it might've been a bear's, it had five toes but the shape and claws didn't align."

Obsidian blinked. "What shape were the toes and pad?"

Coyote stepped forward. "I got a good look at it. The toes and claws were long, and the pad was too wide around. Also, the back footprints were too similar to the front."

Obsidian narrowed her eyes. "Dragon."

Everyone listening looked confused. Way up here? The Dragon Kingdoms resided far from the Redwood Mountains. Even if they were going to meet with the gryphons, those from the south would have just flown across the sea instead of walking through here.

"Other than Ben, why would one be up here?" Coyote questioned.

"I'm not sure," Obsidian shook her head. "Perhaps if they stick around we'll find out. It's either a forest or volcanic dragon."

Obsidian took a few steps towards the prey but halted and spoke again. "They might be injured. If you see them around, try talking to them. I may go see things for myself later. Now, no need to keep the herd waiting," she carried on her way and the hippogryphs that swarmed began to join her.

Ben trotted over to Obsidian, she stood near the fallen buck. Normally she would catch rodents for him, but he was getting old enough for larger animals. She had already torn fur away from a spot for him to rip at. As he sank his little fangs into the deer and pulled away, he found it was much tougher to him than squirrels or rabbits.

Sunflower appeared at his side opposite of Obsidian. "How do you like deer?" she asked

The hatchling only squeaked gleefully when he lifted his head, but his face said it all. Sunflower nickered.

"Tell you what, if Mom goes to look around for the dragon later, why don't we go explore up the river?" Sunflower offered.

Ben raised his head again for a moment and nodded quickly.

After he had eaten as much as he wanted, he curled up between Obsidian's front legs and waited for her to finish.

Two foals tussled in the valley, a bay colt and a silvery filly, while Komodo ran circles around them. Rearing up and flapping their wings at each other, their hooves and talons were never still. Ben was laying in the grass, watching, twisting stems around his claws on one foot, not even realizing it. The foals were much bigger than him so he wasn't sure about joining. He didn't feel left out though, watching them was entertaining enough. Komodo broke off and stood to the side of the wrestling two, however, he was ready to come hurtling towards them again at any moment. A short while later, he noticed something coming up behind Ben. Ben craned his neck to see. Sunflower was ambling towards the young dragon so he got up and prepared to explore the riverbank.

"Are you ready?" she asked.

He nodded and weaved around her front leg.

"Why does Mom want to find the dragon, again?" Ben wondered.

"If there's one up here, it's just a little strange. Normally dragons would fly across. I think she's worried about them," Sunflower explained. "Now, let's get going!"

Now that he thought about it, he had never seen another dragon before. Sunflower headed towards the river with a slow trot. Ben looked at the foals again before running off.

"Bye!" He called and then dashed after his dam.

Komodo just whinnied in response, not in pain, but because the two got fed up with him pulling their feathers and started to wrestle with him instead.

The pair headed upstream along the shore, set on going beyond where the river entered the valley. Ben could see the towering stones ahead, tall and looming, like a gateway to their home with a miniature waterfall that caused the water to speed through the trench. They went around the obstacle, Sunflower could've flown between the boulders and over the river, but she didn't want to risk it. She guided him around the wall and up the hill. The pathway narrowed, exiting the valley and turning into a thin pass split between the mountains by the river. Conifers with skinny trunks grew on the sheer cliffs. The flow was much calmer back here.

Ben carefully stepped down the soft slope of the riverbank. He sniffed around the edge, looking into the river through the reflections. Sunflower joined him. Underneath the glassy surface were a few medium-sized fish who did not have to put up a fight to stay in place against the current. Ben's ears raised. During the few times he had been to the river, he hadn't seen these before! He stretched out his palm and dipped it into the water, the fish scattered and fled. Ben looked around confused.

"How did they do that?!" Ben asked with surprise.

"Do what?" Sunflower replied.

"Be under the water!"

"Fish have gills, the little slits behind their heads."

Ben blinked at her, then back at the river. "Why don't we have gills?"

"Because we live on land. You may not have gills but when you're bigger you'll be able to fly above the clouds!" Sunflower lowered her head to him. "If you're lucky, you might catch a fish to eat."

Ben looked up at her once more then searched the river more determinedly. Obsidian would surely be proud of him if he caught one. His eyes scanned the sheet of pebbles along the shallow end. For a moment, he took his focus away from what lies beneath the water and instead saw the reflections atop. He saw his face wobbling with the river. He had seen his reflection a few times before, but his featherless, beakless image always caught him off guard. He knew that he was a dragon but he never felt any different. He always imagined himself as a hippogryph.

They strolled along the winding path through the mountains. Only the sound of the river and their steps were heard. He spotted more fish, which were smaller and hiding around stones. Sunflower saw Ben's body tense up, ready for a strike.

"You have to be quiet and careful with fish, don't let the pebbles shift too much," she told him softly.

Ben's neck arched, then he lunged his jaws into the shallows, though he only got a mouthful of water. With a splash he lifted his head high up, his lips drawn back in a snarl, snorting out a misty spray of droplets.

"Oh! Are you okay?!" Sunflower trotted over.

Ben shook his whole body. His ears drooped as he stared back at the river, the fish had swum away seemingly faster than a blink.

"It's alright if you didn't catch one, it was only your first attempt," she tried to cheer him up. "Not even all of my hunts are successful!"

He wanted to show Obsidian that he could catch one, but his failure left his confidence feeling low.

"Do you want me to show you a better way to hunt fish?" she asked.

"Okay," Ben murmured and followed her, ready to go upstream.

"The fish in our river are tricky and don't feed many hippogryphs, so we usually don't bother. But, it's best to use our talons to try and scoop them up. The way you tried it was like a heron, we don't have beaks like theirs. They can also feel the vibrations in the water from your steps and notice your shadow," she told him, facing the water and gliding one of her claws through it as a demonstration.

That made Ben feel a little better, that if he were to try again he wouldn't have to use his mouth. Getting a snout-full of water was freaky.

"I don't know if we will, but if we find more small fish do you wanna try again?" his dam asked.

"Maybe," he mumbled.

Sunflower came over to him with her head at his level. "Listen, don't sweat it. You just gotta keep going and try again sometimes," she groomed his scaly withers softly.

Ben pressed his head to the underside of her jaw. She raised her head and looked above him. It wasn't long before the sun would disappear behind the mountains. The days were getting shorter, too.

"Do you want to head back?" she looked back down at him.

Ben met her gaze and considered it for a moment, then trilled softly and stretched his neck forward. He began to continue walking along the shore. Sunflower turned herself in his direction and followed.

The first stars appeared, glimmering in the growing darkness. Obsidian stood on a mound in the valley. From where the river entered her home, she saw Sunflower and Ben on their way, just passing the boulders. Ben was holding something in his mouth but she couldn't tell what from the distance. They were making their way towards her. Ben's trot was jaunty, his tail swayed side to side.

Obsidian greeted her mate, touching their beaks together. Ben curled around her leg, and she saw that he was carrying a small black feather in his teeth.

"Why do you have that?" she asked curiously.

"I like it. It looks like you," Ben answered.

Sunflower could practically see Obsidian's heart melt.

"We tried fishing but ended up hunting feathers," Sunflower nickered. "Did you find the dragon?"

"No. Nothing," Obsidian lifted her head from nuzzling Ben.

"Maybe they went on their way?"

"Probably. But I haven't been able to shake this feeling since I got back. It's...unsettling."

Ben listened curiously to them, and asked, "Where are the dragons? Why don't they live here?"

His dams looked at him. "Their kingdoms are just elsewhere. They usually live within their own territories rather than alone and all the way out here," explained Obsidian.

"But, what do you mean by 'unsettling?'" Sunflower continued speaking with Obsidian.

"It's why I was standing here. I don't feel like the herd is alone right now," the dark mare's eyes narrowed, fixated on the dark, forested edges of the valley.

They stood for a moment, not even a chirp from any creature was heard.

"Is someone watching us?" Sunflower whispered, gazing out at the shadows.

"That's how I feel, but maybe I'm just paranoid," Obsidian sighed.

"Hm. I'm going to take Ben to rest, but I'll be awake," Sunflower told her.

"But I wanna see, too!" he peeped.

"I don't think you do. There may not even be anything out there, and it'll be a lot of standing around," said Obsidian.

"Come on, if he's still up, we can show Komodo your feather," Sunflower called him along quietly. That seemed to change his mind and he bounded after Sunflower.

It seemed like most of the herd was going to their nests, too. Obsidian stood alone like a statue, her ears were the only part of her that moved, but nothing broke the silence. She may have been only imagining things, but at the same time, she wasn't sure about that. She decided to walk out farther, maybe there was a cougar stalking and waiting for its moment to strike. She stamped her feet heavily while flicking her tail and raising her hackles. She prowled back and forth a few times, huffing and hissing. Nothing seemed to react. Perhaps she should give it a rest. Her coat smoothed out. With one last deep breath, she turned away to go to her cave. Still, the silence remained. Until a thick conifer began to creak and rustle.

CHAPTER 5

Obsidian's eyes darted back to the trees, quickly spinning herself around. She was right, something was there. She ruffled her feathers again and fanned her wings. She wasn't sure whether to stay where she was or to run and get her herd. The noise settled and it was quiet for a few heartbeats, then two gleaming eyes appeared. They were not a hippogryph's, but too large for any wild cat. She pinned her ears flat against her head. Both stood unmoving for a while. Obsidian was the first to speak.

"Come out," She commanded, not knowing if this beast could even understand her.

At first, it did not move. The animal hesitated, then stalked out from the shadows. Hulking claws slowly entered the valley. Six gold horns grew from the creature's wide head, staring back with umber eyes. In the low light, Obsidian saw thick black stripes trailing along its body. She was face to face with a soot-gray volcanic dragon, their scales melted in with the dark. For such a large beast, they had been very stealthy. Neither of them spoke for a span of time, just looking at one another.

Once more, Obsidian broke the silence. "Why are you here?"

They continued staring, almost as if they were thinking of an answer. "I was checking something."

She didn't expect a younger voice, this dragon sounded no more than if he were a few four-seasons old. He seemed to have several narrow scars dragged down his neck.

"And what is that?"

"You have something I need."

Obsidian raised her chin with narrowed eyes.

"Let me explain first," he took a few steps forward. "I am Fossil. Do you know about the last prophecy from the unicorns before they vanished?"

Obsidian blinked, caught off guard by the question. What relevance did this have to anything? "No."

"It was vague, but they felt that it had a strong possibility to be true. The only thing they had received were visions of great power being used and…"

If he was trying to be dramatic with that pause, Obsidian didn't care for it. "Get to the point," she snorted.

Fossil raised his head back looking offended. "…Blinding white. You have that albino hatchling."

Obsidian felt her heart begin to speed.

"How long have you been watching us?" she demanded to know, keeping her cool for now.

"It's not that important. Now, I-" Fossil began, Obsidian cut him off.

"I'd say it is important!" she stomped, fanning her tail out.

Fossil's tail spines rattled as he flicked it to his side. "Maybe a moon-cycle. Anyways, that prophecy just stuck with me since I was young. Quite the coincidence that I'm in the area when an albino hatches."

How full of himself. "So, you're suggesting that my son has powers."

"If the prophecy's true, yes."

"He doesn't. Go away."

Obsidian turned around and began to walk away. Fossil shook his neck as if reeling from her words. He tried to get her attention again.

"He's young, maybe he just doesn't know that he does yet," he tried to call her back.

"Dragons cannot possess powers of any kind," Obsidian didn't waver in her stride.

"If he does, you will be keeping me from saving a kingdom."

Obsidian stopped and glanced back, the distant amber dots that Fossil could see were her eyes seething in fury.

"You are very stupid to expect me to believe a centuries-old prophecy and allow you to take my son to who knows where for however long," she hissed bluntly. "Sorry if your kingdom is in a bad state, but he cannot help you."

"Well, I don't want to *take* him, I would only need his powers to manifest and then use them. No one said you couldn't come."

"How thick are you? What's even the problem with your kingdom?!"

Fossil only glared and looked to the side. "It's personal."

Obsidian turned away again. "Get out of my territory. I don't want to see you again."

Fossil just stood there, his tail swaying. Without even looking behind her, she could tell that he was still thinking of a way to try and convince her. Obsidian whipped around and lunged at him.

"GO!" Her whinny was earsplitting.

Fossil reared back and twisted around to flee into the woods. Obsidian galloped after him, hissing and clacking her beak. She stopped at the edge of the pines and waited for the dragon's fleeting steps to vanish into the distance.

She halted and stared into the darkness. She heard the cantering of a few herd members approaching a couple of moments later. She looked behind and saw Char, Avalanche, and an older stallion named Fire closest to her, other hippogryphs stood in the distance, glancing at one another anxiously.

"What in the world are you doing?!" Avalanche questioned.

"What's got you so worked up? What happened?" Char asked.

"Char, you did indeed find dragon prints on your hunt," Obsidian confirmed. She started toward her cave, "The dragon came out to speak with me. But I must talk to Sunflower about this."

The herd members who were awake followed her as they made their way across the valley.

Ben was already sleeping, Sunflower's eyes opened as she heard the beating of hooves drawing near. She lifted her head and flicked her ears. She saw the silhouette of Obsidian entering their cave with several hippogryphs stirring outside.

Sunflower blinked. "What's going on?" she whispered.

"My weird feeling was right. I met a dragon," Obsidian told her.

Sunflower blinked a few times more, surprised by how riled up Obsidian sounded. "What did they say?"

"He thinks a prophecy from the *unicorns* is about Ben! Claiming that he'll gain powers and be able to stop a threat to the Volcanic Kingdom that was so vague he wouldn't even tell me about it when I asked him! Unicorn prophecies are much more likely to be false. If it were true, it wouldn't be relevant five centuries after they went extinct!" Obsidian fumed, it was a shock Ben wasn't awoken by this. "Not only that, apparently he had been lurking around our territory for a moon-cycle *watching* Ben!"

"Ooh, that's unsettling," Sunflower pinned her ears back. "He sounds out of his mind. Dragons don't have powers, no beast does."

"That's exactly what I told him, yet he persisted and kept trying to convince me to let him take Ben with him."

"What did he look like, did you catch his name?"

"It's Fossil. He's a dark gray volcanic dragon with black stripes. I chased him into the forest and made sure he ran out of earshot. I don't want Ben going without any adult around him until we can be sure the dragon has left for good."

Sunflower nodded. Avalanche pushed her way past the crowd, and into the cave.

"What will you do if he doesn't listen? What if he turns violent?" she pressed.

"I won't jump to that conclusion, but if it comes to that then we *will* fight him," Obsidian's voice was collected as ever but held rage within her words. She shook her mane. "Everyone, don't worry about it for now. Unless he comes back, nothing will happen."

Obsidian dismissed the hippogryphs with a tail flick. They departed and headed back into the valley. Avalanche went past Obsidian to her own nest and settled into it. Anger still coursing through Obsidian. *The nerve that young dragon had.* She laid down beside Sunflower in their nest with a thump. Sunflower rested her head, Obsidian stared through the cave opening while hoping that Fossil would not show his face here again. She had difficulty sleeping that night, her thoughts latched onto what she would do if he returned.

In the morning, Sunflower was already up and about. Obsidian laid next to Ben in the cave, being the only two still in there. He began to stretch and roll over onto his chest. Obsidian turned her attention to the hatchling.

"Good morning, Ben," said Obsidian.

Ben made a soft trill noise through his nostrils.

Obsidian gathered herself in a straighter posture. "I need to tell you about something."

Ben relaxed his head back down but kept his focus on her.

"You remember yesterday when I went to search for the dragon who left footprints?"

Ben nodded.

"After you and Momma had gone back in here, I met him," Her tone was serious but not droning. "He was... He had his own agenda and wouldn't listen to me. He told me that, supposedly, a long time ago unicorns foresaw that a white beast would have powers. He thinks you are that beast, but I think he's wrong. Dragons cannot have powers."

Ben took in her words, twiddling his claws slowly. "What kind of powers?"

"I don't know. But unicorns were the only beasts who had powers. There is absolutely nothing that confirms his idea."

"Then why doesn't he just find a unicorn?"

Obsidian paused. Her ears drooped. "Ah… They've been gone for a long, long time. No one knows what happened to them. One day they all vanished."

Ben sat blinking for a moment.

"I don't think I have powers," he shook his head and stood up. He started to walk but was stopped by Obsidian.

"One more thing, I don't want you to wander far from or even within the valley alone. I don't trust that that dragon has given up and left the mountains. I want at least one adult with you near the outskirts and beyond."

"Okay."

Ben crawled out from the cavern. Obsidian watched him as he went. The sky was overcast, the way he liked it. He padded through the grass, which felt slightly different somehow, the texture beneath him seemed crunchier. The breeze that blew over him gave him a small shiver, everything seemed to be a little off today. Looking up at the sky, he could see darker clouds past the peaks, probably rain. He hoped those clouds wouldn't come his way, he hated the way mud would get all over his feet.

His herdmates were going about their day, as usual. They didn't seem to care about the strange-to-him things Ben had noticed. In the corner of his eye he saw movement, Ben shifted his gaze and saw Komodo bounding towards him. His cousin carried the same energy as always, bright and fun.

"Hey, you're finally up!" he nickered, swishing his tail. "Do you know what everybody's talking about? Because I don't."

"Uh," Ben started.

"Everyone's whispering and being weird about the woods."

Ben blinked at him for a moment. "Mom told me she met a dragon last night. He thought I had powers."

"Powers?" Komodo looked at him with tilted ears.

"She said he believed a… A properly…? One from unicorns."

Komodo seemed even more confused. He quickly shook off this expression. He looked around their surroundings though Ben didn't know why.

"If everyone's worried about the dragon, we need to guard the mountains," Komodo said. He was ready to spring off immediately.

Remembering what his dam told him, Ben stopped the foal before he could. "Wait! Mom also said I can't leave the valley without a grown-up hippogryph!"

Komodo relaxed his muscles. "Then let's bring Avalanche, she's all about defending the herd," he sprang away towards the center of the valley.

Avalanche? She didn't talk to Ben much and she seemed kind of standoffish. Ben slinked up the hill that a few of their herdmates were chatting on. Avalanche was laying down, her legs tucked beneath her body. She tilted her ears halfway back when she saw her brother.

"If you're going to ask me to toss you into the river, my answer is still 'no,'" she grumbled.

"That's not it, we need to protect the mountain but Ben's not allowed to go away from the valley without an adult right now," Komodo explained.

"Why?" she narrowed her eyes.

"Everyone's being edgy about that dragon, so we have to make sure he's not here."

"Hmm. No," she said curtly. Komodo's ears lowered. She continued, "Not just because I don't want to, but nobody's going to let you. He is a full-grown dragon that we don't know, and you're both short."

"What if *weeee* only went through one pass," Komodo asked.

"No."

"Then how 'bout…" he looked around, his sight caught by a large hill close by in the woods. "Only to the peak of that hill?"

"Why can't you just get ours or his dams to go?"

"You hardly do anything with Ben!"

"Do I *have* to?"

"You should!"

Avalanche groaned. Rising on her legs, she shook her coat. "Fine. But I don't want to be up there all day."

"Okay!" chirped Komodo.

He sprinted towards the base of the hill almost immediately, spinning himself around and stopping in his tracks, he waited for his family to catch up. Avalanche let out a long nicker and followed the colt. Ben hurried after Komodo. Komodo began to heave himself up the side in bounds. Ben would rather take his time walking up. Avalanche came alongside Ben and slowly passed him. He felt awkward with Komodo being ahead, and left alone with Avalanche. She didn't seem hostile, but she wasn't the most pleasant hippogryph. Ben looked up at her face, her expression grumpy. She flicked her brown gaze down, catching Ben staring. He quickly turned away, the brief eye contact gave him an uncomfortable shiver.

"So you still can't breathe fire yet," her words were a statement, not a question.

Ben shook his head, still not turning to her but could feel she was still looking at him

"I'd rather you not breathe it at all, at least nobody'd be in danger of getting burned," she grumbled.

Ben didn't answer. Breathing fire wasn't something he often thought about. Hippogryphs can't do it, so why should he? He looked around at the tall pines. He'd never seen fire but he knew trees burned. What if he accidentally lit a tree on fire and their forest burned down? He shuddered at the thought and quickened his pace to reach Komodo. Large stones varying in size were jutting out of the hillside with some almost as big as Ben. He heard Avalanche's voice behind him.

"You know that if we somehow see the dragon up here, we're not going near him!" she called to Komodo.

"I know!" Komodo shouted back.

Ben hoped they wouldn't see anyone at the top, but he had to ask. "What do we do if he *is* there…?"

"Very unlikely, but we get help and wreak havoc," Avalanche said in a fierce tone, not aimed at Ben.

"But we have to make sure anyway, herdmates look out for each other!" Komodo said nobly.

"That is true," Avalanche replied, speeding her pace a little. "But we don't send foals into battle, do we?"

"Yeah, I know."

Komodo remained ever eager to climb to the top. Through the trees, Ben could see gaps in the clouds letting in sunlight.

"Do you think the rain clouds will come this way?" he asked with concern.

Komodo searched the sky. "Well, I don't see any now, so maybe they moved on."

Ben felt relief waft over him.

"The top's not far now, just a little more," Komodo's stride shifted into a canter.

Ben still fell behind him, but not as far as Avalanche. Ben was slowed by the stones and had to pull himself up over a few. Avalanche had caught up to him, though she kept stopping shortly ahead of Ben, only continuing once he got over the rocks. They reached the peak after Komodo. Avalanche gazed over the land, too, a particular area caught her attention. She saw what looked like a mostly-eaten mountain goat, it had been ripped apart by whatever killed it.

"Did that wolf pack come back?! Ugh, remind me to tell Obsidian later," Avalanche groaned irritably.

Komodo turned to her, wide-eyed. "You fought *wolves* and didn't tell me? What happened?!"

"It wasn't really much of a fight, we just ran at them being loud and big, but apparently, that wasn't enough."

"What battles *have* you fought?" he asked curiously.

Avalanche turned back to the mountains, looking for anywhere familiar. "Char, Dandelion, and I had a skirmish with a cougar down between those cliffs down that pass. It'd been getting too close to the valley for comfort. Of course, strolling into a herd of hippogryphs would be a very stupid thing to do, but better to just deal with it before it got worse."

"What was the fight like?"

"A lot of running around and jumping. Cougars are quick and have deadly claws and fangs. Three against one made it easier, don't go trying to fight cougars alone."

Ben listened to Avalanche's story quietly, then it clicked. Avalanche's attitude, why she would go places with a party of hippogryphs but rarely come back with food.

"You're a fighter? Is that why you don't hunt?" Ben asked.

"Yeah. I *can* hunt, but I don't function well in hunting parties. Chasing intruders though, I handle that better," Avalanche said casually. After only a short time, the initial intimidation Ben felt from her died down.

"I like being away from the herd sometimes, anyway," Avalanche turned back in the direction they came.

Ben and Komodo's eyes followed her. Komodo went beside her and observed the land over there, too.

"Well, if nothing's here there's only one thing left to do," Komodo trotted over to the edge of the flat top. "We run downhill!"

"But we haven't even been up here that long," Ben tilted his head.

"There's nothing to do up here except look, and we looked!" Komodo trotted in a small circle and leaped down the slope, cantering tall with each stride.

Avalanche joined him, without jumping. Ben watched them go for a moment, then decided to come along. He, too, trotted down the hill. He took a small leap, jumping downhill was strange enough to fan out his wings for support, making little hops down most of the way. He was enjoying himself and leaped into the air higher than he had before. He glanced at the sky above, a streak of harsh light flashed in his eyes through a parting in the clouds. He shut his eyes tightly.

"Hey! Stop!" he heard Avalanche's voice call out. Before he could even get a moment to look for her, he was suddenly pushed out of the way of where he was headed.

Ben rolled onto his side. He blinked the pain away, dark blobby shapes cluttering his view.

"You were going to crash straight into a boulder!" Avalanche snapped.

Ben stood up and shook himself. His stance was more balled up, shaken by Avalanche's tone. "I couldn't see it… The sun came through the clouds," he squeaked.

"Are you okay? Light seems to bother you a lot," Komodo asked.

"I guess. I don't know, does it not bother you?"

"Obviously if the sun was in my eyes it'd hurt, but I'm fine otherwise."

"Oh."

Ben thought perhaps his eyes were sensitive because he was a dragon, but he couldn't think of a reason why that would be. He looked at his claws, Avalanche shook her mane and closed her eyes slowly.

"Don't take my shout personally. Just be more careful," She huffed. "Let's keep going. I need to report to Obsidian."

The three made their way back to the valley more carefully. Komodo stuck closely to Ben.

"Sorry I thought running down was a good idea," Komodo said, feeling at fault.

"It's okay. You didn't push me into the boulder or anything," Ben replied kindly.

Avalanche stepped quietly down the mountainside, dead pine needles littered the forest floor. She was followed by Swallowtail, Dandelion, and Spruce under the starlight. Avalanche searched for where she had spotted the mangled goat earlier. The woods didn't smell of wolves though, making it harder to track it down.

"What's the plan once we get there?" Dandelion, the palomino stallion yawned.

"Obsidian wanted us to run off the wolves again if they've come back," Avalanche explained, her voice low.

"The same pack?" Swallowtail whispered.

"Probably," Avalanche replied.

"Do you think they'll put up a fight this time?" asked Spruce. "I hope so, there's never anything going on out here."

"They should just run away with their tails between their legs…" Dandelion hoped.

"They may not be a big pack, but wolves are smart. They obviously know that they're stronger together, the same as we are. If it's a battle, we need to split them up," Swallowtail instructed.

Avalanche's ears darted around. Silence. The mountains grew colder as the season turned. She saw the familiar clearing where the carcass was laying a moderate distance away. Swallowtail was the first to take flight towards the clearing. The others followed her lead. The possibility of the wolves being there right now wasn't a big one, so they didn't worry too much. There wasn't a beast in sight besides the goat. Still, no scent of wolves, nothing even similar. Only the stench of the fallen animal beginning to go bad.

"Oh, this place? I passed here earlier but I was going too fast to stop and take a closer look. I only caught a whiff of the smell," Spruce said.

Avalanche was looking around for any trace of the pack, Swallowtail examined the goat closely. Dandelion and Spruce stood off to the side, keeping an ear out for anything.

"This kill can't be more than a day old but I can't find anything. It didn't rain, yet there's nothing. No wolves," grumbled Avalanche.

Swallowtail raised her head and met Avalanche's gaze. "No wolf scent, no tracks. Are you sure it was wolves?"

Avalanche came over beside the chestnut mare, taking a good look at the goat. It certainly seemed like it had been torn apart in the way canids would have, but had long scratch marks along it, too. Too deep and wide to be the result of a wolf's claws. Especially around the back of its neck. Avalanche pulled it over to get a better look at its back. Long wounds were slashed horizontally across.

"Maybe the wolves did get the message…" Swallowtail said.

Dandelion and Spruce raised their ears.

"I'm not sure these are from them," she continued.

"Then who?" Spruce asked.

"The dragon," Avalanche growled through her breath.

Dandelion tensed up. Avalanche caught sight of dry blood on the ground, which she hadn't noticed at first. Her eyes followed it as far as she could see. It seemed deliberately smeared on the ground. Focusing harder, she saw it was splattered all around them. A certain area had much more unusual stains on it. It trailed back towards the direction they had come from, towards the valley.

Avalanche snorted loudly. "What's this supposed to be? A threat? Because he can't have a dragon? How pathetic."

Spruce noticed what she was talking about. "*Oh watch out, hippogryphs, I'll show you a thing by killing this goat and painting with its blood!*" she mocked.

"It *could* be unintentional but that's a pretty big 'if'" Swallowtail flicked her ears.

Avalanche turned to the border of darkness that rested beneath the branches of pines to her right. "Should we go after him?" she seemed ready to jolt down the path. Spruce was prepared to join her.

"Maybe not, we know little about him, so I don't think it's a good idea to try and find him with just the four of us," advised Swallowtail.

"Fine," exhaled Avalanche.

"Let's get back to Obsidian and hear what she thinks," Swallowtail trotted towards the edge of the clearing and took off. The others followed behind.

Obsidian wandered the valley patiently, awaiting her search party's return. She fanned her wings for them to spot her as the four came home. They landed a small distance away from her and slowed their strides to meet after reaching the ground.

"Well?" she prompted. They had returned much sooner than she anticipated.

"We only found the dead goat. No wolf tracks or even an old scent trail," Swallowtail answered. "Avalanche and I got a good look at the way it had been killed and it didn't fit the way wolves would. There were large gashes from claws on the back of its neck."

"It's the dragon. There was dried blood smeared all over the dirt, a lot of it was pointing toward the valley," Avalanche interjected.

Obsidian's ear twitched but her expression remained neutral.

"What do you think we should do?" asked Spruce.

Obsidian thought for a moment. "Nothing for now. Give it some time. If we see more suspicious activity, we will act out."

Spruce and Avalanche appeared disappointed by her words. Dandelion immediately broke off from the group.

"Good to know cause I'm really tired. Goodnight," after he spoke, he trotted away.

"Alright, we'll keep an eye out," Swallowtail said to Obsidian. She turned to Spruce and Avalanche. "Goodnight," and then she began to walk away.

Spruce followed her a moment later. Avalanche remained. The two mares stood alone in the field, Obsidian shifted her eyes over to meet her niece's. Her face was aggravated. Obsidian waited for her to speak.

"If things do take a turn, don't do nothing again. You've done nothing for too long. I know that you didn't feel well, but it wasn't an excuse to ignore us," Avalanche's voice was cold, her ears firmly pinned back.

The young mare then left without another word. Obsidian watched her go with narrowed eyes but did not reply. Obsidian had stayed in the valley a while longer before going into her cave, everyone else inside it was asleep, except Avalanche. Avalanche wasn't in her nest at all. Obsidian stepped into the young mare's nest for a moment, it wasn't warm. She hadn't paid attention to where she snuck off to. She knew Avalanche had complicated feelings towards her, and she wasn't in the wrong for doing so. Obsidian *did* just ignore her herd all that time, she had felt guilty about it ever since. She stepped over into her nest beside Sunflower. She hoped Avalanche just needed some time to cool down. The worst-case scenario was that she went after Fossil herself, but that didn't seem like her. She may be a difficult mare but was not foolish.

CHAPTER 6

After Avalanche had seen the shredded goat, herd life mostly continued as normal. Perhaps Fossil, if he did kill it, was only hunting, though he had done a sloppy job of it. A whole moon-cycle had nearly passed now. The morning air was chilly, the sun wouldn't touch the valley for some time, unfortunately. Obsidian was awake but kept her head tucked into her winter down that was beginning to grow. She didn't feel like getting up, it seemed everyone else felt the same way since they all were still in their nests, too. The cave now had one less member after Ben and Komodo had gotten too large for all of Obsidian's family to fit comfortably in, Avalanche had moved into a cave with Spruce and a few other young hippogryphs. Ben was catching up to Komodo fast, his shoulders were already nearing Komodo's elbows.

Obsidian didn't know how big Ben would get but he certainly was going to outgrow an equine. Her nest had to be expanded even more. It was starting to look like a giant eagle nest. Obsidian felt Ben move at her side. He was curled up, wedged in between his dams. He stretched his body out and yawned. From nose-to-tail, he was easily the same length as them now.

"You're up early today," Obsidian whispered.

"It's so cold," he curled back up into a ball, covering himself with his wings.

Obsidian opened her eyes and saw the valley under a sheet of snow. "I see why now."

Ben lifted his head, blinking in surprise. "What happened?!"

"It snowed during the night."

"Doesn't that only happen on the taller mountains?"

"No, winter just comes sooner here. It'll be like this for the next few moon-cycles."

Ben stared at the glistening fresh snow. No tracks nor grass could be seen but it didn't look deep.

"Will it ever be warm again?" he asked.

"Eventually. The seasons repeat themselves every four-season, hence the name."

The bedding shuffled as Sunflower began to wake. She stared out of the cave with tired eyes. She then laid her head back down.

"Good morning," Obsidian nickered.

"'Morning," she replied. "We got our first snow?"

"Yes."

Sunflower gathered her legs beneath her and rested a wing over Ben.

"This is both of the boys' first snow, huh?" she realized.

"How can I stop being cold?" asked Ben.

"You can move around or this would be the perfect time to learn to breathe fire," Sunflower pushed herself up on her feet and shook her coat.

Ben felt anxiety jab his ribs. He didn't want to be freezing though, so perhaps it was time he did. He slowly rose from the nest with her. Sunflower made her way out of their cave, snow crunching beneath her feet. Ben followed behind closely, taking his first steps into the snow. It was colder than the air and a consistency he hadn't experienced before. It went from a soft layer to being packed under his claws. He kind of liked it. He sped into a trot to Sunflower's side, kicking up dusty snow each stride. Obsidian accompanied them too, emerging from behind. Ben was now hopping around, lifting all four feet at nearly the same time. His dams watched him bound. He dove his snout into the blanket of snow and flipped his head up. Glittering snowflakes scattered through the air, landing on his back. He looked over to where the mares stood side by side.

"How...do I breathe fire?" he asked sheepishly.

The hippogryphs looked at each other.

"I'm not entirely sure myself. I don't know what age dragons learn to use their fire crop," Sunflower told him

"My fire crop?" Ben tilted his head.

"Under your jaw, where you have loose skin and soft scales. That's where you build up your fire," Obsidian stepped forward. "Dragons have their crops long before they hatch. We just don't know where you should start."

Ben tried to focus on using his crop, trying to make something happen, but he just kept holding his breath instead. Standing still let the frigid temperature of the snow set in his legs, how was he supposed to heat up his crop in this weather?

"I can't," he sighed. "I'm too cold."

"Hmm. Maybe if you warm up a bit," Sunflower nickered.

She started into a trot, her steps high. Ben followed her and matched her speed. They climbed up a mid-sized hill that would eventually lead them up to the wall of mountains behind their cave. Obsidian remained where she stood, her gaze followed them along their path. She stayed in place for a while but then joined them. A trail wrapped around the side of the cliff and followed a shallow arc, not nearly as steep as the mountain itself. Once Sunflower and Ben trotted up to a point that was about the height of two hippogryphs, she spread her wings and leapt from the ledge. Ben hesitated, then unfurled his own and glided down. He wasn't taking any long journeys at this age but he could fly a short distance. Obsidian soared down but landed with more of a thud onto her feet.

Ben broke into a gallop once he reached the ground, turning in a tight circle. Sunflower chased after him, snowflakes flying up around them. A pile of snow was coming up in his path. He readied his legs and jumped over it. When he expected to land, he just kept going, plunging into the tiny snowbank. Only his wings and tail were sticking out.

Sunflower slowed to a halt. "You okay?" she whickered.

Ben shot up into the air swinging his wings, landing and flopping down to roll around. He felt a rush of heat swell behind his jaws. Surprised and caught off guard, he scrambled to flip himself upright. Small wisps of black smoke trailed from his nostrils. The feeling was unusual, his head and mouth felt so hot yet it did not harm him. He ran back to Sunflower.

"What happened?! Did I do it wrong?" squeaked Ben.

Sunflower seemed happy, both his dams did. "No, I don't think so. You didn't quite breathe fire, just smoke, which always comes from a fire," the palomino mare whickered.

Ben blinked. His face became more concentrated, flaring his nostrils, trying to do it again. The idea was still odd to him, breathing fire felt out of place. The warmth in his crop had not died down even after he exhaled the smoke. He wasn't really sure what he was doing but he managed to create another tiny plume of smoke. Igniting the fire was proving to be more difficult though.

Ben shook his head, snorting out more smoke. "I can only do smoke, I guess."

"You only just started. You'll figure it out," Sunflower came over to his side.

The small joyful expression from Obsidian had faded as quickly as it came. Ben's ears fell back. She wasn't acting differently, but something seemed off about her today. Ben started to worry it was because he couldn't make fire. He took soft steps through the snow to his dam with his head low.

"What's wrong?" he whispered.

Obsidian's ear twitched like she hadn't even noticed him walk up to her. "Oh. Nothing new," she didn't sound upset with him or in general, her tone was rather soft.

Ben folded his wings against himself, he glanced away and flicked his ears for a moment. "Did I do something wrong?"

Obsidian faced him. "No. No, I just don't have good memories of winter," she lowered her neck to gently rest her fuzzy jaw on top of his head.

"Why not?"

Obsidian stared out at mountains for a moment. "A long time ago, I had a different mate and egg. His name was Cedar. Three four-seasons ago now, I used to live in a cave higher up in the mountain with him. One winter, an avalanche happened there. Nobody could've stopped it. He tried to escape with the egg but he wasn't fast enough and he died. While that's how I began to feel this way, there are many more reasons I do now."

Ben soaked in her words, then asked, "He died?"

"Yes. Just as hunted prey does, so do we. You have many four-seasons to live, so don't fill your head with worry," Obsidian brushed the tip of her beak down his neck.

Ben went under her and then curled around her front legs. "We can make new good memories then."

Ben started towards Sunflower and continued past her. He slowed his stride and looked back at them, beckoning them to come along. Obsidian appreciated Ben wanting to make her feel better, she went into a trot and joined her family. Ben pranced through the snow, at a distance, his white scales would easily allow him to blend in. Obsidian trod alongside Sunflower, the dark mare's expression still seemed gloomy.

"I know it's hard and I understand how you feel," Sunflower said softly. "But what's happened, happened. We're always working through it together. Let's go catch up with Ben."

They sped up their pace to be just a short length behind their son. Ben bounded along, lifting all four feet again. Sunflower chased after him, tossing her neck. He twisted around and reared up at her, and so did she. Their front legs touched the ground again at nearly the same time. Obsidian found the energy to lift herself in the air with a flap of her wings and leapt forward, but her feet dragged through the snow. She plowed a small wave at the two. A little bit landed on the bridge of Ben's snout. He shook himself off and playfully hopped around in a circle. Sunflower shook her coat and was glad that Obsidian joined them.

Ben took off again, running in a huge ring around them with a springy gait. Obsidian lay down and spread her wings flat out. She shook and flipped bits of snow onto them, then lowered her head. Ben came over to check on her, he slowed to a curious stalk up to her shoulder. When he came closer, she lifted her wings, sending snowflakes up into the air and falling onto them both. Ben opened his wings and made an excited snort. Obsidian whickered. Ben trotted and weaved around her, rearing up a few times.

Back near their cave, a shape moved within it. It caught Ben's attention as he stood below Obsidian with perked ears. Komodo exited, looking around at the valley, moving one foot, followed by picking up another uncomfortably. Ben cantered over to meet him.

"It snowed!" Ben called to his cousin.

"It sure did," he was still taking in the sight. "I didn't think it'd be so much so suddenly."

"I almost learned how to do this!" Ben huffed out a little jet of smoke.

Komodo's ears raised and his eyes lit up immediately. "Wow! How did you do that?"

"I don't know, I was just running around then it happened! But I don't know how to breathe fire yet."

"Avalanche isn't gonna be happy," Komodo joked, clawing questionably at the snow again. "But why does it have to be so cold? I don't even feel like moving."

"Momma told me that moving around a lot will make you warm again, and it did."

Komodo shook his coat and exhaled, his breath visible. He took a few stiff steps. "Well, okay."

Ben skipped ahead out into the open, he looked over his shoulder a few times, waiting for Komodo.

"Not like that, you have to run!" Ben urged.

"But it's too cold," Komodo fluffed up his neck.

"It won't be if you run. Come chase me!"

The colt began to trot sluggishly after the hatchling, then made himself canter. He caught up quickly, trailing close behind the dragon. With a heave of his wings, Komodo flew over Ben's head. He slid across the snow as he landed, so did Ben, stopping to watch him fly above. Komodo sank to the ground with the unexpected loss of traction, his legs splaying out under him. Ben reared to pounce at him. Komodo gathered himself and clambered to get back on his feet. He hopped with an excited buck, seeming to not mind the cold anymore. Obsidian and Sunflower watched the two blaze through the frosted valley.

"Sometimes it doesn't even feel like he's a dragon. He moves just like a hippogryph and fits right in," Sunflower said warmly.

Obsidian nickered. "You think they'd let me appoint a dragon as the lead?"

Sunflower tilted an ear. "Now don't say that."

"I'm only kidding."

"I mean don't say that as if you're going to die soon."

"Who said I was going to die?" Obsidian bumped her with her wing.

"No one I hope!" Sunflower turned to groom Obsidian's withers.

They watched the pair play for a few more moments. The once pristine, untouched field now had spiraling trails of footprints.

Obsidian sighed. "But, you know, I've thought about stepping down for a while now and passing off my leadership. I'm not ready to, but I don't feel like my position is deserved at this point either. You deserve it more than me after all you did while I sat around."

Sunflower turned to her, ears angled. "I did all that *because* you weren't feeling well, I'm not after your role and I wanted to do you a favor. If the herd didn't want you as the Lead Mare they would've done something about it. I remember the way you were, so level-headed and wise for your age back then. I'm sure they all want you to make a comeback."

Obsidian let the breeze ruffle her feathers. "It's so hard to convince myself that I can be that again."

"I know you can. You've got time."

Running around all morning had worn Ben out, he returned to his nest after a while and napped, he was the only one there at the moment. The sun now started to hide away behind the peaks once more. Ben stretched his wings out to the sides and raised his head. When he looked outside and realized how much later it was, he was surprised he managed to sleep that long. Suddenly, he remembered the other day when his mothers had told him they wanted to begin practicing his hunting skills soon. He wondered if today would be a good time to start. He sprung up, and after a few strides, he halted. Scanning the land for his family among the herd. The evening was quiet, his herdmates huddled close together to endure the icy wind, which made him realize that he hadn't felt cold ever since this morning. He just carried on his way, like the snow wasn't there at all.

On a hill, he spotted Obsidian's midnight plumage. She and Sunflower were standing together in the last of the sun's beams. Obsidian had her wings angled in a way around them that blocked the breeze. He ran toward them, when they saw him, they walked to meet him.

"We were just thinking about coming to get you," Obsidian said, stopping when she came up to him.

"I'm ready to practice hunting!" Ben told them.

"Right now? Then let's head out before it gets completely dark," Sunflower trotted and glanced back to watch Obsidian and Ben follow as they made their way into the coniferous forest.

Padding close behind, Ben stared up at his dams. "What could I catch?" he asked.

"Whatever you find. Keep alert of your surroundings, spot your prey before it sees you," Obsidian whispered.

Ben didn't often go into the woods, they mostly took him around the river. He liked it there and knew what to expect— fish, he had caught a few minnows there now. Out among the trees, there were so many possibilities, it was intimidating. He took Obsidian's advice, his eyes darting around, listening closely with perked ears. The snow seemed deeper, it had only fallen last night but a lot of space at home had been padded down by hippogryphs' steps. They moved quietly, as to not startle nearby creatures, but they were all searching together. Ben inhaled deeply and took in the scents. The soft smell of pines was most prominent but he didn't mind, it was comforting; the smell of home.

Ben's attention had been tapering off as they walked, his focus was brought back by a tail signal from Obsidian. She fanned her tail feathers out to halt them. Sunflower and Ben stopped beside her. Their eyes followed the direction her beak pointed, leading them beneath the branches of a pine. A dove scratched and pecked at a patch of exposed dirt. A perfectly sized catch for a young dragon. Ben flicked a glance to Obsidian for guidance.

She lowered her head to him and whispered, "Don't approach from this angle. We'll go around. Come along."

They hid behind some tangling shrubs dusted with snow. Sunflower and Obsidian laid down to be less noticeable. Ben still wanted direction.

"Take careful steps," Obsidian looked over and saw some fallen branches large enough for Ben to walk along. "You could climb on those limbs so the snow doesn't sound beneath your claws. But don't pounce from too far away. Claws out, jump from the strength in your hind legs."

With Obsidian's advice, Ben lowered into a crouch. He slinked onto the thick branch as softly as he could. Step by step, gently stalking the bird, though his heart pounded. He worked hard to not let his claws tremble with both anxiety and anticipation. At a distance that he felt he could trust himself to pounce from, he held his breath and took the jump. His talons sunk past the feathers and stabbed into the dove. He landed on his elbows and slid with it, it flung out a wing, smacking Ben in the face but he didn't let go. Clutching it tightly, he wasn't sure what would be the right way to take it down if his initial attack didn't do the job. But shortly after, it stopped struggling and the flapping of its wings ceased.

"Yes, excellent!" the sudden volume in Obsidian's voice made him jump a little. He twisted his neck around to see his dams rising out from behind the bush. They trotted over with loving, proud expressions.

"You did a wonderful job!" Sunflower whickered.

The praise from his dams made him feel even warmer, he squeaked at them excitedly.

Sunflower began to speak, "I didn't wanna mention it while Ben was stalking, but that branch he climbed isn't from a pine."

Obsidian looked back at where it was resting horizontally across the ground, just tall enough to be seen above the snow.

"It's deciduous. It's bare and has no needles," Sunflower rolled it over, revealing twiggy appendages growing and splitting off from its side. two frosty, dry leaves still clung to a stem. "There are no deciduous trees nearby."

"Wind from the snowfall perhaps?"

"Maybe, but that'd have to be some fierce wind to move a branch this big over here. Or it might not be recent at all. I don't know, it's just weird."

Ben listened but said nothing, he didn't see why a limb from a different kind of tree here would be a big deal. He grabbed the dove in his mouth as he prepared to head home.

CHAPTER 7

Another quiet moon-cycle passed Obsidian with the familiar, bitter winter weather she'd experienced many times before. On this sunny midday, she dragged herself out to join a hunting party, they had only taken flight a short time ago. She was joined by Spruce, Dandelion, and Chasm; the young hippogryphs awaited her guidance.

"Lead the way, but are we just heading north?" Chasm asked as they soared up beside Obsidian.

"Yes, mostly. Avalanche and Monarch had reported to me a few days ago that herds of deer were passing through there. If we dive into a group and catch multiple, we can make this a shorter hunt," she explained to her herdmates.

Another snowfall happened recently. As they flew at high speeds, Obsidian watched the land below her zip past her. She tried to hide it, but she felt nervous that she may be rusty. It had been some time since she was last on an actual hunting party. She, Dandelion, and Chasm were a quiet trio, preferring to spend their flight in silence, only speaking up when it was time to take down an animal. Spruce, on the other hand, kept pestering Chasm.

"Come on, isn't there anything to talk about? Keeping our mouths shut until something happens just feels awkward," she glided above the chestnut hippogryph, tilting her head to look at them.

"Not really," they responded.

"Nothing at all? What about the herd? It's boring when I get put in a group without Avalanche, she's always got things to talk about."

"Are we talking about the same mare?" Dandelion blurted.

"Yes! Whether it's just talk or giving orders, she never misses a beat," she gushed about the mare.

"You might be the only one who gets along with her," Chasm nickered.

Spruce took it as a compliment, and their words made her feel proud of herself and continued to talk about Avalanche. Obsidian had tuned her out at some point, just listening to the wind whistling around her ears. She could only describe her relationship with her niece as...distant. She didn't dislike her, but it was complicated and she never really could tell if Avalanche did care about her like family. She couldn't say that Avalanche's feelings towards her weren't valid either. She can't change Avalanche's mind overnight though, it was going to take time to mend any bond they may have had when she was a filly.

Now that they were near where the herds of deer had been, she and her herdmates traveled much more slowly. The density of pines grew greater here in the north which was both an advantage and a hindrance for all animals involved in this hunt. The land dipped into a small wooded valley, a place deer would probably enjoy. Down there were a few patches of oak trees mixed with the conifers. The four landed atop a mountain ridge.

"Search through the trees for deer. We'll attack together," Obsidian told them.

They all kept a watchful gaze and prowled about to get a better angle of the ground, searching for even a glimpse of movement. Chasm caught sight of a doe walking by, only noticing her as she walked behind an oak that had been wrecked and reduced to a mere stump, creating a gap. They turned their head to their herdmates and clacked their beak to grab their attention. The three trod over next to Chasm.

"Do you think we'd have a better shot from the ground?" Chasm asked Obsidian. "Diving through pine branches could give the deer enough time to escape."

Obsidian tilted an ear and examined the trees for a moment. "Maybe not. We could still be seen much more easily down there. I think it's best to take our chances in the air," she replied. Chasm nodded.

Obsidian opened her long wings and soared above the forest, her party quickly joining her. Once they glided close to where the destroyed oak was, the hippogryphs awaited their Lead Mare's signal. They were spread apart but still close enough. Obsidian shifted her wings to descend diagonally, then folded them beside her to dive. She'd already found a deer to go after. The others lingered in the air a little longer. Obsidian braced herself, claws forward, and quickly took the creature down. The deer barely put up a fight, stunned by the sheer impact, before falling limp. Obsidian gathered herself, her front feet pinning her catch. Her attack had immediately sent the rest into a panic, but Chasm and Spruce weren't far behind her and managed to take down a pair. Dandelion was the last to strike and the only one to have missed. He trailed after one for a bit before it dashed away into underbrush branches that were too thick for him to squeeze past. He snorted and flicked his tail as he watched it vanish into the woods.

"Oh no!" said Chasm.

"Guess I'll try again," Dandelion huffed annoyedly.

"Should I come along in case you need someone to close it off from running?"

"Sure, why not."

Dandelion took flight again, Chasm glanced back at Obsidian for approval before following him.

"Go ahead, we'll wait here with your deer, too," she told them. Chasm hurried after the stallion.

As Obsidian and Spruce waited around for the two to return, Spruce was unusually quiet and just staring around at their surroundings. She seemed focused on a certain spot. The broken tree.

She finally opened her beak. "I swear someone has it out for oaks. Avalanche and I keep seeing busted trees like that one around the mountains."

Obsidian twisted her neck to look at the nearby oak. "Hmm?"

"We've seen specifically oak or other deciduous trees. At least...maybe eight this past moon-cycle and a half."

Obsidian blinked. "Do you know why? The weather can't have been *that* bad."

"No. After we spotted the fourth one, we checked it out but didn't find an answer. They've all been stumps with no branches left."

Obsidian stared at the remains of the tree, there were splinters scattered behind it, so it hadn't been a fire. But the oak's limbs weren't around, not even hidden under snow.

"You know, on the day the snow first fell, I took Ben to hunt with Sunflower and we saw a singular branch that could've been from an oak," she recalled.

"But what would be ripping apart trees and throwing the pieces around?" Spruce dug a claw into the snow and tilted her ears.

Obsidian then noticed large shapes in the air, it was Dandelion and Chasm.

Chasm came down to the ground to take their catch. "We're finished and ready to head back," they stated while grasping the deer back in their talons.

The three on the ground pushed themselves into the air with strong flaps of their wings. Spruce looked like she wanted to say more, but kept silent. The thought would remain on Obsidian's mind.

"Let's get going!" Komodo whinnied with a joyful buck. He paused and looked towards his sister. "Where are we going?"

"Only around the outskirts of the valley," she answered.

"Really?" his tail drooped.

"It's your first time watching for intruders. You'll start small."

Conifer readily came trotting up beside Avalanche. Their dam had pure pride for Komodo all across her face, he had grown much. He was looking like an adult hippogryph, but still had room to mature. Avalanche unfolded her wings and began the search, it would be short and easy, just a quick flight around home. Only Komodo and Conifer were accompanying her today. They didn't go as high as Avalanche normally would, the winter temperatures only got more freezing high above.

"Where do we start?" asked Komodo.

"Just here, we'll make a big oval around. All you need to do is keep your eye out for anything weird," explained Avalanche.

They flew towards where the river entered the land and the base of a mountain. They'd circle back to the woods on the other side of the herd. Avalanche knew she'd be doing most of the work, but didn't care much. Conifer rarely went to survey the territory, she wasn't the kind to battle and Komodo had only just begun. All seemed to be in order by the river, though it was rarely eventful over here. They were coming up to mountains that reached higher than they were flying, Avalanche wasn't feeling motivated enough to go over them.

"Let's go around those peaks, we can still see a lot of them from just the side," she instructed.

She soared above the slope of the mountains. Komodo couldn't seem to stay focused on any one spot for more than a moment, amazed by the view. Avalanche scanned the forested cliffs. Boring. Just silent woods swaying gently in the wind.

"If we do find something, will we have to fight?" Komodo questioned, he had once seemed raring to go out into the territory and tussle but right now concern edged his voice.

"Don't get it in your head that we will, we're still near the valley. Nothing with any common sense comes this close. We're just checking if anything has been damaged lately," Avalanche called to him.

"If anything is broken, do we fix it ourselves? What exactly needs fixing?"

"Rocks or trees that have fallen in potentially dangerous spots we can usually do by ourselves, and we thinned out snow piles on the cliffs recently enough."

They carried on, reaching the edge of the taller summits. Descending lower to the ground, following the curve of the mountain but remained fairly high up to get a good look at the woods. Conifers and snow coated the rugged, uneven land. Avalanche watched the forest and tried to see past the wedges of branches. It seemed quiet down there until Komodo had spoken. "What's that?"

Avalanche turned her attention to where her brother stared, farther out than they would have flown around in this group was *another* decimated tree. She let out a hiss.

"Come on. We're going there," she growled, she knew that just like every other tree she had found, it would yield no answers but this was unnatural and couldn't be ignored. She darted off in the direction of the trunk.

"What is it?" Conifer asked. She and Komodo scrambled to fly after her.

"A smashed tree, but I've been seeing too many just like it. I have to know why they keep appearing!" Avalanche shouted over the wind.

She dove above the trees like a dart. When she reached it, she landed with a thump on her talons and examined what remained of the oak. The top was spiked and splintery where all the limbs had been removed, a very unclean cut. Though it was more like it was barreled into and snapped off through pure force. Conifer and Komodo landed behind her after a few moments, panting as they caught up.

"What is it?" Komodo asked Avalanche.

Conifer studied the tree, then said, "Oh, I saw one like this out hunting a few days ago. I didn't think much of it but perhaps I was wrong?"

Avalanche gave her neck a rough shake and paced as she explained, "Yes. This is the *NINTH* one I've found! They're all scattered around and always non-coniferous. They've all been mangled the same way, sharp and branchless, nothing but half a trunk is left. Other than twigs, the top half is nowhere around. Sunflower said she saw an out-of-place deciduous branch a few days ago! Cougars, wolves, and bears are out of the question, they *can't* pull off something like this and wouldn't even want to."

Her family was just as stumped as she was. The three were all silent and in thought. Until it dawned on Avalanche.

"The dragon's still here," she hissed in a whisper.

Komodo seemed confused. Ben? Surely not. Though Conifer remembered what had happened a few moon-cycles prior.

"The dragon Obsidian met a while back? Why would he still be here? There have been no real signs of him around or even faint scent trails," Conifer asked.

"That's what he would want us to think. Not long after Obsidian discovered him, I had found a mutilated goat carcass with blood painted towards our herd. Now I see these trees. We don't know him at all, so there's no reason to not think he's the one doing this," Avalanche theorized.

"But, then how would he be masking his footprints and scent?"

Avalanche didn't have a clear answer. She looked around, there were zero prints in the snow, not even trails of wood being dragged away. "I don't know. I'm looking into this further. I will tell Obsidian but I'll do it regardless of if she wants me to figure it out or not," she took flight again, "Let's hurry and finish this."

The snow gleamed bright enough beneath the clouds later that night to see moderately well. Avalanche soared through the sky, undeterred by the cold, Conifer had come along with her. They watched the ground below, searching for deciduous branches. They were only able to spot a few pieces from above, but Avalanche couldn't help but wonder how many they may see on foot.

Avalanche slowed. "Being high up isn't doing us any good. We need to walk."

"Won't it be hard to find them down there, too? We'll see less of our surroundings and have to pick through shrubs and twigs," asked Conifer.

"More to sort through but it'll be easier to see what is what."

Avalanche didn't wait another moment to sink to the ground, her momentum carried through into her landing and she began trotting once she touched the snow, stopping after a few strides. Perhaps it wouldn't be as tricky to find the branches as Conifer had thought. No large snowfalls had happened for a few days. They stood near the one they found earlier while soaring, Avalanche glanced around, hoping to locate more. She wanted to find a trail, whether it be footprints or a path of branches. Conifer let her wings hang and submerged her wrists into the snow, she pushed them outwards away from her body to reveal the hidden grass and sticks that weren't tall enough to poke through. Most of the pieces may be visible, but some could've been buried. Avalanche did the same and brushed the area with her wings.

"Have you figured out how the dragon wouldn't have left any footprints?" asked Conifer.

"He must've flown but that can't be the only answer, there's no way he could have hovered low enough to the ground to pick up the branches," said Avalanche with her beak just above the snow.

"You'd think somebody would have run into him by now if this has been going on for more than a moon-cycle."

"He's definitely elusive…"

Avalanche continued shoving away sheets of snow, she wandered the length of about two hippogryphs east from where they landed when her foot bumped into something. She dug it up. Conifer came over to her filly's side.

Avalanche ran her talons across a small oak log. "There's one."

"Do you think there's more around?" Conifer lowered her wings again to plow the snow.

"Probably."

They had created a big clearing in the snow, searching farther east but to no avail. The two they found seemed to be the only ones nearby or others were just lost beneath the frost elsewhere. They could have spent the whole night out here searching but it probably wasn't worth the effort. Snow clouds were creeping in, thick snowflakes began to slowly waft around them.

"We're not going to make any progress if snow starts falling faster, we need to go to Obsidian," Avalanche grumbled. "It's all just going to fill back up."

Conifer lifted her head and folded her wings back up. "It'll be a shame to lose these under the snow, but I guess you're right."

She expected Avalanche to take off merely a heartbeat later, but she remained still, staring at the ground silently.

She flicked her ears. "What is it?"

Avalanche's ears flattened. "He does leave footprints, they get covered by the snowfall," she realized. "He must be masking his scent with another and the wind blows away anything else."

Conifer could see the way Avalanche was bunching her muscles. It was snowing harder now, he was going to come out, and she wanted to track him down. She moved in front of her.

"There's only two of us, we aren't going after him. We don't know where he is," Conifer said, trying to discourage her.

"He's planning something. He doesn't want to be found which is why we need to," Avalanche replied firmly.

"Think sensibly! We need to be careful and get help first. We can start by taking these branches somewhere he didn't intend them to be."

Avalanche silently accepted that. Conifer grabbed the log where they first landed. Avalanche took hold of the second one. They took off with the wood and kept flying past the valley, up the wall of mountains. On the other side of the ridge, they dropped the branches. Avalanche gave both a nudge and the thick pieces tumbled down the cliff. They then returned to the herd. Once they landed, Avalanche wasted no time trying to find Obsidian. She cantered towards the cave that she herself once lived in. Avalanche prowled into the opening, gleaming eyes opened as she stepped in. Sunflower's opened too, as narrowed slits. Ben and Komodo were asleep. Obsidian stared at them questionably, they had not told her beforehand that they headed out.

"Hmm?" Obsidian awaited for the mares to speak.

Conifer stepped closer into the entrance. "We went out looking for pieces of the destroyed trees and found a couple close together."

"They may look randomly placed, but I find that hard to believe," said Avalanche after her dam finished, her ears tilted back. "Fossil is doing this. He has to be doing it only during snowstorms, he flies and the snow fills the footprints he would have no choice but to leave. He's trying to do something."

Obsidian's gaze became more focused. "If you think there's a reason the branches are there, did you remove them?"

"Yes, we took them to the mountains facing away from us," nodded Conifer.

"Keep doing that, but put all of them in different places. In the morning, I'll tell everyone else to do the same whenever they find one."

"I can get searching tomorrow, too," Sunflower yawned, resting her eyes.

"I won't want Ben to be alone anywhere again," Obsidian looked at the sleeping hatchling and lowered her ears.

Conifer nodded again and walked in to lie down into her nest. Avalanche still stood halfway in the cave.

"Fossil comes out in snowfalls. We can run him off for good," she said in an icy tone.

"I will keep it in mind," Obsidian whispered, locking eyes with her.

Avalanche flicked her tail. She backed out and flew away, snowflakes drifting down off her back. Obsidian and the rest of her family went back to sleep.

The next morning, Obsidian had called together the hippogryphs who were able to fly confidently; she had ordered them all to take the branches elsewhere when spotted. If they were unable to carry it back at that moment for any reason, they needed to mark the area and alert another herdmate. Over a few days, they continued to dismantle the vague, sprawling trails of wood, chucked away far from the herd's home. As more and more were uncovered, the wooden limbs became scarcer. Though new ones had appeared one day, only a few, but if the dragon was going to stubbornly keep at it, they would need to take further action.

But now sunset was drawing close, heavy gray clouds blocked out the sky. The wind blew from behind and ruffled Obsidian's coat. Snow had begun to drift down once more. Out from the gloomy haze came Avalanche, almost blending in completely. She moved up next to her aunt. It was dark, windy, and difficult to see, a golden opportunity for Fossil to strike. It would be surprising for him to not be creeping around. Obsidian faced the young mare.

"Are you prepared?" she asked.

"I've been waiting for too long," Avalanche said with her head held high. "But are you actually going to take care of the problem?"

"I want to hear what he has to say first, but he will likely fight us."

"It's obviously Fossil. I don't see the point in hearing out someone who won't do the same for you."

Without another word, the mares flew away and kept as low as they could.

"Where would he be?" asked Avalanche.

"He usually breaks apart trees far from our herd, doesn't he? The only deciduous trees that are still close enough for him to use are always in small groups," said Obsidian.

"We can't search every single patch."

"I know, but we need to hit as many as we can."

The wind knocked their wings around as they fought to keep themselves leveled. They inspected multiple small clusters of trees, but there was no sign of the dragon.

"We can narrow it down by only checking ones where he hasn't already destroyed a tree, I don't recall him ever taking down two from the same place," observed Obsidian.

Avalanche nodded. They continued their flight across their territory. Obsidian had been leading initially, but Avalanche overtook her after some time. She glanced back at her.

"Pick your pace back up," she grumbled.

Obsidian flapped her wings strongly but barely sped up. Avalanche clacked her beak once, she pointed an ear back towards her.

"What? *You* called for me to come out here with you," the young mare said gruffly.

Obsidian shut her eyes and exhaled through her nostrils. "May I confide in you just this once?"

"Fine," she begrudgingly accepted.

Obsidian was hesitant to speak for a few moments, she didn't seem to be looking where she was heading. "Truthfully, I don't want to have to fight him but I know that's bound to happen after all we've seen."

"You were furious after you first met him. Wouldn't you want to rip into him?"

"I was. And I should, I'm not afraid of him."

"Then why?"

"I'm afraid to fail."

Both mares fell silent for a short while. Obsidian continued, "Just as I thought I was starting to feel better, Fossil never left. Whatever his plan is, it's dubious. And if I fail, Sunflower will have to go through the same loss as I did. No matter how disconnected I may have felt these past four-seasons, the herd and my family have always been there in the end. I want to fight for them but I'm scared to lose them."

Avalanche wasn't sure what to say. She didn't feel much of a close bond with her aunt, she wasn't very good at helping others either.

"You won't fail," was all she said. She wished she knew what else to say, but Obsidian probably wasn't expecting a heartfelt response from her.

The two hadn't said a word since. They kept on searching the woods for Fossil. It was late into the night and both mares were growing tired, they had only found a few spots without a broken tree. Obsidian was jolted fully awake by a sharp cracking that came from down within the woods. She and Avalanche staggered in their flight then they froze and hovered above. They looked at each other, both knowing what the only thing that sound could've come from was. *Fossil.*

They darted to where the sound had emerged from. They saw a large figure below, he really was right there. Avalanche flapped away to hide and wait for a signal from Obsidian. Obsidian took a deep, quiet breath. She had to go down there and speak with him. They were lucky enough to actually find him, she couldn't pass up the chance now. The snapping of tree limbs muffled her wings as she fluttered down, the snow chilled the bottom of her talons, her whole body felt like ice. He didn't notice her as he was recoiling from charging head-on into the bare tree. Obsidian took one step forward and gathered her composure.

"Fossil," she began. The dragon whipped his head around, his tail spikes rattled. Pure soundless surprise crossed his face. "What on Veynekan have you been doing?"

He had no answer.

"I told you 'no' moon-cycles ago. You are not welcome here. You could have been putting your persistence and stealth to use solving whatever your kingdom faces," said Obsidian firmly.

Fossil remained speechless, still as the trees he destroyed.

"What are you doing with the branches? Answer me."

"...I *need* his power," he finally murmured.

Obsidian puffed up her neck feathers as she spoke. "We went over this when we met. My son has no powers, he is a normal dragon who happened to be albino. How can you be so dense while at the same time sneaking around as long as you had?"

"But how can you be sure?"

Obsidian stomped a foot. "Stop trying to take me in circles. I won't help you and I will not budge."

Fossil narrowed his dark eyes and lashed his tail. "You will. I am not unfamiliar with using force," he started drawing near. He moved slowly and intimidatingly, lifting his wings gradually. "The Queen cannot stay in power, she will suffer for what she did. I will ignite the branches-"

As fast as lightning itself, a beast shot out from the twisted foliage with a screeching whinny. Obsidian scrambled back. Fossil roared as Avalanche clung onto him and ripped her talons down his neck right into the scars that lined it. He swung out his wings and threw himself around wildly. Avalanche let go and flew off before he could crush her under his side. Obsidian shook off her shock and leapt to her niece's aid. She hooked her beak into his shoulder and jerked away, kicking him with her hind legs as he scrambled to get off his side. His fire crop began to glow with embers.

"Get away!" Obsidian shouted to Avalanche, flying up into the air.

He shot a small blast of fire but the desperate panic caused him to aim poorly, he didn't manage to graze either of them. As Avalanche reached out her claws to strike again, Fossil fled in a weaving path, quickly vanishing into the darkness of the storm, a crimson trail was left along with his footprints. The mares landed, Avalanche raised her hackles, prepared to go after him. Obsidian shook her head.

"Will you at least do something about him now?" Avalanche huffed.

"Yes. From now on Fossil is to be attacked on sight," Obsidian's eyes held anger like Avalanche had not seen before.

CHAPTER 8

New branches stopped being scattered around the mountains the day after Obsidian and Avalanche had confronted Fossil. There were few still left lying around, but they had become so rare that the herd didn't continue to pick them up anymore. Fossil had not been seen recently either. The hippogryphs had spent a whole moon-cycle after that night, searching to no avail. Obsidian and Avalanche remained wary, they wouldn't let go of their suspicions, Avalanche especially. She would still drag out a party into thick snowfalls to hunt down the dragon.

Ben was now four moon-cycles old and the same size as Komodo, he would surely surpass his height in the coming moons. Ben and Obsidian were sprinting down the side of a mountain with a shroud of snow flying up around their feet. They were engaged in a mock battle, bounding around each other and gliding on their wings momentarily as they swiped. He got a few feet ahead of Obsidian and moved beside her, then tried to buck. But his tail blocked the way of his kick, only landing a hit on himself. As he started to stumble, Obsidian reared and tried to stop, she quickly flew over him to prevent their crash. Ben accepted his fall and passively let himself slide down the snowy hill on his side. Obsidian landed a short distance away from where he lay. She came over to him, he stayed down and laughed snortily.

"Are you alright?" his dam asked.

Ben pulled himself up. He nodded and shook snowflakes off of himself.

"I know it's not how you think of yourself, but you can't buck. Your body just isn't built for it."

Ben arched his neck and kept his head lowered, flicking his ears.

"It'll make you a better fighter if you find a way to battle that works for how you move," Obsidian cooed, running her beak along his withers.

"But I don't know how," he said, scooping up snow on his tail spikes. "I thought Fossil hadn't been seen in a while, though."

"He hasn't been, but I have clearer memories of him than you do and I find it hard to believe that he has fully given up. You need to be able to defend yourself and figure out your fire crop too."

Ben sighed. He felt proud when he first blew smoke and he could keep himself warm now, but what use would fire be surrounded by trees? He didn't really feel like he needed to learn more. He rose to Obsidian's side.

"Fossil was the only dragon I've fought and it was only for a few moments, so I, unfortunately, don't have any ideas of how you *could* fight," Obsidian nickered, turning around to walk. "Maybe in the summer, we can fly to the Forest Kingdom and learn a few things from them."

That piqued Ben's curiosity. He knew nothing about how the dragons of Veynekan lived. But he felt confident that he'd still want to stay in the herd despite whatever he may discover. The two made their way towards the valley, the branches of pines swaying gently in the wind. It wasn't far away and they could both see their home at the base of the mountain. Though the sun was out, Ben didn't mind. The sun had been beating down for the past few days so the snow had thinned and was not so glaring to his eyes right now.

"Your dam should be back soon," said Obsidian, looking up at the sky.

They padded down to the edge of the land that dipped into a trench with the frozen river. They flew over and back into the valley. It was a lazy kind of day, only one group of hippogryphs were out at the moment, which Sunflower was on. Their herdmates hung around casually with the slightly warmer weather. Komodo was watching Ben and Obsidian return in the way he'd always raise his tail when he was attentive.

"Hey!" Ben greeted, trotting towards the colt.

"Hello, Komodo," whickered Obsidian.

Komodo pranced towards them on his spindly legs. "Where did you go? I forgot," he admitted.

"I went to teach Ben more fighting, though we're back early," Obsidian told him.

"Ah, I've just been hanging around here, Avalanche wouldn't let me go along with them," Komodo lowered his neck.

"It's for the best for now. I know you want to, but you need more general experience."

"How am I gonna get experience if I barely go?"

"You are welcome to join me and Ben when we practice. But still, you aren't a whole four-season old yet, we're just looking out for your safety."

"I know that," Komodo sighed and joined in their stride beside Ben. "I wonder if they'll actually find something today."

"Would we want them to find traces of Fossil?" asked Ben, nervously glancing at his dam.

"I both do and don't want them to. I don't want him to still be lurking, but if he is, we need to chase him away," answered Obsidian. "For good."

As they reached the clearing around the center of the valley, Komodo was throwing his head, inviting Ben to play. He joined him and the boys ran after each other. Snowy slush splattered with each step. Obsidian watched them sprint around. She looked up at the empty sky and saw six beasts flying together towards the herd. She was ready for their report and unfurled her wings so they would take notice of her. The group steered towards her, all giving a good distance between one another as they prepared to land. Sunflower and Avalanche were at the front of the group. Avalanche seemed to be worked up and in a huff but that wasn't unusual. It made it hard to interpret what their findings may have been, however. Sunflower's expression didn't give her any hints either.

"Anything?" asked Obsidian.

"No," grumbled Avalanche. "It's like he vanished."

Sunflower spoke, "He could've actually left though. He couldn't have stayed airborne forever and would need to hunt and rest, too. There's no way he could cover tracks like that."

"He would want us to think that, wouldn't he? He could be hiding farther from our territory, waiting until the time is right," said Avalanche.

"But is he *that* desperate? To wait around this long for Ben, who isn't even that interested in breathing fire, to gain some weird power he's never shown any signs of having?" questioned Sunflower.

"I can't shake the feeling that he *is* waiting."

Obsidian exhaled through her nostrils. "Let's hope he is nothing but a coward as he was when we attacked him."

She wanted to, but it felt wrong to assume he truly fled. She didn't want to be in fear every day. Despite Fossil's activity going completely silent, she worried that the whole herd wasn't safe.

"Most of Fossil's branches were taken care of, right?" asked Obsidian.

"Yes. I haven't seen one in a while," nodded Sunflower.

Avalanche began to walk away, she had nothing else to add. Sunflower stayed by Obsidian. They watched Ben and Komodo run through the clearing.

"If only we could find him. I wish I had chased him when I found him before," Obsidian flattened her ears.

"It was only you and Avalanche then, wasn't it? I think letting him go was the right call, he could've easily gathered himself and fought back," Sunflower reassured her.

"I know. But I feel like I've made the wrong choices again."

Sunflower leaned onto Obsidian's side, "We'll get him next time. Let's just relax for now."

Life continued to be quiet for the next two moon-cycles. Obsidian, Avalanche, and Sunflower were the only ones who still seemed to worry about Fossil. There were no traces, no scents, no trails. Nothing. They even temporarily expanded the distances they would fly during searches. Still nothing. Any lead on Fossil was a dead end. It wasn't good for any of them to feel like this but Obsidian didn't know what to do to stop it. How many more moon-cycles would go by until this would pass?

Conifer, Char, Swallowtail, and Spruce glided across the sky. The winter winds rushed beneath their wings.

"Is there even going to be anything out here?" asked Spruce.

"We'll see," said Conifer.

Char huffed. "It's just a lot of snow down there."

"Let's just keep looking, deer are usually out and about this time of day," Conifer straightened out her wings.

The woods seemed as if they had gone empty, the only movement they could catch was the rustling branches.

"I hear Fire's wing is getting better, he might be joining hunts again soon," Swallowtail spoke up.

"About time!" nickered Spruce.

"Well, I can't imagine winter is doing him any favors," Conifer joined in.

"We're nearly to the end of it now though. I miss spring," sighed Swallowtail, perking up at the thought of warm weather returning.

"But it does mean we're all going to shed like mad," Char said in a dry tone.

They continued soaring and scanning their territory, it remained so strangely quiet. It felt like they were the only inhabitants left.

"I don't think there's much out here. Should we maybe try the woods more to the east?" advised Swallowtail.

Conifer tilted an ear toward the chestnut mare. "You might be right."

The four mares soared in a semi-circle and headed to the eastern forests. They picked up their pace, there was nothing to catch in this area, so no need to move along leisurely. They were speeding over the mountains. Then suddenly, something startled Spruce, she stopped and hovered in place. Her herdmates frantically flapped their wings to slow down and check on her.

"What's wrong?" asked Conifer.

The young mare's face had panic scrawled across it. "Do you not see the smoke starting to billow?!" she squawked.

Their attention darted to where Spruce was staring in terror. Gray clouds of smoke started to rise from behind the trees on the horizon.

"Forget the hunting party! We need to take a look then immediately report to Obsidian!" Char took charge, rushing to the location of the smoke. The mares bolted after her.

Spruce couldn't keep her wings straight, shaken by the sight and they were now flying straight towards it.

"What do we do?!" whinnied Spruce.

Char didn't even glance back at her, "We'll see how bad it is then go home."

The billows grew taller and extremely quickly, another one roared up from another nearby spot, too far to have spread from the same flames. As they came closer, they could see the hot glow. The pines were swiftly becoming set ablaze, the fire taking advantage of the unusually sunny weather. It was soon obvious that this wasn't a natural forest fire, this was intentional, and the source was alive.

Even Char seemed ridden with horror, "Nevermind, GET AWAY!" she whinnied.

A dark silhouette of a beast exploded through the branches. Piercing, gleaming eyes immediately spotting the hippogryphs. They scattered away but regrouped shortly after, heading towards the valley. They heard the woosh of great wings coming from behind them. They dared to look back and saw him. *Fossil.*

Once thought among the herd as a foolish young dragon, he now seemed utterly terrifying as he began to pursue them, closing the distance between them uncomfortably fast. His fire crop brimmed amber, smoke trailed from his nostrils and mouth. The burning light of the flames revealed his bared fangs in the growing darkness. He spat a stream of fire directly at Conifer. She dodged his attack just barely, the mares scattered again.

"WHAT DO WE DO?!" screamed Spruce.

"Get away from him! Get to the valley!" called Swallowtail from a distance.

Conifer was separated from the others, she spotted Char and tried to move towards her. Fossil's wing beats drew near again but Conifer couldn't see him hiding right in her blindspot. Another blast of fire came tearing after her, one she hadn't been prepared for. Hitting the tip of her right wing, she fell from the sky and into the snow. The singed feathers were put out under the frost. She hurried up back onto her feet and briefly studied the wing. The flight feathers burned off at the ends. She would eventually molt and regrow them, but wouldn't be flying away now. However, she could still run.

Char noticed her and landed by her side, galloping beside her. "Are you okay?" she asked.

"I can't fly right now!" answered Conifer, shaking herself off.

"I'll stay with you."

The mares sprinted together, Conifer undeterred by the pain surging through her wing. Bounding through the clutter of naked underbrush.

Swallowtail, who was followed closely by Spruce, had found them. They matched their speed and soared above them.

"What happened?" shouted Swallowtail from above.

"He got my wing but I can still make it," panted Conifer.

"Should we all stay together on the ground?" Swallowtail looked to her and Char for approval. "I don't think Fossil is still chasing us but that's not a good thing either, he must've gone back to burn the forest again!"

"I'm going to stay beside Conifer, you can join us if you want to. But also," Char looked over to Spruce who had all of her hackles raised, "Spruce."

She was snapped out of her fright, staring down at Char.

"You go ahead and keep flying. Get to Obsidian and alert her now!"

"Y-yes, Char!" squeaked Spruce. Without waiting another moment, she thrust herself higher into the sky and flew out of their sight within moments.

Now that Fossil had returned with an attack to ravage their home in flames, Conifer realized her filly was rightfully on edge and wished she'd listened more closely to her. She wondered what action Obsidian would take.

Spruce soared faster than she ever had before, shocking herself with her own speed. She could see the caves in the mountainside, but that also meant that the fire was too close for comfort to their home. She hoped the dark, overcast sky would let down snow but it didn't look like it. She raced past the edge of the valley and landed recklessly, nearly falling over from the shakiness of her legs. Her wings quivered with fear and fatigue. Her herdmates' heads shot up, they watched her stumble across the field. She huffed with each stride of her gallop. Intrigued hippogryphs lagged behind, more coming along when they saw that she was tearing straight towards Obsidian's cave. Once she reached the cavern, she attempted to stop abruptly but was moving too fast and her legs slipped out from under her. She slid just inches away from the opening, barely keeping herself from falling flat.

Obsidian jolted up, sitting on her hindquarters. Sunflower and Komodo were startled by everyone, too. Spruce panted heavily, she didn't even bother gathering herself. The awakened hippogryphs in the cave stared at her.

"It's burning…" Spruce breathed. "We have to go! We have to do something!"

She was already twisting around, she flapped her wings wildly. The herd outside backed up away from her wings. Obsidian stood up fully.

"What? What's happening? Tell me," asked Obsidian. "Catch your breath!" she continued, Spruce was about to gasp out more exhausted words.

She took in a few heavy breaths and lowered her wings in a neutral position, fear dominated her face. "The forest is burning! Fossil set it on fire! You have to do something!" she shakily whinnied.

Obsidian blinked and lunged out of the cavern. Sunflower woke Ben. Komodo followed his aunt out.

"Wait, you were with Char, Swallowtail, and Conifer too. Where are they?" Obsidian asked.

"Conifer's wing was struck, they're all galloping back now!" Spruce glanced back into the woods behind.

Obsidian's hackles raised. "I need them to return before I make any decisions!" she exclaimed, bolting off towards the trees.

Ben crawled out from the cave with Sunflower, he blinked the drowsiness from his eyes. He was fully awoken when he saw Obsidian running away through the snow, Spruce chasing after her.

"Wait, what's going on?" he asked.

"Fossil has set our forests on fire," whispered Sunflower, though quiet, her voice was bitter.

Ben's head darted around, searching for fire. He couldn't see the fire for himself. *Yet.* Only the smoke that spewed from it. The fear rising in him kept his voice from working.

"Conifer has been injured but she and the rest of our herdmates are almost back. Let's follow!" explained Sunflower, sprinting after her mate.

Ben, Komodo, and the herd followed the pale mare. Other hippogryphs flew away to gather the rest who were in their caves. Ben could see that Obsidian was stopped at the border of the woods, she then reared back with her wings fanned. Conifer, Char, and Swallowtail burst through the foliage, slowing their pace and reuniting.

"How did this happen?" Obsidian demanded to know.

Conifer shook her coat, panting. "Spruce spotted smoke starting to rise. We thought it was only a forest fire so we went to investigate. Fossil rushed towards us and we tried to fly away but he went after me in particular, that's when I got burned. He stopped chasing us after that but he has absolutely not stopped burning the woods."

Looking at her sister it was plain to see, Fossil must've targeted her because she resembled Avalanche so closely. Obsidian saw the herd soaring in. Everyone was here.

Avalanche did not hesitate to speak her mind. "Now is our chance to kill him! He's out there, with the strength of all of us we can end this!" Avalanche growled, flicking her tail, wings raised in an intimidating manner.

Obsidian considered their options. While taking him out now was ideal, it was also dangerous. "That won't go well," she said.

Avalanche's ears flicked. "You gave us the order to attack on sight!" she hissed.

Obsidian stomped her foot, "The most likely outcome of fighting him right now is that he will lead us into flames and we suffocate from smoke or be burned! The other is that we risk our home being set on fire further!" she thundered.

Avalanche did not continue to speak, she only glared.

"Then what do we do?" asked Sunflower, stepping forward.

Obsidian's head drooped, she tried to think of something. "Even if we drag him away from the fire, he can still ignite more trees. Even in an area with very few, he can still burn us."

The herd looked around at each other, their tails swishing uneasily. Fighting Fossil, even with the full force of the herd, was undoubtedly going to leave hippogryphs with severe wounds. Themselves, their territory, and their home were all in jeopardy. But *everyone* going up against him was unrealistic, some were too old, some were too young, inexperienced or just were unable to. But… the dragon had no interest in harming the herd itself. His quarrel was with Obsidian. He wanted Ben. A new plan appeared in Obsidian's mind. One that was most likely to leave her herdmates unharmed. But that plan came with a price, one that would make her heart ache. She didn't want to let the words leave her mouth, but if it meant that everyone else would be safe…

Obsidian looked into Sunflower's eyes, she stared back. Obsidian's did not gleam the fiery amber they always did.

"Sunflower," she said.

"Yes?" Sunflower responded attentively.

"I have to take Ben away from here."

CHAPTER 9

The herd fell silent, frozen in place.

Sunflower stared back at her. Her voice was only a whisper. "What?"

Avalanche stomped forward, not giving Obsidian a moment to respond. "You're going to abandon us *again?*" she growled.

Obsidian shook her head, "No, that's not it. Fossil doesn't care about any of you, he's after Ben. If Ben and I stay here, we'll only continue to put you all in danger."

Avalanche's face seemed to soften.

"I don't want to go!" squeaked Ben.

Obsidian looked at her son with a dreary expression. "I know. But we're not leaving forever, we can return once Fossil is taken care of."

"I have to come with you!" Sunflower whinnied, pushing forward.

Obsidian turned to face her mate, her ears set back in dejection.

"No. I'm sorry. I need you here," she told her, wishing she didn't have to. "The herd will need guidance. They need your wisdom, your intelligence, even your humor. I know you're the perfect mare to fill in my absence."

Sunflower stood as if she were stone. Her gaze was hurt but seemed to shift into understanding.

"Please," breathed Obsidian.

Sunflower closed the distance between the two of them, nuzzling her withers.

"Yes… I can," there was hesitation in her voice.

"Thank you," Obsidian whickered, returning her affection. "I will always return to you."

Komodo had weaseled his way to the front of the crowd. He came up to Ben, disbelief in his eyes.

"How can you...just be *leaving?*" he said to Ben.

"I don't know," Ben whispered, looking at his claws. "I don't want to leave."

"Can't I come?" Komodo pleaded to Obsidian.

She sighed sadly. "I am afraid not. The herd will need young hippogryphs to recover from this fire."

She looked across the treeline where black smoke rose into the air. Crimson spilled over the sky as the flames grew and the sun fell.

"There isn't much time left," stated Obsidian.

The herd shifted around uncomfortably. Sunflower straightened her posture. "What's the plan?" she inquired.

"Get everyone out of the valley, find somewhere to hide. I'm going to lure Fossil away!"

Avalanche jumped into action, beckoning the herd to follow her as she trotted and tossed her head. The hippogryphs began to follow. Sunflower, Komodo, and Conifer waited a moment before going along.

"And one last thing, Avalanche," Obsidian started, catching the mare's attention. "Don't be reckless. Don't go after Fossil when I leave."

She said nothing but Obsidian could see a small, reluctant nod from her niece.

"Where will you go?" Sunflower asked.

"Somewhere in the Forest Kingdom. It's far but the cover of the woods will help us. I think we'll search for the help of other dragons," Obsidian told her.

Conifer took in a sharp breath, brushing her wing against Obsidian. "Stay safe, I know that you'll make it back. We'll be waiting."

The sisters exchanged short mutual grooming before she parted to join the rest of the herd. Komodo lingered.

"Promise me you'll be back?" he asked Ben with hope in his eyes.

"I promise," replied Ben.

"How long will you be gone?"

Obsidian answered, "I'm not sure."

Komodo nodded slowly, he started following his dam but looked back at them, "Goodbye for now…!"

"I'll see you!" Ben called to him. The glimmer of positivity he felt had faded as he watched his family go, not knowing when he would see them again.

"Well," Sunflower began. She glanced up at the smoke coming ever closer. "This is it for now, huh?"

"We'll come home when we can," breathed Obsidian. "I won't show Fossil any more mercy tonight."

"I love you both. Just...whatever you do, come back safe," said Sunflower in a soft, sorrowful whicker.

"We will," affirmed Ben.

Sunflower groomed his scaly withers.

"Goodbye. I love you too," whispered Obsidian.

"So long, I'll wait forever if I have to," nickered Sunflower.

Sunflower began to walk away, she started to trot but her ears remained pointed back at them. Ben and Obsidian watched her catch up to the rest of the herd, who were almost out of the valley but awaited Sunflower.

Obsidian took a deep breath. "Alright. I'm going to drag Fossil away from the forest, I don't want you to help me with this. Fly south from here until you find the dropoff of the mountains, you'll know it when you see it. There's a vast grassland down there with small forests dotted around."

Anxiety spiked Ben's chest at the thought of being separated, but he agreed. "Okay. You'll find me, right?"

"Of course. Wait there for me."

He hesitantly spread his wings. He heard Obsidian shout one last thing to him, "And keep low to the ground!"

He trilled in response, lowering his altitude. Ben couldn't help but stare at the ground, taking in the last view of his home, completely unsure if he'd return. He tried to stay positive, imagining the future when he and Obsidian would be flying back over the mountains. He was going to sprint across the ridge of mountains with Komodo again, he was going to see Avalanche and her party of hippogryphs fly into the valley, Conifer would be soaring through the air again, he was going to hunt with Sunflower and feel her soft down against his scales as he rested between his dams in the nest again. Everyone was going to be okay.

He entered the southern parts of the Redwood Mountains where he had never flown before. Despite his size, he hadn't been ready to join any hunting parties. The land was getting steeper and unfamiliar. It was dim in the twilight as he got farther from the flames, but he saw ahead where it looked as if the whole world disappeared beyond the peaks. As he descended and crossed the wall of mountains, the plains Obsidian spoke of came into view. It was blanketed in snow. When closer, the mounds and rolling hills became more clear. Ben drifted down to hide in the trees while he waited for his dam. It had taken him a while to get here, so perhaps she would come soon.

As Ben flew out of the valley, Obsidian whipped around and galloped through the woods to locate Fossil. The smell of smoke was clear, the flames had spread closer. His scent would be masked by it but she remained determined. She needed to get into the air before it was too late. Opening her wings, the rising heat lifted her into the sky. Though, she needed to stay cautious and refrain from inhaling too much smoke. It was a devastating sight, her territory set ablaze. She searched for the dragon, her anger as ferocious as the fire. In the distance, there he flew. Swooping low to the ground blasting flames at the trees, making little effort to hide himself.

A rush of adrenaline surged through Obsidian as she soared steadfast towards him. Time itself felt like it stopped for an instant as Fossil glanced behind and saw her. After what seemed like no more than a heartbeat, he jerked his body around and rose up, charging Obsidian at full speed. The glow of fire spilled from his jaws. Obsidian sharply turned back around and sped away, flying in crooked paths while ascending and falling randomly. Fossil's wings and legs were smacking into branches but he didn't react or care.

Fossil attempted to get in front of Obsidian and cut her off. He wasn't even bothering with trying to aim at her. She pushed herself through the sky as fast as she could, the wind whipping past her. She just needed to stay ahead until she reached the meadow, it was at the end of her sight. Getting Fossil off her tail didn't seem like it was an option anymore. She didn't know where Ben was hiding, but she knew fighting Fossil was the only way to stop him from reaching her son. If Fossil wanted to get in front of her now, then so be it. Obsidian waited until they were just above the ridge that bordered the plains, she slowed and let the dragon blast ahead of her.

He whipped around, his crop swelled, and he prepared to lunge at her. Obsidian folded her wings, allowing herself to fall. Fossil paused in surprise, and hurriedly plummeted after her. Obsidian flared her wings just before reaching the frost-covered grasses. She turned to see Fossil plunging after her.

"This is the last chance I will give you to leave or I'll kill you!" she warned in a deep, screaming whinny.

"How could you win against me?" Fossil growled, landing with a thump onto his claws.

Obsidian began to circle him, their eyes were locked. "Brute strength is not the key to victory. I will tell you again, your persistence was wasted here. Leave now and return to your kind, use that determination to find the solution to your kingdom. Would they still see you as a hero after this?"

"It's not about being a hero," he snarled, pouncing at Obsidian with outstretched claws.

Obsidian fled from his grasp and managed to kick his shoulder.

"Then what do you want?!" she hissed, turning around immediately and rearing to attack.

She swiped her talons at Fossil, scratching a few scales off as he backed away.

"The Queen must die!" he roared.

Fossil lashed his tail spines at Obsidian, grazing her shoulder enough to draw blood before she could dodge into the air. She dived down and slammed into him, causing him to stagger off his feet. She bit and twisted into his neck, breaking into his muscles. He threw her off, scrambling to his claws. Obsidian tried to land upright but one of her hind legs slipped away from her, she pulled herself back up hastily.

"And you're a selfish enough bastard to destroy someone else's home to do that?" she spat.

"Had you agreed, I would not have," he rumbled.

Obsidian rushed towards him, rearing and viciously raking slits into the webbing of his wing but was smacked in the face by it. She stubbornly clung to him, she twisted her neck down to pierce the soft underside of his belly with the hook of her beak. He jumped back and she wasn't fast enough to avoid being thwacked across the head by his massive palm. She slid backward across the snow. Fossil charged at her again, the mare leaped up and darted to escape his attack. She bucked at him, her aim wobbly as she simultaneously swerved away from his claws.

"In what world would I have *ever* agreed to that damn request?!" she yelled.

Obsidian flew into the air and struck Fossil once more, grabbing onto the back of his neck, digging her talons in deep. She reached and lashed across his eye, his roar echoing off the mountains. Fossil shook around violently as she clawed the same eye again, the dragon flung himself down to the ground on his side. They both grunted, Obsidian made the mistake of unfurling her left wing close enough to Fossil's face, his jaws snapped around the end of it. He yanked and flipped her over his head, she wheezed as the wind was knocked out of her. Even with the pain of her wing and lost breath, she stretched her face to his untouched eye, gouging it with her beak. Fossil screamed in anguish. She was willing to pull it from its socket if she must.

Then she felt heat on her wing and the smell of smoke began to flood her nostrils, it was time to let go. She jumped away but Fossil still had his teeth locked around her wing, she struggled to break free. Fire had risen into his mouth as she could feel her feathers start to burn. She screeched and slashed her talons over his eyes again, stomping on his snout repeatedly. He finally loosened his grip and Obsidian slipped free, black feathers were shredded off between his fangs. Her limb was scorched and bleeding gruesomely. Panicked, she fled into the darkness, leaving Fossil to bleed in the snow. He lay panting shakily, making no effort to chase after.

Small snowflakes started to fall. Obsidian needed to find Ben *now*. She limped around the hills, looking around for forests. She waited until she could no longer see Fossil to call out for Ben.

"BEN!" she shouted.

There was no answer.

She moved into a slow trot. Her injured wing sagged off her side.

"Ben, where are you?!" she called again.

He would be able to stop her wing from bleeding. Though, the only way would be intensely painful.

She spotted movement within the bare woods, like a snow pile itself began to walk. She drew closer.

"Ben?" she asked.

The beast crawled forward. "It's me."

Obsidian was relieved, her head flopped down in exhaustion.

"What happened?!" asked Ben, the fright in her son's eyes was unbearable to see.

"I fought Fossil," she panted. "And I need you to help me. You're not going to like it, but if you don't, I may die."

"What is it?"

"You need to burn my wing," she raised the shredded wing. "It will stop the bleeding."

"Wh- I don't want to hurt you!"

"I know. But I only need you to do this once."

Ben was hesitant, could he even breathe fire well enough? He worried that he wouldn't be able to. His jaw quivered.

"NOW!" she demanded.

Ben jumped and ignited his crop. He didn't enjoy the feeling of building up fire, it didn't hurt but it was like he inhaled an ember. His flames glowed, Obsidian stretched out her wing for him to aim. She shut her eyes. Ben reluctantly exhaled fire onto her wound. She held still as long as she could bear, which wasn't long. She snatched her wing away and screeched in pain, waving it around. She buried it in the freezing snow. She snorted and sighed.

"Thank you," she panted.

"You're welcome, I think," Ben mumbled, feeling guilty even though she had asked him for this.

Obsidian lowered her head again, she looked ready to collapse. "Let's find somewhere to rest, I can't go much farther tonight," she breathed.

CHAPTER 10

Ben and Obsidian traversed deeper into the frozen grasslands. The falling snow had stopped during the night. Obsidian awoke long past dawn. When she opened her eyes, she didn't see Ben beside her. She jolted up instantly, looking around frantically. Her mind was soon put at ease when she soon spotted him sitting over to her left. She stared out into the frost, thankfully for his eyes, it was still overcast. There was a dead hare lying next to him. Obsidian stood up and shook her coat, her wing began to ache and she quickly regretted it. Ben looked over his shoulder.

"Are you feeling better?" he asked.

"My body still hurts," she exhaled.

A soft rumble sounded through his snout in response.

He was looking away, shifting his wings. Obsidian creakily got onto her feet and came over to his side.

"I caught this earlier," he pointed to the animal with his snout and pulled it closer between them.

"Ah, thank you."

He gestured with his tail for her to eat first.

"Are you sure?" asked Obsidian.

He nodded.

She lowered her head and tore through the hare's pelt. Ben gazed out into the distance again, watching closely.

"Where was Fossil?" he asked.

Obsidian lifted her head. "I fought him closer to the foothills and ran away after my wing was shredded. I left him there lying in the snow, I don't know where he may be now."

Ben looked back at her. Now that they were in the light, he inspected his dam's injuries closer.

"You can't fly," he acknowledged sadly.

Obsidian shook her head.

Ben looked south. "How far are the dragons?"

"It would have been only a little over a day to fly there, but to walk… it will take some time."

Ben sighed softly.

"However, Fossil could have gone blind for all I know. I clawed at both of his eyes. So he may not be able to track us so easily," continued Obsidian.

Obsidian continued to eat. Ben's tail tip flicked while his sight was locked onto the horizon where the Forest Kingdom would eventually come into view, nervous about meeting other dragons. Obsidian raised her head and pushed over the rest of the hare toward Ben.

"Here, you have the rest," she insisted.

"But I'm fine," he replied.

"The plains are vast and we need energy if we want to get across. Eat."

Ben accepted and laid down with his catch between his claws.

"If Fossil might not be able to find us, why don't we go home?" his head popped back up.

"I need treatment for my injuries. We don't know how to use herbs or weave bandages like dragons," she explained. "He still has his nose too. But I also wish we could go back now."

Ben slumped back down. Obsidian stood guard until he finished eating.

"Let's not waste any time. I will run as fast as I'm able to right now," she began trotting out from the patch of woods.

Ben followed beside her. The hills rose and fell like miniature mountains, it went on longer than the distance he could see. How vast the continent was only began to hit him.

"You know, this is where I found your egg. Somewhere out here, I caught a glimpse of it in the grass," Obsidian spoke. "We can't see it now, but there's also a lake not far from here."

Ben observed the area around them. He never really thought much about *how* Obsidian had found him, but he didn't care that much about who left his egg there in the first place. The clouds above him showed no signs of clearing, but that would inevitably change. Ideally but unlikely, it would stay gloomy long enough for him to cross. They had tuned out the sound of crunching snow, the rhythm of their canter faded into the background. Obsidian limped in her stride, Ben considered telling her to slow down, but she seemed too determined at the moment. The least he could do was remind her to take breaks with him. He bumped her side with his snout as they ran side by side. She glanced back at him.

"We should rest," he suggested.

His dam whickered and slowed herself down to a walk, then stopped in place. They stood beside each other, panting hard.

"We should at least find some trees," said Obsidian as she began to move forward again.

Ben strolled after her, there were a few birches ahead.

Obsidian spoke again. "You're quieter than usual. Are you alright?"

"It's a lot," Ben exhaled. "It's a lot to take in right now."

"I understand."

Ben leaned his head over. "What's the Forest Kingdom like?"

"Truthfully, I have never actually been there. I've only met forest dragons who were passing by."

"Oh… Well, what do you know?"

"There are definitely forest dragons."

Ben whickered softly.

"But," continued Obsidian. "The trees there are bigger than any you've seen at home. I hear they regrow leaves even before spring."

"What about the dragons?" Ben asked.

"They look like you but with boxier heads. Their scales are brown or green with varying patterns and markings. And as we go towards them, the snow will get a lot thinner."

Ben remembered the initial question he kept forgetting. "How long will it take to run there?"

"Well…" Obsidian began calculating in her mind. "We gallop about half the speed we could fly, but combined with resting and hunting, it could take around a quarter-moon-cycle."

He sighed.

"Though, we don't need to get to the palace. There is a village—similar to a herd, closer to where the prairie and woods meet," she finished.

Obsidian picked her pace back up. Ben sped up to stay beside her.

"We need to keep moving, though. The sooner we get there, the sooner we can go home," she nickered.

They had taken a few breaks during the day, now a pink sunset was painted across the horizon. Obsidian's stride started to look pained, she clearly wanted to reach their destination quickly but Ben worried that she would overwork herself to do so. His own legs were sore and exhausted, too. He slowed to walk without warning, catching Obsidian off guard. She skidded to a halt through the snow, and turned around, stepping toward him.

He waited for her to come a little closer. "Shouldn't we take a break?"

Obsidian stopped a few feet away, she flicked her tail and huffed. "You're right," she said, though Ben knew she didn't actually want to.

"Do we hide in the little forests again?"

"Yes, let's go down there."

She trotted down into the basin between the hills, Ben followed behind. They scanned the area for a safe spot to rest, but there were only small hideaways beneath the thin cover of bushes.

"We're not going to fit there," snorted Obsidian softly.

She turned away from the clump of trees. Looking out into the uneven field, there was another space not far away. They trod over to the more suitable shelter. The trees were taller and more numerous, a few elms were grouped closely and formed a clearing between the roots large enough for the both of them.

"I think this is fine," said Obsidian.

Ben nodded but stayed on his feet.

"Should I try to hunt?" he asked.

Obsidian looked up. "You don't have to unless you want to."

"Well, I think I will."

Ben hurled himself into the air, the gust from his wings shaking the branches. Obsidian watched him go, wanting to soar along with him again. Even when they get to the Forest Kingdom, she'd still have to wait for herself to recover. A feeling of dread nagged at her. A feeling that she would never fly again. When she looked at the state her wing was in, it seemed too plausible, but at the same time, she felt acceptance.

Ben returned in the night with another hare, he was not experienced with hunting large animals. He descended through the trees near her, holding his catch between his jaws. As she read his body language, she saw his ears flick with what seemed like embarrassment.

"You're fine, I don't expect you to bring down a whole buck," she told him.

Ben still pawed at the ground bashfully, he brought the animal over and laid down across from her.

He exhaled. "Momma caught deer a lot, I wish I could bring you one, too."

"We hadn't trained you to hunt like that yet. I appreciate what you have caught very much, Ben. Without you here with me, I would be dead," responded Obsidian, her voice warm.

His eyes were closed but he seemed content. He nosed the hare and scooted himself toward Obsidian to eat with her.

"When we go home, will you teach me to hunt deer?" he asked.

"Of course," whickered Obsidian.

They remained in the small wooded area and slept. When Obsidian woke, she noticed that the sky had cleared. It was still early enough that the sun and snow wouldn't be too bright for Ben. She got onto her feet and yawned, turning her head to where Ben was curled up with his nose tucked under his wing. She pressed his shoulder with her beak. He twitched and lifted his ears, just barely opening his eyes.

"We should start moving again before the sun is high," she whispered.

He groaned softly then slowly sat up, sleepily resting on his hind legs. He yawned, bearing his long fangs. She started to walk away and Ben quickly got off his hindquarters and padded next to her. Ben sighed as they reached the edge of the trees, he had hoped to see the silhouette of the Forest Kingdom in the morning haze.

"What will it look like when we get close?" wondered Ben.

"You'll know. The trees that we'll pass through first are average looking, but the deeper you go into the center, the taller they'll get," said Obsidian, looking up at the horizon.

Neither of them saw gargantuan trees yet, though Ben could see the shape of a few faraway mountains that stood out the most among the rest, it was not where they had come from. Ben thought the trees surrounding the herd were already giant, he couldn't imagine just how big they would be in the kingdom.

The sun was slowly climbing through the sky. The snow became scarce, the grass grew higher freed from the weight of ice. They had each other but their trek through the grasslands was lonely, they had seen few other beasts, filling them with a sense of emptiness. Ben thought Obsidian's gait was looking odd before, but now it was obvious. Running beside her, he prodded her with his snout again.

"You've been running for too long, I can see it in your stride!" he told her. "Will you at least not go faster than a canter?"

Obsidian let out a soft sigh, her breath steamed in the freezing air. Not wanting to worry Ben was a greater concern to her than getting there faster, and she knew he was right. She slowed way down, her soreness and wounds crept in instantly.

"Alright, I'm sorry. I won't try to push myself like that," she panted.

Ben chirped with ease quietly.

He gave more attention to his surroundings again now that they weren't bolting past everything. He could see some large figures out in the distance, there were about a dozen of them. He tried to squint to see them better. His eyes widened.

"Hey! Who are they?" he blurted.

Obsidian gazed over at the animals. "Hm? Those are horses."

"Not hippogryphs?" he asked. "Then why do they look like us?"

"Horses have many of the same features, but no wings, beaks, or talons. Their tails are also hair, not feathers."

"Can we talk to them?"

"No, they'll probably run away. They say that ancient equine beasts spoke to horses, but not anymore."

Ben stared at the herd as he trotted past. One horse lifted its head and watched them until they were far away. The excitement that rose in him swiftly trailed away.

They began sleeping through the day more and traveling at night for Ben's comfort. Tonight, the soft moonlight guided them, stars glittered above. Both could faintly see that the clear sky seemed obstructed down on the horizon by a lumpily-shaped wall. Ben suspected it was only some thick clouds but they never floated away.

"What is that?" he whispered.

Obsidian blinked and twitched her ears, she had been zoned. She looked up and observed the rough line ahead.

"Hm?" her ears perked up. "Oh, those are the forest's foothills! If we can see those, we're about halfway across."

Both of their strides became more energetic, speeding into a canter and continuing south. The way the ground had felt under their feet had changed, there was even less snow and the dirt was hardening as they approached. Ben was growing impatient, anticipation to see the woods beaming greater within him. His legs ached but he didn't want to stop.

Finally, after one more day, they arrived at the edge of the foothills. Rocky terrain sprinkled with grass and snow. Ben tried to stretch his neck high enough to see over the mounds but he was unable.

"Almost there," Obsidian breathed.

She started up the hill, Ben joined her despite his stiff legs. He could've flown above his dam when she cantered and galloped but he didn't want to make her feel alone.

"How will we know how to get to the village?" asked Ben.

"We can probably just ask someone from it, wandering dragons are supposedly common," she nickered.

They climbed up, almost to the top. It wasn't a large hill but their tired muscles made it much more challenging. When his view was no longer obstructed by the ground, he could see their destination. The Forest Kingdom sat just a canterable distance away. The front trees were tall, similarly to the ones at home, but the branches elegantly weaved around each other, creating a sturdy canopy. The roots were large and twined around the leaf-covered surface like snakes. At first, he thought there were more mountains behind it, but no, it was foggy, monstrous trees standing in the deepest parts of the forest. He couldn't believe any tree could grow to that size.

"We're so close," Obsidian panted with relief.

She mustered the strength to continue cantering through the hills. Ben joined her and used his wings to boost himself up the hillsides. They could smell the scent of oaks, maples, sycamores, and all sorts of trees along the wind. As they loped down the last row of foothills, their path was now free of obstacles. They excitedly took their first steps into the Forest Kingdom.

Chapter 11

They finally arrived, neither of them could care about their aching legs right now. The soft ground, the scents, the diffused light through the canopy, it was all so unfamiliar but exciting. Ben stumbled over surface roots but managed to catch himself. The woods became darker the farther they stared in, barely any snow had reached the ground. Obsidian never saw such lush foliage before the winter was fully finished. As the adrenaline wore off, they started to slow their stride and relax, plodding down into a walk as they panted.

"Look for worn trails, or sniff out dragons if you can figure out what they smell like," Obsidian said.

Ben scanned the ground, no paths in sight. "What do they smell like?"

"I'm not exactly sure."

Ben tried sniffing for something that might stand out, but the whole forest overpowered his senses, so much all at once. He was only accustomed to coniferous woods. Obsidian felt aimless, surrounded by unknown plants as strange birds called from all directions. The underbrush rustled as animals scurried away from the visitors. She picked up the scent of deer, fresh too, but was determined to find the village. She didn't like hunting on foot, anyway.

"I'm so tired," groaned Ben.

"I am too. But we'll get there today, just hold on a little longer," Obsidian assured him.

She knew it was close by somewhere, but the forest began to feel like a maze.

Ben quietly started mimicking the call of a mourning dove off in the distance, only half paying attention to where he was going, just following behind Obsidian. His foot suddenly fell into a large groove in the ground worn down by footsteps.

"Whoa!" he chirped.

Obsidian stared left to right along the dip in the land.

"This must be one of their pathways," she said. "But which direction will lead us to the dragons?"

Ben glanced around. He hadn't noticed it until he was standing on the path, but there was a potent, yet faint, scent lingering. Unfortunately, it was old enough that the direction it was heading became unclear.

"What now?" he asked.

"Let's just try this way first. If the scent starts to disappear, we'll turn around," she started down the trail.

"When we get there, do we just ask someone to help?"

"Perhaps. We'll figure it out," she told him. She wasn't sure of much right now.

They followed along the pathway for a while and the scent trail remained consistent. What lay ahead of them was obscured by a small hill. Walking along the bend, Obsidian noticed a figure walking toward them in the shadows farther up. She paused abruptly, Ben halted beside her.

It was not a dragon, the animal also stopped in their tracks. The beast was winged, they flicked their tail with uncertainty.

A feathered tail. Obsidian blinked once in confusion.

They all stared at each other for a few moments.

"Hey," she, the beast, addressed them with a neutral tone.

"Hello?" Obsidian responded. She took a few steps closer.

All three of them were twitching their ears. Neither Ben nor Obsidian knew what this creature was. She started inching toward them, as she came closer, her features were more clear. It was uncanny, her head was equine-like with an upright mane but thick fur covered her neck. She had legs like a hippogryph and there was a single talon on the wrists of both wings. Stepping out of the shade, her coat was hues of blueish silver broken up by a white underbelly and head.

"What *are* you?" Ben's words slipped out.

"I'm half hippogryph, half gryphon. Not common, I know," she answered, not sounding offended.

"Who are you?"

"I could ask the same about you," she nickered. "I'm Flossie."

"I'm Ben."

"Obsidian," the mare replied.

Flossie didn't appear to be a threat to them. She sauntered closer, carrying dandelions in her beak. She was rather short. Her eyes were seafoam green, typically an impossible color for equines.

"You're the first actual hippogryph I've seen," she looked up at Obsidian, then to Ben. "And I told you, now you tell me. What are *you?*"

"We think he's a forest and volcanic dragon hybrid, he just happened to also be albino," Obsidian answered.

Flossie perked up. "Finally, somebody who will understand!"

"Understand what?" Ben took a step back.

"I don't know, being a hybrid, I guess," she picked at the ground with a talon. "What brings you this far out, though?"

"That is a long story. Right now, I'm looking for a healer, we're trying to find the village nearby," said Obsidian.

"Setiir? Well, you're in luck, I'm from there and know just the dragon," Flossie started to trot past them, looking back after a moment. "But you're going the wrong way."

"Is it okay to follow her?" whispered Ben.

"Ah, I suppose," Obsidian breathed.

They followed behind her, Flossie started to canter when they came close enough, but her feet didn't stay on the ground for long. She hopped into the air and flew low to the ground ahead of them.

"Who is this dragon?" inquired Obsidian.

"Hamara, brown and spotty, I live with her. Almost everybody in Setiir knows a thing or two about healing, actually, but she and a few others specialize in it,"

Flossie answered. "I say 'almost everyone' because the one who doesn't know is me."

"Why not?" Ben asked.

"Remembering plants is hard."

The way Flossie flew was different from how a hippogryph would, her wings were broader too. She was flying a few feet above Obsidian's shoulder height, making staying in the air this low look easy.

"Are you from the mountains?" asked Flossie suddenly.

"Yes. We had to run all the way here. I'm very tired," sighed Obsidian, lowering her head.

"Are you from there too?" she turned an ear back towards Ben.

"Yeah," Ben panted as he ran. "Are you?"

"Maybe, but I didn't hatch there."

"But aren't you part hippogryph?"

"My egg might've been laid there, but I've never set foot on any mountain."

Ben blinked. "How'd you get here?"

"Hamara was given my egg, I don't know who handed me over but who cares?"

He felt a familiarity with her words, "My dam found my egg. I don't care who left me there either."

There were only a few moments of silence before Ben asked, "How big is Setiir?"

"Decently sized, lots of dragons like to live there because it's closer to places outside the kingdom. Nobody likes flying through the woods alone for half the day just to get anywhere," she told him, "Except Hamara, maybe."

"Did Hamara hatch you? Why do you call her by name?"

"I dunno, she doesn't really mind."

"What's she like?" Obsidian rejoined, her voice questioning.

Flossie gestured with her talons. "Social skills are so-so, but she can sure treat a wound!"

"Sounds charming," Obsidian nickered tiredly.

"How do you track anything here? There are so many smells!" Ben spoke again.

"Not sure! I can't actually smell very well," she admitted. "I got the short end of the stick with my gryphon half."

A few moments later, Flossie lifted her ears to listen ahead. "We're almost to Setiir," she realized.

Ben tried to peer farther up the path. The trees were stretching taller than before and he couldn't see the hidden village but noticed the crabapple trees lining the trail ahead along each side.

"Did those trees grow there naturally?" he studied the oddly specific placement of the trees.

"No, they got planted there by dragons," explained Flossie.

"Oh!"

They began to see flashes of movement through the gaps in the oaks barrier, their bodies were the colors of the woods, melting into the environment. Flossie landed and hit the ground trotting. Ben and Obsidian slowed to match her stride. An archway opening the wall was formed by branches that had been manually weaved into the shape.

"We're here!" announced Flossie.

They passed through the entrance. The trees that cast deep shadows grew high towards the sky, rivaling the height of the redwoods that stood in the mountains. A few were large enough to house dragons within carved-out cavities, most had a burrow dug beneath the roots. Forest dragons were plentiful, their green and brown scales filled the village. Ben noticed that they did look a lot like his own reflection. He and Obsidian heard rustling leaves and wings flapping from above. They lifted their heads and saw platforms with giant nests cradled by branches, occupied by more dragons. It wasn't long until the residents of the village spotted the two travelers, then they watched and sniffed curiously.

Ben felt himself shrinking back as they walked through. "Why are they looking at us?" he whispered.

"It's probably your scales, and they've only ever seen half a hippogryph. You've gotta admit, you're an interesting pair to see," answered Flossie.

Ben still kept his wings folded tight against his body.

Obsidian glanced around. "Where is Hamara now?"

"That's our den under there," Flossie directed them to one of the trees farthest from the rest.

She jauntily padded down into the tunnel. Ben looked over the edge into the burrow.

"We have visitors!" called Flossie from within.

An older, raspy voice replied. "Why?"

"Why do you think?"

Flossie appeared back at the opening. "Come in," she beckoned them.

Ben went down and was followed by Obsidian. It was larger inside than they anticipated. A couple of thick roots of the tree above poked down from the ceiling into the floor like columns. Three nests were placed around, one didn't look frequently used, the two at the back contrasted each other in size. The smaller one had bones stuck around it like decoration.

Bundles of drying plants were organized and hung neatly from roots. Lying on the floor was a brown, nearly olive green, dappled forest dragon with a lighter underbelly. A necklace hung around her neck with a small satchel attached. Her jaded green eyes met theirs, an old burn mark covered her nose.

"This is Hamara," Flossie told them, bounding over to the dragon and then looking back at Ben and Obsidian. "I'll let you tell her what you need."

Obsidian flicked her tail as she stepped forward. "I am Obsidian. My son and I ran across the grasslands all the way from the Redwood Mountains. I fought a volcanic dragon right before we started our journey and I need my wounds treated."

Hamara lazily walked over and wasted no time to inspect Obsidian's injuries. Her neck craned around, lifting the mare's fur and feathers with a long claw when she needed a better view. Obsidian stood still with her ears halfway back.

"Nothing's infected, surprisingly," said Hamara. "What about the hatchling?"

"He's fine," Obsidian replied.

Hamara eyed Ben for a moment, checking regardless before walking off back to where she was sitting.

"Just some time needed to heal, but I can make something to help the process," Hamara shrugged with the wrists of her wings.

Obsidian twitched an ear, the dragon hadn't spent much time assessing her wounds.

Hamara looked around. "Speaking of which… Flossie."

Flossie's head popped up.

"I thought you were bringing back plants that I needed for this exact kind of reason," she continued.

"I did!" replied Flossie.

"But where is it?"

"Right there," Flossie aimed her beak where she had left the flowers she was carrying.

Hamara turned her neck and stared down at the yellow flowers sitting next to her root shelves.

"Flossie," she sighed. "I asked for marigolds. These are dandelions."

"Listen! I don't even know the difference between a crow and a raven," squawked Flossie. "What's wrong with dandelions, anyway? I thought you used those too."

"They are not what I asked for."

"It's still cold though, can I even find marigolds yet?"

"Maybe, I was hoping there would be some blooming early."

Flossie sighed. Ben and Obsidian still stood at the entrance awkwardly. Hamara glanced toward them for a moment.

"Lie down in that nest for now," she said, going right back to sorting her plants.

The two slowly moved over to the empty nest, laying down in the forest dragon-sized bedding. Hamara gently picked out herbs and gathered them together in her palm, using her wings in place of her front legs. Flossie fluttered off toward the smaller nest. Obsidian let her injured wing rest unfurled. She quickly let her exhaustion put her to sleep.

Finally, no more traveling. For now, they could just relax. Obsidian was in a shallow sleep with her ears kept active. She flinched awake when water trickled onto her from a small piece of wood carved into a bowl that Hamara held, the dragon cleaned around the wound with the droplets. It made it sting again but she drew in a breath and bared it. After she finished, Hamara smeared something made with the herbs onto the mare's injuries.

"There is nothing more I can do for that wing. It doesn't look like you'll be able to fly again," Hamara's tone was flat.

Obsidian raised her head. "We can't be sure of that, it has only had a few days to heal so far," she said defensively

"If anybody would know, it's me," Hamara rumbled quietly and turned away after she finished.

Obsidian felt annoyed that the dragon simply walked away to end the conversation, but she chose not to re-engage. She just wanted to sleep.

CHAPTER 12

The forest was bathed in gloomy light at the crack of dawn, songs of birds were already filling the air. Ben lay next to Obsidian with his eyes shut but still awake. He could hear faint shuffling from the corner of the den. He tried to ignore it and keep sleeping but combined with the birds, it was difficult to fall back asleep. Though he had been sleeping since daytime yesterday, he didn't feel like getting up. The sound of something brushing against the ground continued.

Ben opened his eyes slightly, Hamara's silhouette sat surrounded by the roots she kept herbs on and was the source of the noise, her tail sweeping from one side to the other. Ben blinked. Hamara was staring down at her plants intently, doing the same thing she had been when they got here and picking at the bundles with unbreaking focus. She huffed softly. Ben pushed himself upright to lay on his chest and continued to watch her work.

"What are you doing?" whispered Ben.

Hamara froze for a moment.

"I forgot I had guests," she said, continuing to pick through her supplies. "I am sorting my herbs."

"This early?"

"I haven't actually slept yet, perhaps I'll do that soon."

Ben flicked his ears. "How have you been sorting them that long?"

"I removed ones that were too withered and no use, and I had gotten up to gather new ones during the night."

"Are they all for healing?"

"Of course."

Hamara went silent again, remaining hunched over. Ben's eyes flicked over to the sky through the tunnel, a bird fluttered by. The wistful coo of a dove sounded outside.

"Are you *truly* not hurt? I find it hard to believe after your journey," Hamara spoke again.

Ben turned his attention back to her, shaking his head.

"Hmm." Her tail swept across the dirt again. "But I must ask, how did you end up out there? A dragon in the Redwood Mountains?"

"I don't know, I just hatched there," Ben's ears bent back anxiously.

Hamara finally looked at his face, away from her herbs. "I don't think I ever caught your name."

"...I'm Ben."

"I've never seen a dragon have so many equine mannerisms, it's interesting," Hamara said tilting her head. "Nice to officially meet you, I suppose."

Ben shook his neck awkwardly, unsure what to make of her. He thought she was equally interesting, but mostly strange. He didn't pester her further, she wasn't much like how he had expected a healer to be. Ben turned and laid his head on the ground, peering up at the leaves high above. Flossie had rushed them to their den so quickly, Ben wanted to explore Setiir, but thinking of going out alone made him feel shy. He silently waited for Obsidian to wake up.

Some time had passed and it was growing brighter outside, Hamara had gotten up and left the burrow a while ago. Ben opened his eyes and rolled onto his side, his back against Obsidian. He picked at the dirt with a claw, contemplating the idea of trying to wake her. He knew he would feel guilty if he purposely tried to...but he was itching to look around. Not to mention lonely. He gently poked Obsidian's shoulder with his nose. He lowered his ears back for a moment, she didn't react. Ben laid his head down and inched closer, nudging her again. She stirred, then relaxed. In the back of the room, the sound of nesting rustled as Flossie rose off her side and preened.

Ben stretched his neck up, Flossie nipped at her feathers a while longer before noticing him. Ben accidentally made eye contact, which he never liked, and flinched back. Flossie shook her pelt as she started to walk over, and stretched in a feline-like way.

"Good morning!" she cooed. "Did you see when Hamara went out?"

Obsidian's ears twitched back at the volume of her voice.

"I think she left earlier," Ben told her. "She said she hadn't slept yet either."

"When did you wake up?"

"A little while ago, but I was up for a moment earlier."

Flossie continued to groom her feathers. Ben's gaze drifted back to the entrance of the den.

"I'm bored…" he sighed.

He glanced at Obsidian, then to Flossie as she paused her preening again.

"You'll find something to do outside, no one said you couldn't go out," she said.

Ben backed down at the idea, pulling his tail closer. He turned to his dam again, snorting softly and flopping his head down next to her. He gave her another prod on the wing.

Obsidian twitched and slowly started pulling herself together. "Alright."

Both she and Ben lifted their heads.

"What is it?" asked Obsidian.

Ben sat up. "We never got to look around the village," he whispered.

Obsidian exhaled, "Just give me a moment."

She slowly got onto her feet, her injured wing was held against her ribs slackly.

Flossie's ears were perked fully forward. "Are you sure you should walk around?"

"I'm fine to walk, you needn't worry about me," Obsidian told her, although her sore stride was plain to see.

"Well...let's just hope Hamara doesn't show up or she'll flip."

Obsidian began climbing to the surface, Ben padded after her. They emerged from the tunnel followed by Flossie who invited herself along.

Obsidian flicked her eyes to Ben. "Where to?"

Ben glanced around Setiir. "Uh."

Forest dragons crossed their view, some still glanced at Ben and Obsidian but kept moving. He wasn't sure where or what anything was here, too overwhelming.

"I'm not sure," he said, pointing his ears to the sides.

"Just poke around wherever looks interesting," Flossie ducked under his tail and came around on his side opposite of Obsidian. "Though there isn't much within Setiir unless you're looking for a chat."

Flossie began trotting down a pathway through the village, the two joined her. There was a trio of dragons sitting near each other and speaking, but Ben couldn't hear their conversation. The three dragons wore matching wooden pendants with a tree carved into the center. Flossie continued on her way, she would flash the dragons a look with perked ears. She didn't mind them and they didn't look opposed to the newcomers either, but their eyes all on them made Ben feel uncomfortable in his own scales.

"Good morning, Flossie. Seems like Hamara's still a beacon for unusual beasts!" an emerald dragon greeted her as he passed by.

"I swear it's her hidden talent!" she nickered.

The forest dragon made a chuffing sound in return as he proceeded.

Ben caught himself staring as the other dragon left, he was so tall! He wondered if he would be that size when he was an adult.

To their left was the beating of wings and flashes of umber scales through the branches. A heavy thud sounded as a dragon landed, carrying an entire doe in their jaws. They trod across the clearing and two young hatchlings bounded up excitedly from a den. Large shadows moved over Ben and Obsidian, two smaller dragons leapt across the wobbling bridges set up in the branches above.

Flossie caught them eyeing the higher level of the village. "You can go up there if you want."

Ben looked at her, then Obsidian.

"If you want to, go ahead. I can wait down here," Obsidian urged him.

"Are you sure?"

"I won't feel left out. I'm still tired."

She tossed her head forward, giving him the approval to go. Ben trilled to his dam, stepping aside to spread his wings and spring into the air. His wings felt a bit stiff, he gathered himself and flapped to hover just inches above the layer of wood before landing softly. Flossie came up across from him. Ben gazed at his surroundings, he could feel cold air radiating off of the snow on top of the canopy. The platforms were much larger than they looked from the ground. The sprawling branches looked like a tangled forest of its own. He saw the boards and the narrow paths loosely connecting them, supported by vines that had been twisted together into ropes.

"Mostly young dragons come up here, a lot of adults are too big," Flossie told him. "It makes a good spot to watch over the woods, too."

Ben stared along the suspended bridges made of tree trunks, he reached out to place a foot on it. As he pressed weight onto it, it tilted and swayed, he snatched his leg back. Not feeling confident about it, he crouched and readied his haunches, springing over to the next tree. The impact of his landing made the branches shiver. Flossie trotted over to him across the bridge, it teetered as she crossed but she barely reacted.

"I know it's freaky but it won't fall, you just keep moving," Flossie said, passing him to peer over the edge. "You're checking out my home, so may I ask what the mountains are like?"

"Not as warm as this, it's so nice here compared to my valley," he started.

"You should see it in the summer. I personally don't love the warmth like everyone else here," sighed Flossie. "The bugs suck, and my coat is naturally thick."

"I can't remember anything about summer in the mountains."

"Really? Wait, how old are you?"

"Six moon-cycles."

"I thought you were at least a four-season old!" she said, surprised. "You're not much shorter than your dam."

He whickered in reply.

"So, how does your herd function?" she asked.

"Uh," Ben thought for a moment, "We all live in a valley, most of my herdmates are mares. I didn't get to go on any before we had to come here but they would go together to hunt, and watch over our territory. We were pretty isolated, bears, wolves, boars, and cougars are most of our threats. I've never met any other hippogryph herds."

Flossie nodded as she listened. "It's a little similar here except we don't have to guard the territory since we're a part of the kingdom. We usually all hunt for ourselves and our own families, and there are three of the Queen's guards, but they live here."

She pointed to where the dragons wearing the pendants sat.

"Though, they're more like hunters than guards. Hunting for those who can't themselves. Speaking of which…" she paused.

Two of the dragons looked around and back to each other, the third started to move ahead. The others got onto their feet and started toward the archway.

"There they go," observed Flossie.

"Who is the Queen?" Ben asked.

"Queen Reka. I've never met her and I don't know much about her," she said. She lowered her voice. "Some say there's a rumor that she's looking for something secretly through her guards in the villages, but I'm not sure how true that is."

"What kind of thing?" He questioned.

"I dunno. But don't let me fill your head with the local gossip, do you want to see anything else up here?" she asked.

Ben looked back at the treetops. There was a fork in the paths beside them, one leading to a branch above the canopy, thick enough to climb. He padded over, his eyes following up the limb.

"What's up there?" he asked.

Flossie came up from behind him. "It's sort of a lookout spot."

Ben gingerly lifted a front foot to cling onto the bark. The sudden beating of wings startled him as Flossie boosted herself up. He began to climb, there were grooves from previous claws that he wedged his own into. He stretched his neck up through the roof, squinting then opening his eyes but quickly shutting them again as the sun shone harshly. He ducked back under the leaves. Flossie peeked down at him.

"Can you see the mountains north of here?" he asked from below.

Flossie gazed out, fixated on the pale blue horizon.

"No. But I can see mountains to the east somewhat," she answered.

"Oh. I just wanted to know if you could see my home."

"Why did you hide?"

"The sun and snow. It's too bright and I've always had problems with it."

"Ah," she nickered, and hopped back down onto the platform, her hind legs almost looked like they wanted to buckle when she landed.

Ben carefully slid down.

"I want to go down now," he murmured.

They hadn't been up there long, but Ben felt bad leaving Obsidian alone on the ground. He and Flossie glided back toward the forest floor. Obsidian whickered to her son, getting onto her feet and staggering slightly.

"What did you see up there?" she asked.

"There was a wobbly tree bridge and a lookout, but I couldn't see anything since it's sunny above the forest," Ben told her. "We saw three of the Queen's dragons go out to hunt, too."

"Was that who they were?"

Flossie began to explain, "Yeah, they bring back food for those who can't hunt for themselves."

Before any of them could say another word, a gruff shout cut through the air. "Hey!"

Ben, Obsidian, and Flossie's attention whipped over to the sound. Hamara was plodding towards them with marigolds tucked into the pouch around her neck.

"What are you doing out of my den?!" she said, staring down Obsidian.

The dragons nearby seemed like they wanted to walk away and stay out of this.

"Standing," Obsidian replied simply.

"You shouldn't be, I've had many moon-cycles to learn that equine beasts' bodies are no masters of healing themselves," she rumbled.

Obsidian snorted with her ears laid back but followed Hamara's demands. She limped back to the dragon's burrow. Flossie and Ben came along but he followed farther behind, slinking nervously. As they went back down into the den, Hamara returned to her herbs and plucked the plants from her satchel. Obsidian laid in the nest. Hamara got up and moved toward Obsidian, using a wing in place of a leg as she held herbs in her palm.

Flossie's tail flicked. Ben looked at his dam and crept over, kneeling and resting on his elbows to meet his dam's face.

"I want to hunt. Can I?" he asked.

"You don't have to ask for my permission," whickered Obsidian.

Ben nodded once and climbed back up the slope. Flossie glanced around and went after him, whether because she wanted to help him or didn't want to deal with an agitated Hamara. Obsidian exhaled and lay still. She would just try to fall back asleep for the time being.

CHAPTER 13

Obsidian lay in her nest, eyes closed yet restless. A few days had passed since she and Ben had come to Setiir. Though the exhaustion of their trek had faded, soreness persisted in her wing and joints. She glanced back at her injured wing, unfurled at her side. It didn't look any better. She wanted to believe she was going to make a full recovery but the claws of reality refused to unhook themselves. Hamara was lying down near where she kept her herbs, Obsidian wasn't sure if she was awake or finally fell asleep. Ben had gone out into the woods a short while ago, accompanied by Flossie. Obsidian was glad that they quickly became friends, she'd rather him have fun than be bored sitting in a nest.

Obsidian drew in a breath. Setiir felt as lonely as the plains. Hamara rarely spoke. She was without her herdmates, her sister, her nephew, and her mate. Obsidian hadn't socialized with the dragons much and she didn't know where to begin. Ben probably hadn't gotten far yet, so she began considering getting out of the burrow for a while and finding them. Achily, Obsidian got onto her feet. For a moment, she wanted to lie back down and not bother, but she knew that Sunflower would've told her 'it wouldn't make her feel better in the long run.' Obsidian knew that was true.

Hamara seemed to be sleeping, she didn't notice as the mare stood. Obsidian plodded up to the surface, making her way through the village and out the archway. The forest was a whirlwind of scents but, always able to distinguish her son's trail, she veered left and followed it through the underbrush. The ground was cluttered with all sorts of plants this far into the woods, she made her way through saplings and low-growing plants, burrs clung to her fetlocks. As she wove around trees, she noticed the weather had been getting warmer much quicker than it did at home.

Ben's scent was getting stronger but now stretched across a linear path through the oaks, he had been running. Obsidian's anxiety never hesitated to act up, she quickened her pace, worried that something had happened. Fossil *did* still have his own sense of smell. She picked up another trail, one very near to Ben's. It was not Flossie's. She sped into a canter, she knew Ben was close and she smelled fresh blood. Her heart raced. She leaped over a log in her path that she soon regretted, failing to catch herself with her aching legs.

She landed and scrambled to her feet. Looking up, she, thankfully, saw Ben and Flossie standing unharmed, but alarmed to see her suddenly burst through the foliage.

"Mom!" exclaimed Ben in surprise, muffled by the animal he held in his jaws.

He was carrying a red deer, a young one.

"Ben...!" she panted, "I'm so proud of you!"

He responded with his snorty whicker but was still obviously perplexed. Flossie looked up at her.

"Are you alright?" she asked. "Why were you charging through the woods?"

Obsidian shook her coat, twigs sprinkling off. "I got up to follow you, then I noticed you had started running, then blood."

"I'm okay," Ben assured her.

"I see now. Your first deer caught, and in unfamiliar territory no less."

Ben trilled softly, beaming with pride.

"I know you just got here, but we should bring this deer back now," said Flossie.

Obsidian nodded. Flossie took flight, Ben clamped his jaws tightly and cantered after her. His dam watched them bound away.

"You go ahead," she called. "I shouldn't be running."

Ben glanced back and slowed himself. Obsidian followed at a distance, trotting along. Flossie adjusted her speed to remain near Ben, she was speaking to him but Obsidian's footsteps drowned out her voice. Then she began to worry again. Would Ben be happier living here? Where the temperatures rose sooner and the canopy hides the sun? He was half forest dragon, after all. If that was what he wanted then...she wouldn't stop him.

They soon returned to Setiir, taking the deer near Hamara's den. The beasts of the village would eat outside of their burrows and hollows to keep their homes clean. Ben set down the deer then didn't proceed, just staring at it.

"What is it?" Obsidian asked.

"I was waiting for you," he replied.

"Oh, but you don't have to. I've been one of the beasts having a share from the Queen's hunters."

Ben turned his head down, his eyes shone with disappointment. "But we would always share prey at home and we haven't lately… I don't need the whole deer."

"Well, that's true. If you want me to join you, I will," nickered Obsidian, as got down beside him.

Ben pulled the doe closer between them. He turned his eyes to Flossie.

"You can join too," he offered.

"Oh, thanks!" She chirped, finishing up grooming her front leg.

She trotted over in a few choppy strides.

The three beasts tore at the deer. After a few moments, Flossie raised her head to speak.

"From the way you spoke about Ben's catch, I'm assuming you have lots of deer in the mountains too?" she asked.

Obsidian responded, "Deer and elk are our main prey."

"It's about the same here. But once I saw the hunters bring back a bear," she finished.

Ben and Obsidian looked at her in surprise.

"Hamara brought in a wolf once before," Flossie found their shock amusing, but her words were honest.

"Both of those animals are threats at my home," said Ben. "But I've never actually seen one myself."

"If dragons here don't hunt other large predators from time to time, the deer would plummet fast.

"Understandable," Obsidian spoke. "We're rather secluded in my herd so we don't have to worry about others hunting."

Flossie nodded and went back to ripping a shred off the animal.

After they finished, Ben rose to his feet inspecting the bones in front of him. Normally Hamara would've just eaten the bones with her share, but she was still sleeping.

"What should I do with these?" he asked Flossie.

"Hmm, take them somewhere outside the bramble wall, other animals will do the rest," she gestured to it with her wing. "But I'd like to keep that skull and clean it."

As Ben took a few trips to scoop up the rest of the skeleton, Flossie took the deer skull and carried it to the top of Hamara's tree, nestling it between the branches for later. Ben had finished clearing the area and they were about to head back into the den. Just then, Hamara emerged from beneath, causing everyone to back up. She said nothing as she passed them.

Ben flicked his tail and watched her take flight. "Where's she going?"

"Probably to hunt," Flossie answered.

They proceeded down. Obsidian kneeled back into the nest, Ben wrapped around her side closely. Flossie moved to the far end, tidying up her nest. Obsidian took a deep breath and exhaled, closing her eyes. Though she still felt bored and restless, the company of her son made it more bearable.

A blanket of clouds hung above the woods, filling it with dense shadows. Ben and Obsidian rested against the base of Hamara's tree, a cool breeze rustled the branches. They sat in silence and Obsidian was just glad to be outside. Hamara had brought Flossie along with her for some scavenging, which they returned from and were now sorting their findings inside the burrow. Ben and Obsidian heard the beat of a trot coming up from behind them. Flossie climbed out with withered plants in her mouth, she sprung and flapped over the barrier, disappearing for a moment beyond it. She quickly returned with an empty beak, landing back inside the village, and stepped closer to the two.

"Are you finished?" asked Obsidian.

"*I* am, in there anyway," Flossie sighed. "Hamara's still doing her thing and wants me to go gather some more."

She started to turn away but made a semicircle back to them.

"Do you wanna come?"

Ben looked like he was going to speak but held himself back, he glanced and flicked an ear at Obsidian for approval.

"Why are you asking permission?" she looked at him with a softened gaze.

"I thought you'd want to spend some more time together," Ben replied, shifting his claws.

"If you want to go, I don't mind. I suppose I'll join you."

Ben and Obsidian got onto their feet.

"The more the merrier," chirped Flossie, then she glided over to the archway and waited for them.

"What kind of herbs are you looking for?" asked Ben after they caught up with her.

Flossie lifted a front foot and showed them the underside, revealing a dry plant clinging to her fur. "These, but not dead."

It was a little hard to make out, but it looked like it once had tiny magenta flowers and ridged leaves.

Obsidian tilted her head at the ambiguous stem, "We'll try to keep an eye out."

They trod out of the village boundaries. Flossie took short bursts of flight along the trail rather than maintaining a steady trot.

"Do you know where it grows?" Ben wondered.

"Hamara told me usually under small overhanging things," responded Flossie, as she glanced around the woods.

Ben nodded and searched too. They carried on down the path for a while longer. The forest felt quieter today. Flossie suddenly started leaving the trail. She landed and turned, trudging through the flat leaves of the low foliage.

"We probably won't find them unless we go out of our way," she said, looking back. "But I know of a place where there's a dip in the land with an uprooted tree."

Ben and Obsidian took high steps as they followed, the underbrush was particularly thick here. The ground was beginning to curve downhill, the land at the bottom of the slope was more level. An umber mass blocked a large portion of their view ahead. As they approached, Ben realized this was where Flossie was going to check first. The fallen tree was the same size as all the other towering oaks. The roots were a snarled mat, like claws cupping over the pit that it left behind. Flossie dived down and disappeared beneath it where other plants were taking over at the bottom and climbing the sides, she searched through the clusters intently. Ben and Obsidian tried to spot anything that looked like the flower

Flossie showed them, but nothing caught their eye, all they saw were the sprigs of budding plants.

"Hmm," hummed Flossie, she poked around low to the ground with her beak. "I don't think there's any here."

She leapt out of the cavity, the footing of one of her hind legs slipped away but she quickly recovered.

"We can keep looking, there's plenty of shadier places," she started moving again.

They pursued close behind her. Flossie was trotting with this time, Ben couldn't help but notice how her stride looked inconsistent. In fact, this was one of the rare times where Flossie didn't take flight when moving faster than a walk.

"Why do you trot like that?" he asked without thinking.

Her ear flicked and she glanced back at him, "My hind legs have just been like that since I hatched. It's probably because I'm a *very* uncommon hybrid."

Obsidian tilted an ear in Ben's direction. Even though Flossie didn't appear to mind the question, he should've phrased it a little differently.

"Does walking hurt you?" he asked.

"It will, I fly around a lot so it won't, but sometimes I need a break from flying too," Flossie responded. "I can't really run though."

Ben gave her an understanding nod.

The overall appearance of this part of the forest was different from Setiir, not drastically, but noticeable enough. It felt much more untamed as they strayed from the trail, which was to be expected, the underbrush grew wilder and numerous saplings crowded between the full-size trees. Flossie soon took flight again, all of them quickening their pace. Obsidian kept her head forward but her ears and eyes were focused on the forest as it passed them by.

"The woods seem silent today," remarked Obsidian.

Flossie looked back and then around at the trees. "Really? Maybe I'm just too focused to realize."

"I may not get out as much as you two, but the lack of bird calls feels out of place," Obsidian's gaze trailed off to the treetops. "The weather seems nice though."

"Guess it's a lazy day," nickered Flossie.

As they traversed farther in search of the flowers, the emptiness hanging over them grew stronger. There didn't even seem to be any fresh scent trails from other dragons, they hadn't even wandered that far from Setiir. Still, they went seeking out the plants.

"How hard is it to find a little flower?" grumbled Flossie with her head inside a hollow tree trunk.

"Why couldn't Hamara just have told you where she found it before?" asked Obsidian.

"Good question, she can be so needlessly vague. Like, you do want these herbs, right?" Flossie backed away from it. "I'll give a couple more places a shot and if we don't find anything, oh well I guess."

Obsidian came trotting up quicker. "Well, let's get it over with."

After checking two other places, a hollow and under a small ledge, neither of which were successful, they paused a moment.

Flossie huffed. "Guess we're coming back empty clawed 'cause I can't find anything."

Obsidian softly nickered in relief. Ben nodded slowly, he wasn't even the one assigned with the task but he felt slightly ashamed about bringing back nothing. But, perhaps now they could race through the trees as they returned to the village.

"Can we run back?" Ben requested. "I'm bored."

Flossie leaped into the air without hesitation. "Yeah!"

She sped off. Ben reared and swiftly broke into a canter, followed by his dam. Leaves rustled and the wind whistled past their ears, they chased Flossie as she wove through the trees. Obsidian took her strides gingerly from the lingering soreness. Ben loved being able to dash across the land without worrying about the sun hindering his vision. He quickly bounded around huge oak trunks that he had naturally learned to do by watching other dragons.

The hill where the trail sat atop was in their sight now. Ahead, Flossie tilted her wings to descend and she vanished behind a wide tree. Ben and Obsidian continued, slowing to a trot. Ben peered around the base of the oak, Flossie stood past it a few feet away, frozen in her stance. He stared, then drew closer. Flossie suddenly pointed her tail down, signaling them to stay quiet. Her ears shifted, Obsidian wanted to ask what she was listening to but kept silent. When Flossie's ears settled, both Ben and Obsidian took another few steps closer.

"What is it?" whispered Obsidian.

Flossie took a moment to answer. "I thought I heard wings."

She tried searching for the noise again, but the woods did not respond. Even the birds didn't dare to chirp.

"Maybe somebody just flew by. But it sounded so close above me…" Flossie breathed.

Ben's ears flicked with uncertainty. Flossie slowly crept toward the hill again, as she started up the slope, a scent was carried down to Ben and Obsidian on the breeze. One that was familiar to Obsidian, one that sent a shiver down her spine. She stamped her talons onto the dry leaves.

"Don't go up there," she refrained from shouting but her tone was riddled with urgency.

Both Flossie and Ben froze.

"Why?" Ben turned to ask.

Their attention whipped to the mound where the snapping of branches and leaves rustling arose as a beast came hurtling towards them. The three instantly scattered, Ben followed Obsidian but Flossie ran off in another direction, Obsidian directed him to follow and regroup with Flossie. The attacker skidded to a halt, tearing into the land with his claws. A beast of dark scales and black stripes, bronze eyes stared at them ferociously. Fossil had found them.

"Run!" Obsidian shouted to Flossie.

They took off, fleeing through the woods, Fossil was quickly on their trail. Flossie leaped into the air, Ben stuck close to his dam's side. Obsidian would have loved to turn around and rip Fossil to pieces again, but being flightless and in pain, it would be slanted in his favor. Especially surrounded by trees that could easily catch fire. And that's when she realized something. When she had fought him she had gored his face, she thought she had blinded him. Upon glancing back, he had no visible wounds. But that didn't make any sense, his injuries couldn't have healed fully already.

"We need to get back to Setiir!" exclaimed Obsidian. She looked up at Flossie, "If you can fly ahead, do it!"

Flossie listened and boosted herself towards the village, soon vanishing from their sight.

Ben and Obsidian did not run along the flattened pathway, hoping to slow Fossil down through the underbrush. For a moment, Ben considered igniting a trunk in Fossil's way, but that would quickly go wrong for a number of reasons. As they jumped over fallen trees, Obsidian's tendons stung with each impact but she refused to stop galloping. She couldn't stop.

Taking a swift look at where the trail was, Obsidian recognized this area and felt slight relief knowing they weren't far from Setiir. By now, Flossie could have perhaps reached Setiir. They were breathing heavily but caught glimpses of the archway past the foliage. Obsidian took a sharp turn towards the path, Ben scrambled after her, neither of them looked back but heard Fossil thrash around after the unexpected curve. Obsidian could see some dragons through the entrance between the brambles but not Flossie, one of them was one of Queen Reka's dragons. She was ready to whinny to the beasts, but before she could, a sudden crackle roared from behind them followed by a snarling hiss and leaves flying into the air. By the time they looked back, Fossil was nowhere to be seen. They both stopped dead in their tracks with astonishment.

Obsidian glanced around warily but the dragon had just...*vanished*.

CHAPTER 14

The leaves began to settle, Obsidian whipped around as footsteps crunched through the underbrush. Out from the shadows came Hamara, rushing over to where the leaves had spiraled. She scraped around and then moved away quickly. Ben glanced at their surroundings with confusion and panted heavily. As was Obsidian. The dragons just inside the arch were also watching intently, Flossie crept under them.

"What just happened?!" yelped Ben.

"Hmm?" Hamara looked up.

"What happened to Fossil…?"

"Who?"

Obsidian spoke with heavy breaths, "A volcanic dragon…who was chasing us. He disappeared."

Hamara looked around. "Well, he isn't here now," she shrugged her wings.

She started to walk past them through the gateway. Once she noticed the dragons nearby who watched, she hurriedly trotted away. Still puzzled, Ben, Obsidian, and Flossie stood around outside for a while longer. Flossie's ears fell back, then she briskly followed Hamara.

"He couldn't just…have left without a trace," Obsidian muttered to Ben.

Ben didn't know what to say. Obsidian went back into the village as the dragons dispersed. Ben padded behind her. Setiir's residents were just as bewildered, already murmuring to each other. Obsidian caught a glimpse of Hamara's tail as she slinked through the crowd, and the two pushed their way through the dragons. At her tree, they stood huddled around the entrance and found Hamara by her shelves, poking around in her satchel as they stepped in. She flicked her eyes to their questioning faces.

"Everybody else saw it, why are you acting so nonchalantly?" asked Flossie.

Hamara thumped her tail against the ground. "The dragon had wings, didn't he? He could have seen Setiir's walls as clearly as any of you, and took off," she responded.

"As fast as one could blink?" snorted Obsidian.

"You had your backs turned to him."

Ben's ears flicked. "Didn't you come out from behind him? You walked over to where the leaves flew around."

Flossie narrowed her eyes. "Why were you there?"

"Gathering herbs myself. Which reminds me, did you find what I asked for?" answered Hamara dryly.

"No, don't try to change the subject!"

Hamara huffed and continued what she was doing, pulling stems from her pouch and setting them down, then gave the beasts her full attention.

"Would you rather the dragon still be chasing you? You would prefer the hunters fight him off and risk more injury? Risk him recklessly deciding to set the trees ablaze?" she questioned.

Obsidian flattened her ears. "No."

"Then leave it." Hamara stood up. "You got out of trouble unharmed, the circumstances are odd but consider yourself lucky."

The dragon shoved her way out of the den. The remaining three remained awkwardly as the room fell quiet. Obsidian stamped her talons down.

"The circumstances are more than *odd*, they're unbelievable," Flossie breathed. "You would've heard the beat of his wings."

"What was with her?" Ben asked, facing the other two.

"I don't know, she's stubborn but usually because she's actually in the right. This time though…"

"She weaseled her way out," Obsidian clacked her beak. "I can't say I'll miss her when we go home."

Flossie's head fell slightly, remembering that they weren't here to stay. She lifted it back up. "How's your wing been healing?"

"Some new feathers have grown, but I don't know how long it'll take to get all of them back or if it'll fully heal," sighed Obsidian. "I'm going to lay down."

"I think I will, too," said Ben.

He and his dam went over to their nest. Flossie stood at the tunnel, gazing up at the branches. She climbed out, the other dragons seemed to have settled down somewhat, but Hamara was nowhere to be seen. She took a breath. Hamara would cool down and come back eventually but continuing to pester her about it wasn't something Flossie looked forward to, though she didn't want to let her off the hook so easily. Now that she had a moment to herself, Flossie realized just how frightened she felt after fleeing from Fossil. She decided against trying to follow Hamara and returned to the burrow.

The sunlight began to fade. Obsidian had gotten up only when the guards had brought in prey. Hamara still wasn't back. The diffused light of sunset was prying into the den. Flossie began to worry about the dragon, she slowly rose from where she lay and shook her coat. She walked across the room and returned to the surface. A chilly breeze rustled the forest. Flossie watched the dragons go by, as one crossed her vision, it revealed a dark shape stalking along the path. Flossie soon recognized it as Hamara's silent stride. Where had she gone all day?

"Were you waiting for me?" Hamara asked plainly.

"No, I just got up," replied Flossie. "Where were you?"

"Getting the flowers you didn't."

"This late?"

Hamara nodded slowly. They stood outside in silence for a few moments longer.

"Will you at least tell *me* why you're acting so weird?" Flossie pleaded in a whisper.

A grumble rose through the dragon's throat and she narrowed her nostrils.

"Not on the ground," she breathed, and flew into the branches of her tree.

Flossie quickly fluttered up after her. Finding a spot to perch comfortably on, Hamara turned to face her.

"I saw the dragon but not the moment he vanished. But we know that you did," repeated Flossie.

Hamara snorted softly. "I did see him. As I said, I was gathering plants earlier, which was when I heard something not far from me, so I began to run there. I saw him through the trees, I watched him disappear."

"What happened?"

"If you blinked, you'd have missed it. He was suddenly just not there. I ran over after I saw it."

Flossie blinked. "But *why* did it happen?"

"I wouldn't know. Perhaps the world was just feeling generous today."

Flossie tilted her head, unconvinced.

"Strange things happen sometimes. Maybe there's a reason. Maybe not," concluded Hamara.

"But if that's all it is, then why didn't you want to tell Ben and Obsidian?" Flossie persisted.

Hamara's ears twitched in hesitation. "I was afraid they may tell the Queen's dragons."

"Why?"

"The volcanic dragon's not around anymore, we don't need the Queen sending in unwanted attention."

"How can you be sure that he isn't still in the woods?"

"I don't know where he is, he could be on another continent for all I know," Hamara stood up. "But if he's still here, he's probably very disoriented."

She leapt and started drifting back to the ground.

"Wait," Flossie began, but Hamara didn't hear her.

She flew after her and landed beside the dragon.

"But if they promise not to tell the hunters, will you just tell Ben and Obsidian what happened?" Flossie asked her. "Don't make unnecessary tension."

Hamara exhaled curtly. "Fine."

Flossie bowed her head and slinked into the burrow after Hamara, heading straight to her nest. Hamara went to unpack the flowers she had collected. Something about Hamara's explanation still felt off though. She had so casually confirmed that Fossil disappeared in an instant in front of everyone, and just accepted that. But…that felt too easy. Would other dragons start vanishing suddenly too? Flossie shook herself, she was thinking too hard. She tried to relax and fall asleep, but was jerked awake again by a new thought. *Was it magic?*

Ben was the first to awaken. Feeling a little restless, he got up and crawled out from beneath the tree. He sat in front of the trunk as the dawn air chilled him. Not many beasts seemed to be awake, mainly just the Queen's dragons. There was a particular dragon wearing the same pendant as the others that was unfamiliar to him. This one was sandy-brown with speckles, the usual hunters he saw were shades of green, and one was umber. Ben watched them curiously, but the new beast didn't seem to be doing much.

The events of yesterday came back to him. It was so frustrating, it wasn't fair. Ben didn't believe he had any powers, why couldn't Fossil just leave them alone? He picked at the dirt with his claws, then returned to the nest, feeling irritated. In the darkness, he could see the small movement of his dam's feathers. He softly clicked to her as he lay down.

He wanted to ask Obsidian what she planned on doing now, he tried whickering quietly to get her attention. Obsidian opened her eyes slowly.

"Hmm? I heard you get up," she whispered.

"If Fossil's back, what do we do?" responded Ben.

"The Queen's dragons can fight him off if he comes here."

Ben thought about the way the dragon had charged after them. They had gotten so close to the village before he vanished, despite that, Fossil didn't back down even then.

"But he knows we're here, nothing's stopping him from flying over the wall. What if they fight him and he just heals again?" Ben whimpered.

Obsidian drew in a slow breath. "We'll just have to keep an eye out. If we have to track down how he did it before going home, then so be it."

"How much longer do we have to stay?"

"I'm not sure, I would like my legs and scabs to heal fully before we try. My wing could take a long time *if* it's even able to fully grow back."

Ben's ears drooped.

"I want to go home. I miss Momma," he sighed.

"So do I," Obsidian groomed his withers. "We will make it back."

Obsidian shut her eyes again. Ben sighed and tried to relax.

Flossie popped up from her nest and turned her sight to Hamara who was awake. She glanced at Flossie, then back to her talons. Flossie snorted and pushed her head forward, looking over where Ben and Obsidian were, they were also up, which Hamara was aware of. Flossie flattened her ears.

"What are you doing?" Flossie hopped closer to Hamara.

The dragon grunted, scraping a small pile of dirt out from a claw.

"Is it that hard to say 'I'm sorry, now that I've calmed down let me tell you what happened yesterday'?!" she snorted, making sure the other two heard.

Hamara grumbled and screwed up her snout. She stood up, only putting in half the effort. Obsidian lifted her head to watch, though her eyes held little interest. Hamara and Flossie came over to them, Hamara slumped back down onto her hindquarters across from them. She eyed them and inhaled before she spoke.

"Alright, I overreacted last night," Hamara began, "I did see the dragon disappear. I ran to the spot he last stood on because I couldn't believe it."

Obsidian stared back, her blank expression unwavering. "We know that you saw him, I just want to know why you reacted the way you did."

"You tried telling us that he flew away yesterday though, not disappeared," Ben remarked.

Flossie looked at Hamara, realizing those words slipped her mind when she spoke to her last night.

"I was stressed, worried that you'd tell the Queen's dragons," answered Hamara.

"Why?" asked Obsidian, narrowing her eyes.

"It'll just get busy, Queen Reka will send more over and they'll be everywhere. The village can handle it themselves. The dragon could've been teleported to the other side of the continent for all we know," Hamara explained. "He's only one dragon."

"So what you're saying is: you would rather do nothing about a dangerous dragon who could decide to walk right into the village?" Obsidian stood up, her neck feathers raised. "I've been face to face with Fossil, he set fire to my mountains and tore my wing. From my experience, he has little common sense and will do whatever to get what he wants. If it meant getting to my son, he would burn this place."

"What does he even want with you?" questioned Hamara, glancing at Ben.

"Fossil thinks Ben has powers. I don't believe it one bit. He never told me *what* he wanted Ben for beyond something about a queen."

Obsidian took a step back, she was about to turn around but stopped to speak again.

"I can't go home without endangering my whole herd until Fossil is dealt with. Sorry that you'll be disturbed, but I don't care. It's selfish of you to not inform the village of what you saw," she snapped.

She climbed out through the tunnel to the surface without another word. Ben watched her leave, his ears fell back, then he, too, left.

"Well, I told you to ask if they would promise not to tell," Flossie said meekly.

Hamara growled softly. Flossie lowered her head. She shook it off, suddenly remembering something.

"After I laid down in my nest last night, I thought of something and I wanted to ask you about it," said Flossie.

Hamara didn't face her but tilted an ear down toward her.

"Do you think…" Flossie paused in hesitation, "that it was magic?"

The dragon's head did not move, but her eyes shifted to Flossie.

"I cannot be certain," was all she said.

CHAPTER 15

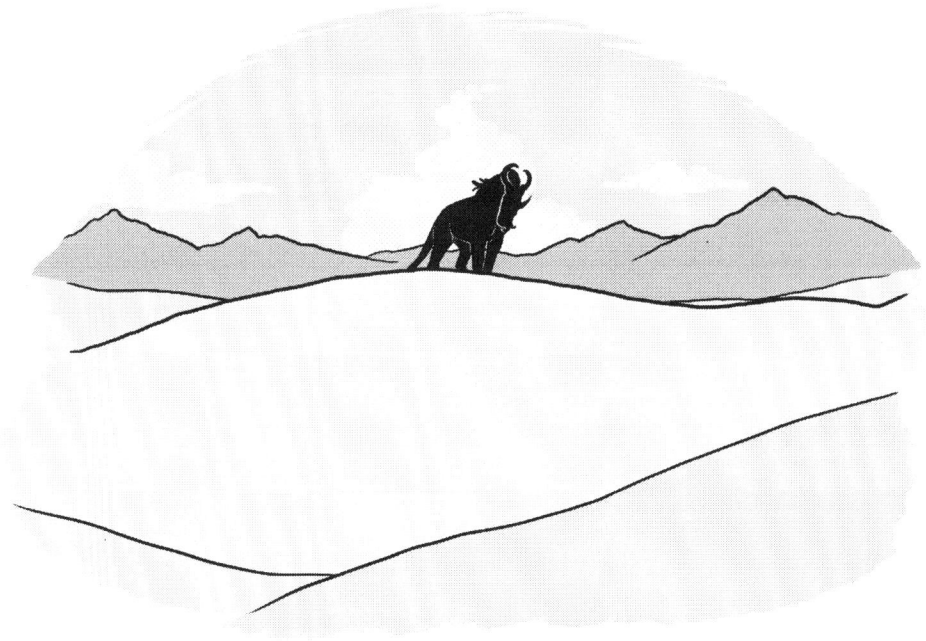

11 days ago

The plains were a blurry sea of snow before him. With only one barely-functioning eye left, the dragon relied entirely on his sense of smell to navigate the frozen grasslands. Fossil wandered through the snow, his wounds stung. He didn't know where he was and had nowhere to let his injuries heal. Was it even worth going after Obsidian again? Even if he looked for someone to treat his wounds, he wouldn't find his way, or he wouldn't be wanted there.

Not the Volcanic Kingdom... Forest Kingdom too far.

He continued trudging along with no direction in mind. He was so close to getting toward his goal, now it was crushed. He wondered how the Volcanic Kingdom was doing right now. Did the same Queen still reign or would somebody else have already stepped up before him? He hadn't stepped foot there in over three four-seasons. He felt a bitterness inside him, whether or not the Queen still lived, his rage was beginning to direct itself towards Obsidian. He wanted to carry on through sheer stubbornness.

Fossil had grown so used to the sound of his own steps and whistling wind. But perhaps the young dragon was not alone out there. An unfamiliar scent wafted through the air, it was similar to beasts he had smelled before. *Equine.* But something was drastically off...almost like a trace of rotting flesh burrowed beneath it. He saw no figures among the glaring white but stopped in his tracks. He shifted his ears, searching for anything. Snow crunched as footsteps began, a four-beat amble. The sound came from behind a small hill to Fossil's left. He turned to face the mound, watching it intently though he could barely tell where the line between land and sky was. An obscure shape began to rise, defining that line. An unclear animal of gray and white stood atop the hill.

They both remained in place, staring each other down. Fossil began to heat his fire crop, small trails of smoke rose from his nostrils.

The beast spoke to him, "You're in quite a state."

The creature's voice was like ice slithering along the dragon's spine. Fossil flicked his tail curtly, his spines clattering.

"Don't act rashly," the equine shook his mane. "I come proposing an...alliance with you."

"Who are you?" growled Fossil.

The gray animal came forward a few steps. "I will tell you if we make an agreement," he said. "I know you can't see me, I think it would be wise to accept my offer. There may be something extra in it for you."

"*What* is it?"

He moved closer. Fossil could almost make out what he looked like, but he wasn't entirely sure.

"I know what you want, I can learn a lot about anyone with just a glance and a bit more," he began with a smooth yet eerie tone. "You want revenge. You have been wronged. You need to put them in their place. You're after something now, or rather, you were."

Fossil stepped back, eyes widened. "The Queen sent you!" he hissed. "Only she would know that!"

The equine nickered. "Don't jump to conclusions. I want to help you if you would listen to what I have to say."

Fossil relaxed his muscles, giving him a signal to continue.

"Your suspicions about me will fade soon enough, if you join me, of course," the beast claimed. "I will help you track down what you're seeking and accomplish your goal if you can get me a little something hidden away in the Volcanic Kingdom's palace."

"What is it?" demanded Fossil.

"A small, white, opaque stone. All I need to know is the location and I can go from there. But obviously, I will assist you before doing so."

"Why would you need that?" Fossil tilted his head skeptically.

The beast flicked his tail. "It belongs to the Queen, all it does is sit around day after day but she keeps it anyway. I wonder why."

"Then what do you need it for?"

"Why not cause a panic? Stealing and getting away with it would be an embarrassment for her, wouldn't it?"

This seemed too good to be true. Could this random beast solve all of his problems by merely following alongside him? Something in Fossil told him to run.

Fossil jerked back from the other's face, "Wait, what *exactly* do you mean by I would get a reward just for agreeing to your offer?"

"Find out," he replied ominously.

Trust a mysterious stranger to get everything he was after? The equine's voice held sincerity but he was hiding something. Fossil remained uneasy.

"So?" he awaited an answer.

"Tell me more, how can you track down who I'm after?" Fossil questioned him further.

"I was born with a gift. Describe them to me well enough and I just might have a lead to find them. If I see said beast at least once with my own eyes, I can track them from anywhere," he explained.

"Show me an example."

"Alright, what should I find?"

"Have you seen a thistle?"

"I'd say so."

Fossil turned his head to the blankets of snow surrounding them.

"Bring me a dried thistle from beneath all the snow," he demanded.

"As you wish," the stranger bowed his head and bounded into the field.

Fossil tried to watch him but he faded into the white after a certain distance away. For all he knew, that beast could have just run off right then. A short while later, he heard the equine trotting back. He carried withered thistle stems but not in any claws or teeth. Fossil couldn't understand how he was doing it. The stallion set them on the bridge of Fossil's snout, where his vision was slightly better, a strange blue glow neared his face too.

"Is that enough proof?" nickered the equine.

"Maybe," snorted Fossil, the stems falling off his face.

"I'm ready for your answer," he said urgingly.

Fossil was still hesitant. "How do I know you didn't just sniff for those?"

"Can you smell the grasslands beneath this frost?" he retorted.

Fossil blinked. He couldn't. The beast tossed his head impatiently. Something still felt wrong, but he was intrigued and worried about what would happen if he refused.

He took in a slow breath and stated clearly, "I will join you."

The animal raised his neck, signifying that he made the right choice. "Oh, wonderful," he nickered. "Are you ready for your reward?"

Fossil's body tensed up. "Yes," he answered cautiously.

The equine straightened himself out, Fossil saw an icy blue mist emit from atop his head. He hadn't paid much attention to the dark spike-shapes on the creature before now. Fossil took a few steps back, wanting to dash away.

"Remain still," he told Fossil.

He watched as the blue billow grew taller, it suddenly crackled like lightning and flashed in small bursts. It flooded over him, wrapping around his body. He shut his eyes tightly, then quickly realized it did no harm, his pain started to fade. This smoke felt like feathers brushing across his body. He looked at his torn wing and saw the tears seal themselves back up under the mist. That was when he noticed he regained vision in both eyes, he stared as all his injuries healed completely. He inspected himself to find that the blood dyeing his scales had also vanished. He whipped his head back at the other beast with amazed bewilderment, it instantly turned to fright after gazing upon his face. He looked as if he had seen a ghost and was almost convinced that he had. He was speechless.

A unicorn. A gray-painted unicorn stallion stood before him. His horns were a deep midnight-purple. There were two long, curved-back horns pointing towards each other at the ends between his ears and one small spike near his snout. His brown eyes held emptiness with vertical slits for pupils, unlike any equine he had ever seen. He was considerably old, bony, and rather unkempt. His hooves looked worn and chipped. The unicorn narrowed his nostrils.

"I finally reveal myself to someone willingly and you have nothing to say?" he huffed.

Fossil blinked and shook his head in disbelief.

"No, I- you're…" he started.

"Yes, I am."

"But you're… Unicorns disappeared centuries ago."

"They did."

The stallion turned away, flicking his white tail tip.

"Now, we have work to do," he said looking back at Fossil. "Anything I've seen before I can find, but I have never met who you're after. Describe them."

Fossil flattened his ears. "You used magic to pick through my past, didn't you?" he growled.

"Yes. I'm surprised you figured out exactly what kind of spell I used despite Veynekan being devoid of magic now," the unicorn admitted. "Back to business."

Fossil frowned. "You can't tell anyone about what you saw from my life."

"A fair request. In return, do not tell anyone that you have seen me."

He began walking back up the hill he had appeared from, his tail lashed again. Fossil climbed after him.

"I'm looking for an albino dragon, I think he's a forest dragon hybrid, he's still a hatchling. He travels with a black hippogryph," Fossil told him.

The tall horn on the unicorn's forehead glowed softly again, he tilted his ears and gazed upon the plains.

"There is something I am detecting, it's far from here and I cannot guarantee it's whom you're looking for," the equine said.

Fossil thought his description was clear enough, a hybrid albino wasn't something you saw every day. He stepped forward, ready to make the journey.

"I cannot fly but you needn't worry about me," he continued.

Fossil tipped his head to the side. "But I thought I needed to follow you there."

"You do, I can keep my pace up for a good distance."

Fossil nodded. Without delay, the stallion sprung off into a canter, running up into a gallop. Fossil launched himself off the ground after him. He stared out ahead of him, his confidence had been restored, he *was* going to get his way now. However, he still felt wary of the unicorn. Trying to stay on his good side was probably his best option for now. He glanced down at him carefully, the stallion ran below the dragon at an equal speed.

"Hey," Fossil called from above. "Of all beasts, why choose me?"

The beast did not return a glance. "I can't just stroll into the Volcanic Palace on my own, now can I?" he replied.

Fossil felt anxiety claw in his chest. He knew he would have to go there at some point, but he didn't have to feel so nervous now with this unicorn beside him. He inhaled slowly. It suddenly hit Fossil that he never asked what this stranger's name was.

"Wait! What's your name?" he asked.

"How rude of me to never introduce myself, especially when I learned your name without telling you," he nickered, then stopped dead in his tracks.

Fossil quickly tried to slow down, he twisted around and landed in front of the halted stallion.

His dark gaze met Fossil's, "I am Komeetta."

CHAPTER 16

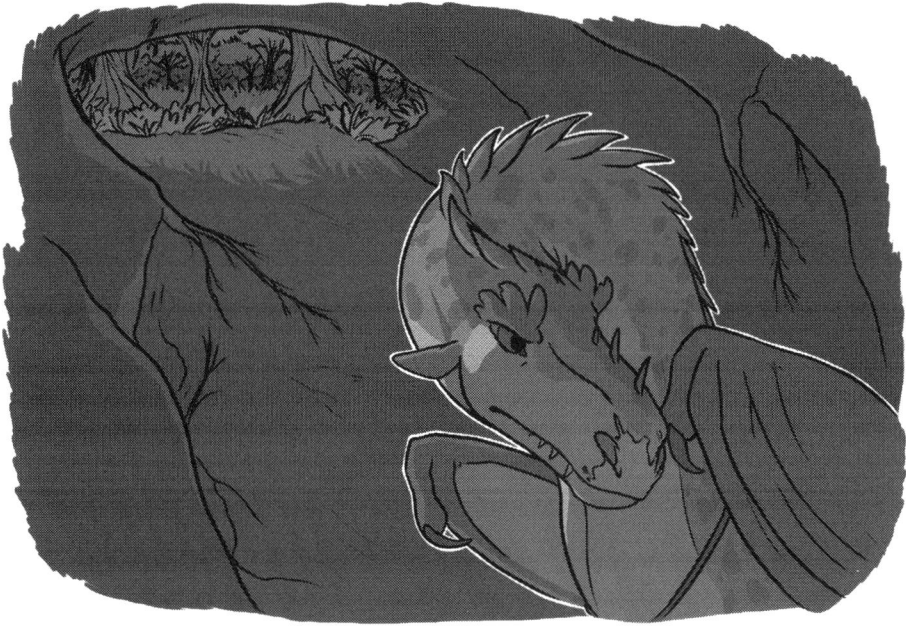

Obsidian rested under the dappled sunlight, still wary of their encounter with Fossil two days ago. She and Ben didn't feel comfortable straying outside the village. She watched the dragons of the village go by, the Queen's dragons were relentlessly active. Leaves shook above, Ben and Flossie began to glide down. On the forest floor, they playfully swiped at each other, rearing up halfway. Obsidian rested her head between her front legs. The beating of large wings sounded from behind the three of them, and Obsidian felt her neck feathers instinctively prickle up. A dappled, beige forest dragon flew through the fork in the tree and over their heads. The pale dragon wore the same necklace as the village's hunters, and they watched as it landed near two other forest dragons.

"I've never seen them before," murmured Flossie.

"Could the Queen have already sent more dragons here?" Obsidian wondered aloud. She got to her feet, "I was not the first nor the only one to tell the hunters what happened. But it does seem fast though."

Their attention was glued to the trio of dragons who were speaking to each other in hushed voices. After a few moments, they ambled toward the archway. Obsidian could only hope that they would find something leading to Fossil and take care of him if he dared to come near Setiir. A flash of another's brown scales through the foliage reminded Obsidian that she had not seen Hamara yet today.

"Did either of you see Hamara earlier?" she asked.

Flossie paused for a moment. Both she and Ben shook their heads. Obsidian let out a sigh and stretched her legs before taking a few steps forward. Another two guards flew above the village together, the treetops swayed dizzily from the drafts of their wings.

Ben's ears flicked. "If they're too busy, I can hunt later if you want," he offered, brushing against her shoulder.

She whickered to him, "You won't be going out there alone, you know."

"I wouldn't want to."

Obsidian gently nipped at her son's withers affectionately. She was expecting Flossie to chime in and join as well, but the mare said nothing. She looked over at her. Flossie was staring up at the sky, her eyes darting around the canopy.

"What is it?" Obsidian asked her.

Flossie hesitantly brought her head down, shooting a double-take at the air.

"I feel like I, at the very least, should have seen Hamara earlier," she murmured. "She seemed upset the other day. I'm worried. I think I'll just go for a walk."

She started into unhurried steps. Ben and Obsidian watched until she made her way toward the center of Setiir. Ben pointed his ears back.

Obsidian took a soft breath. "I'm sure she will feel better once Hamara relaxes and Fossil's dealt with."

She reached back to preen her wing. Ben sat down and lazily brushed his tail over the fallen leaves, when he suddenly asked, "Do you think everyone at home is okay?"

"I'm sure they are, we led Fossil away," she reassured him, lifting her head. "I'd rather it be me than them."

They both longed to return and see their family again. Depending on how things go in the near future, that could either be very soon or far off from now.

"Fossil wouldn't go back there, would he?" worried Ben.

Obsidian shook her head. "He's only interested in us." *Interested in revenge.*

She had enraged Fossil, fought him, and had thought to have blinded him. He would surely try to harm her again if given the opportunity. She would tear him apart if she had to, no matter the circumstances. The dragon was nothing more than a fool. Ben had no powers, she was sure of that. Another concern of hers was just *how* exactly Fossil could have ever healed that quickly while her own wounds were still visible.

Obsidian puffed out her feathers as she inhaled, and flattened them back down as she sighed, slowly releasing her anger.

"Everything will be alright," she told Ben.

Hamara never showed up later that day. Now at tomorrow's dawn, there was still no sign of her. Obsidian began to feel annoyed, Hamara couldn't be that thin-skinned, could she? The possibility that she fled just because Obsidian told the Queen's dragons about Fossil made her scoff. This dawn seemed dead silent, the guards were elsewhere right now, a robin's song echoed through the trees eerily. Outside of Hamara's burrow, Obsidian saw that the village was blanketed in fog.

The trunks of trees were still black as ink in the sunrise. There was no white noise from shivering oak leaves blown by the wind. Until slow footsteps, like the rhythm of a heartbeat, came into earshot. The beast's pads thudded against the dirt outside, low but weathered breaths followed in their stride as it drew closer to the tunnel. Whether the gait belonged to a forest or volcanic dragon was unclear. From below, they saw the dragon place their claws into the passage. Obsidian let her tense muscles relax at the sight, but she now turned suspicious. Hamara's head ducked into the underground, greeted by the three pairs of gleaming eyes. Obsidian huffed, her ears flicking. Flossie rose to meet the dragon.

"Where did you go? Why didn't you come back yesterday?" she asked with concern.

Hamara's hooded eyes sluggishly turned to her. "I attempted to track down Fossil since he was bothering them so much," she answered, twitching her tail tip to Ben and Obsidian, her voice was weary.

Surprise lit up Obsidian's face, it didn't seem like she would have ever considered doing that for them. Though, her thoughts quickly shifted to more cynical ones. *To get us and the guards out of here faster.*

Flossie swept her eyes along Hamara's body, finding no injuries, only exhaustion.

"Did you find him?" Ben whispered hopefully.

Hamara stared at the ground in front of her blankly, shaking her head. Ben sank back down to his bedding.

"I searched far through the forest and found no trace," she said, stiffly walking towards her nest.

Hamara had had no luck, but neither did the guards. Obsidian still felt skeptical though. Something seemed off, or was she only anxious again? Hamara flopped into her nest. The other three clearly had questions stirring in their minds but she wouldn't be answering them right now. Everyone lay in their nests without another word.

All but Hamara were awake. She had effortlessly fallen into a slumber, her breathing still ragged. She needed the rest, but everyone was still upset with how she brushed them off, just like she tried to keep it to herself after seeing Fossil. Something besides the wind made the branches of the trees sway gently, not too far from Setiir was the flapping of plenty of powerful wings. Obsidian tried to tune out all the noises surrounding the surface, the beasts were getting closer to the village. She tried to count how many from each wingbeat she heard. A whaling roar echoed through the woods. Obsidian swiftly got onto her feet, Ben's head popped up, his eyes wide. Obsidian rushed to the top of the tunnel just in time to see seven forest dragons dive beneath the canopy, the Queen's pendants were worn by them all.

"Seven of them?" Obsidian whispered.

Ben peered out past her. Did they genuinely need eleven dragons to find Fossil? The dragons who had arrived glided just outside of the barrier. A jade dragon, the one who lived here, trotted to the archway. Obsidian could see them speaking in low voices. The new beasts attentively watched the green dragon point with her head in three different directions as she spoke, and then separated into small parties, flying off. Ben came up from the den and sat at Obsidian's side.

"Where did the dragons go?" he asked.

"They landed near the arch, said something I couldn't catch, then flew out," Obsidian answered.

Ben brushed his tail across the dirt apprehensively. "Are they really all here for Fossil?"

"I can't say for certain, but that's my guess." She turned back around to return to the cave, stroking a wing along Ben's side.

Ben and Obsidian were lying in the sunniest patches they could find, while Hamara and Flossie had left a while ago to gather more herbs. There was one hunter who had stayed behind and had been gathering large pieces of bark. They weren't sure why she had started to begin with though. A sudden, low bellowing carried through the forest. Obsidian opened her eyes, unable to see the source, but it was getting closer. She began to hear the same barrage of wings again. The three groups who split up came flying over the barrier. The jade dragon took flight, sheets of tree bark in hand, and ascended into the tallest tree near the center of Setiir. The guards followed her up, gathering around on wooden platforms cradled by the great oaks' limbs. It was clear that the villagers weren't too enthralled with the Queen sending this many dragons either as they stared up with lowered ears.

They didn't get to watch or try to listen in for long, Ben and Obsidian's focus was yanked away by Hamara clambering through the entrance, she halted upon reaching the village, Flossie fluttering after her. Other beasts looked over at them, blinking. The dappled dragon was scanning Setiir, looking for something or someone. When Hamara's gaze locked with Obsidian's, her ears flattened against her head. She prowled over in swift steps, her neck low. Obsidian stood up straight, ready for whatever she was worked up about. She stopped a short distance away from the mare.

"*What* exactly did you tell the hunters?" Hamara growled.

"Exactly what I saw happen," said Obsidian flatly, "You should know I am not the only beast to have told them anything."

Hamara looked around at the sky. "But why so many?"

"I know as little as you do."

Hamara flared her nostrils, taking a moment to speak again, "This is too many for one task," she replied, taking a step back. "The Queen can't only be searching for a vanishing dragon."

"Would you know what that could be?" Obsidian asked.

"No."

Hamara sat back, all the tension in her body seemed to melt away. She lifted her attention and watched the guards above again.

Flossie let out a breath of relief. She stared up at Hamara, her gaze hardened. "Will you stop starting conversations so aggressively?"

The dragon's reply was a grumble. She got back on her feet, moving past everyone and toward her tree to deposit the plants. Obsidian took a deep breath and lay back down. Flossie slowly made her way into the den as well.

Things carried on for another two days. The horde of guards went about their business, the only time they didn't seem focused on other matters was when the three who lived in Setiir would hunt for the village. Ben stepped out from the burrow, Flossie wasn't there when he woke, his dam was sleeping, and Hamara looked busy. Frankly, he was too intimidated to ask Hamara where Flossie was. He went up to search for her and inspected his surroundings, her pale coat wouldn't be hard to spot. He saw the same trees, underbrush, and dragons, but not Flossie, then made his way down one of the pathways.

Despite spending many days in Setiir now, it was still strange for him. In the mountains, even with some herdmates he didn't know very well, he never felt timid around most of them like he did with dragons. Something put him off, he knew everyone was looking at him and the different way he moved. Just thinking about it made his scales feel prickly. He decided to fly up onto a platform, steadying himself as he latched onto a strong branch. Glancing around the tops of the trees, Flossie was still nowhere in sight. He glided back down, Hamara had probably just sent her out to gather more plants.

He sighed, and was about to turn back to the den, but noticed the eyes of a dragon watching him from the branches. He froze as their gazes briefly locked, unsure of what they wanted or who this beast was. The dragon began to stand up, casually flying down and stepping into the light. He was a seal brown forest dragon, Ben saw the necklace hanging off them and laid his ears back uneasily. He approached and stopped a respectable distance away from Ben, his face appeared neutral.

"Are you the beast that was chased by the volcanic dragon who vanished mysteriously a few days ago?" he asked.

Ben nodded silently.

"May I ask a question or two?"

He nodded again.

"Besides a disappearing dragon, did you see anything *strange?*"

He shook his head, unable to find his voice.

"Hmm," the dragon nodded. "Do you know anybody who may have seen him while it happened?"

Hamara, he wanted to say, but hesitated. She definitely didn't want to interact with any of these guards, but on the other hand, he didn't like the way she was talking to Obsidian recently.

"Hamara," he murmured, "who lives near the back of the village."

"Hamara…" echoed the guard, something about the name seemed familiar but at the same time completely unknown. He collected himself. "Thank you. I'll keep it in mind."

And with that, the dragon flew off. Ben slinked back to the den, but, again, he was distracted by something. He heard wings drawing close from somewhere outside Setiir. White feathers appeared over the brambles as Flossie descended. She landed onto the trail, carrying some roots with prickly stems in her beak.

"Hey!" Flossie greeted him quickly to not drop her plants.

"Hi! I was looking for you," said Ben, shaking the awkwardness out. "I didn't know where you went."

"Hamara just didn't feel like going out again."

Flossie lowered her head and shoved her bundle of herbs back more securely in her beak. Ben joined in her stride, as they passed a tree on the way back, there was something new stuck onto the side. Ben lifted his head, realizing that it was a slab of tree bark with the underside facing outward. Though what really caught his eye was the etchings of intricate claw marks, he couldn't imagine that they were simply just scratches. Flossie stopped near his side.

"It's dragon writing but I don't do a lot of reading, so…" she tried explaining, tipping her head with uncertainty, "Hamara can read though."

She continued along, while Ben trotted back to her side.

"If it's on the hunters' tree, Hamara would probably be at least a little interested," she mumbled.

Ben nodded softly. They hurried to the den, Flossie sprang into the tunnel and ducked inside, Ben came down after she made her way in. Hamara, busy as ever, did not take her eyes off her plants, only pointing an ear in their direction. Flossie stepped over, setting the roots down beside Hamara.

"Thanks," said Hamara, slowly dragging over the stems closer under her claws.

Flossie gave her a moment to sort her herbs before speaking. "Hamara," she began, finally getting the dragon to look up. "On our way over, we saw a piece of bark on the side of the hunters' tree with writing on it… Can you read it for us?"

After a few moments, Hamara begrudgingly got off her hindquarters. "Alright."

She plodded her way up, the two young beasts trailing behind. She stalked toward the tree and went around to the other side, finding the plate of bark.

Hamara narrowed her eyes. "'*Please report any magical-like activity to the Queen's dragons immediately.*' that is what's written."

Without hesitation, she paced back into her home. Ben and Flossie watched the dragon leave. Flossie slanted her ears back.

"I *know* she didn't tell us everything," whispered Flossie. "I may not know how to read much, but there's more than a single line here."

Ben twitched his tail tip. "Do you think that Hamara has powers?"

"I had asked her if it was magic that took Fossil away, but she told me she wasn't sure. With the way she's acting, you'd think she does have magic. But how?"

Ben considered for a moment that perhaps Fossil was right, about the prophecy, that is. Though maybe he got it a little wrong, maybe it was about Hamara.

Flossie sighed, "Everything's just so weird lately. I wish Hamara would go back to just being grumpy, rather than on edge and grumpy," vented Flossie.

"Maybe she'll be better once the dragons leave," Ben whickered empathetically.

"It's irritating and I feel like she's getting more distant," Flossie flipped over a pebble on the dirt, she started to turn toward the archway before looking back at Ben. "I'm going to fly around the forest to take my mind off it, wanna come along?"

He trilled agreeably. Flossie didn't even wait to get out of Setiir before unfolding her wings and taking off.

CHAPTER 17

The day after, Ben and Obsidian were following the path back to Hamara's. Ben saw a beast emerging from the tunnel, he thought it was Hamara at first, but realized this was the same dragon who had asked him questions yesterday. Ben watched as the dragon sprung into flight into the branches of the hunters' tree. Worry clawed in his chest, hoping that the guard hadn't told Hamara that he was the one who gave them her name. Obsidian padded down into the underground first. Ben was trying to shield himself behind her. Once they entered, Hamara twisted around toward them, looking a bit wild. They flinched back. When she saw that it was only them, her spines smoothed down but her face remained stiff. She was still frenzied. Ben lowered his head behind his dam.

"What?" asked Obsidian.

"You…" she breathed, then gathered herself. "I was just looking for you." Obsidian tilted her ears back.

Hamara snorted. "We're never going to find Fossil just sitting here. We need to leave," she continued, walking toward her herbs.

Flossie practically jumped out of her nest.

"Why? Where?" Obsidian lowered her ears.

"To the Volcanic Kingdom."

Hamara grabbed handfuls of plants and hurriedly stuffed them into her satchel.

"You say this just *after* Ben and I just saw a guard leave your den," Obsidian said suspiciously.

"It doesn't matter," she met Obsidian's eyes. "We can search as far across the volcanic territory as you like, I would like to just be outside Setiir."

"Wait, you're going to leave our home just like that?" hurt filled Flossie's voice.

"...I need to."

"But this is where we *live*. You're one of the most well-trained healers here!"

"There isn't much sentiment here for me, I heal beasts but I'm not interested in bonding. They'll be fine without me."

Flossie's ears drooped. Hamara carelessly scattered around what she wasn't bringing in her satchel.

Flossie spoke again, her expression was stony. "Maybe that's why you're so prone to overreacting, no one knows you well enough to care about your feelings."

Hamara's head snapped up and stared unblinking at Flossie, their green eyes of differing shades locked. The dragon's response was simply a low growl. Ben started to feel uncomfortable. Obsidian was still suspicious of Hamara, but going to the kingdom Fossil hatched in would be much easier than searching the expansive woods. She was willing to give it a shot while keeping a close eye on her.

Obsidian turned her head to Ben. "What are your thoughts on this, Ben?"

His reaction was delayed. He cleared his mind and decided. "I think we should try," he muttered. "But what if other volcanic dragons know about that prophecy too?"

Hamara scoffed, "I can assure you Fossil is the only one who cares."

Obsidian turned back to Hamara, "Fine."

Flossie stood silent for a few moments longer, looking back and forth. "I don't have a choice unless I want to be alone?"

Ben felt bad, but there wasn't anything he could do. He curled his claws into the dirt.

Hamara closed up the pouch and stood up. "Alright, let's go."

She rushed to the top of the tunnel, the others scrambled after her once she was already up to the top.

"Right now?!" Ben called.

"I must!"

They all got to the surface and cantered after the dragon through the village. Flossie flew along with them unenthusiastically. Hamara waited just outside the archway as the other three got closer, she started to open her wings but folded them back up. Groaning as she remembered that they wouldn't be flying there. Obsidian swished her tail, it wasn't her fault she couldn't fly.

"It's going to take a while but I know my way. Follow me," said Hamara.

She sprinted down the path, quickly gaining speed. Obsidian could never have expected this turn of events, but if this is what must be done to get rid of Fossil, then so be it. Things seemed straightforward enough, get to the Volcanic Kingdom, find out who Fossil is and how to deal with him, then head home. That was all she hoped for.

The terrain transformed into rougher gravel as they neared the edge of the Forest Kingdom. Stout, twisting trees flew past them as they sped through the woods, Hamara hadn't taken them down any of the worn trails. Obsidian was well enough to gallop again, but Ben's feet grew sorer with each stride. Hamara continued leading them, she hadn't spoken since leaving Setiir, nor had Flossie. Obsidian couldn't stand the silence between them anymore.

"Where in the Volcanic Kingdom are we headed?" she asked.

Hamara's ear flicked back to listen. "I'm going to the palace first, there's more than enough dragons there."

The mare had never been to those mountains, she wondered if it would at all be like home. Far on the horizon were mountainous shapes. Ben glanced back at Flossie who lagged behind the rest of their group. Regardless, he slowed his pace to fall back near where she flew. She didn't look angry, but blank.

He thought of something to talk about. "Have you ever been to the Volcanic Kingdom?" he wondered.

"No. I've never been outside the Forest Kingdom," answered Flossie.

"My dam hasn't been there either. I guess it's all of our first trips."

He saw Flossie squint her eyes for a moment passively, then looked ahead normally. She probably didn't want to talk about the trip itself.

He continued, "I just hope the volcanic dragons won't be like Fossil."

"Don't worry about it," she told him. "Most dragons are normal beasts."

All three of them remained behind Hamara, proceeding through the pathless forest. Their surroundings didn't change much for a while after reaching these coarser grounds. However, slowly but surely, the canopy above gradually thinned. They sprinted through the trees for what felt like the whole day, but it seemed like they would soon be out of the forest's cover.

As sunset fell upon them, the peach sky became visible beyond the wooded outskirts. The four beasts' pace had slowed to a trot with exhausted breaths. Something caught Hamara's eye, she veered away to inspect it. She stumbled upon a hollow dipping into the land, a fallen elm lying across it.

"We can rest here, then continue in the night," panted Hamara.

The other three approached as Hamara did not hesitate to settle in, Ben got down in the middle, Obsidian chose to sleep while standing. Flossie sat over by the edge. Obsidian relaxed her mind and muscles, hoping that the strenuous journey wouldn't backfire on her still-healing body.

Hamara rose to wake the three at the sight of the moon, a chilling breeze swept around them as unseen birds whooped from afar. Obsidian shook her coat, and lowered her head, whickering to awaken Ben. Hamara waited for them atop the slope.

"We need to get moving," whispered Hamara. "We can hunt on the way."

To everyone's relief, she moved no faster than a walk as they joined her. Silent as they had been during the day, they traversed the last of the woods. The border leading to the open plains and foothills was still far but within sight. The shadowed forest around Ben and Obsidian felt even more disorientating.

They made a chunk of progress before Hamara stopped, fanning her wings halfway to halt them. She raised her ears, nostrils flaring. The fresh scent of deer was carried by the wind. She lowered her head, taking a few steps before launching into the black sky. Her sudden flight startled them all, leaving to track down the creatures without a word. Flossie snorted irritably.

The three of them continued to pad sluggishly toward the edge of the woods in Hamara's absence. Sometime later, wingbeats drew near as she descended from the patchy canopy, a buck in her jaws. Landing with a thud, she set her catch down, allowing them to eat. Ben hopped over and did not hesitate to take a bite. Hamara paid little attention as she began to clean her claws off. After they were done, she only ate what was left. Once again, they trotted onward. Some animals would watch from afar, their eyes gleaming in the moonlight. A single coyote's howl rang throughout the darkness. The dirt became rugged, large stones embedded within it. Ben stared ahead, tall stems of grass swayed lazily with the wind, jagged mountains sat beside the plains.

Ben's heart accelerated with excitement. "We're almost to the meadow!" he proclaimed.

Flossie stretched her neck forward to see, Obsidian looked eager to get out into the open land. When Ben and Obsidian had last been there, it was blanketed in snow, now it had melted away.

"Can you see it?" Obsidian asked Ben.

He looked at his dam, ears tilted. "See what?"

"The Volcanic Palace. It's the tallest mountain in that range."

Ben looked harder at the barrier of stone. The ancient volcano had multiple peaks like spears jutting out from it. He realized that those far-off rocks were entirely black. He'd seen tiny dark pebbles around the rivers, but never bigger than that, especially not one big enough to build a palace on.

"It's a black mountain," Ben said in awe.

"It was a volcano a long, long time ago. These foothills were formed by lava," nickered Obsidian.

Ben looked down and flexed his claws delicately. Hamara had her nose glued to the grass.

"Keep an eye out for komodo dragons. As we get closer, they're more likely to cross our path," warned Hamara.

Ben blinked in confusion.

His dam noticed and explained. "Komodo dragons are a species of lizard that can be dangerous," she told him. "Conifer had encountered one away from home over a four-season ago, and thought it was the most terrifying and amazing animal she had ever seen. So she ended up naming her colt after one."

"But would they be out this early in the season?" questioned Flossie.

"Best not to risk it," Hamara sniffed.

Ben nodded, and after that description, he was not interested in meeting one. He noticed Flossie shuffle uneasily behind him. The four ventured through the night, guided by the silver light of the moon. At least the Volcanic Palace was visible enough. Ben took a long sigh, hoping Fossil would not find him in this land with a great open sky.

Ben, Obsidian, Flossie, and Hamara stopped about halfway through the night to rest again, burying themselves in grasses. Everyone except Hamara slept, she stayed awake on guard. When the dawn spilled pink on the horizon, Obsidian couldn't help but admire it. As they all began their journey again, the imposing shape of the Volcanic Palace was clear, the light shining against the ebony stones. Obsidian could see trees on the cliffs, much different than species she had seen before. They were skinny with ashen bark but had thick foliage. The sudden change in terrain was jarring but exciting to Ben.

They continued to run until they reached the steeper cliffs, Hamara brought her gait down to a trot, then stopped. She stared up along the rocks and all the grooves, walking close to the side of the mound.

"We can't keep running, we need to start climbing now," she said without taking her gaze off the wall.

She found a spot and latched her claws into it, pulling herself up the side, despite being able to fly. Obsidian strolled up, took a running leap and bounded, hooking into rocks jutting out with her claws. Perfectly balancing for a short enough time to not slip, making it up the side in half the time Hamara did. The dragon narrowed her nostrils.

"I know how to climb rocks, where do you think I was born?" she snorted.

Ben and Flossie heaved themselves over the cliff with their wings. It wasn't a tall ledge but they got a better view of the palace from atop. Their gazes following what lay ahead, nobody was looking forward to walking the uneven mountains. Thankfully, the sun wouldn't be high and beating down on them so soon.

"We might not get to the palace by tomorrow," Hamara grumbled, "And we're not getting any closer by standing here."

The smoothest trail they had access to immediately led them across a small ravine, horizontal through their path. It was a cycle, up one mountain, then down, and repeat onto the next. The palace loomed over them as they swiftly began to feel worn out. Obsidian's legs ached, each cliff more exhausting than the last. Nowhere to hide from the sunlight either, but still, they pushed on. Everyone hoped for a creek or prey to be nearby, or that maybe Hamara would be merciful and stop for a break soon, especially since she hadn't slept.

They padded through a canyon, mountains too steep to climb surrounded them on both sides, small caves littered the walls of the ravine. The walls blocked out most noise in the area, only hearing their own claws against the rocks, the quietness putting them on the verge of sleep. Then a new noise attempted to creep in, a limb brushing against the gravel. But the fact that it was heard at all was a mistake on the creature's part. Flossie let out a screech that echoed through the passage. Ben, Obsidian, and Hamara whipped around to see Flossie shoot into the air on frantic wingbeats. Just as she rose, a komodo dragon had lunged forward from the tunnels, snapping its jaws where she formerly stood. Hamara rushed forward, leaping right over Ben and Obsidian's heads, bellowing a roar.

She swiped a front foot and slammed it down just as the reptile backed away with its mouth agape. Obsidian fanned her wing up and backed up towards Ben, urging him to flee. He ran a few strides away, but stopped when he noticed no one was following, he turned and stared back. Hamara was not taking any chances, fire began to build in her crop. Right before she could unleash her flames, the lizard charged at her legs. She pulled her limbs back nearly too late as the animal's teeth grazed her. She hissed and blasted fire into its face. It recoiled and turned to escape after being singed. Flossie and Hamara did the same and ran the opposite way. Obsidian looked over at her son, who was still standing a few wing-lengths away. Her ears pointed back, but not with anger.

"Why didn't you run?" she asked him.

Ben lowered his head. "Nobody was coming with me."

"I need you to be safe," she came trotting over whickering.

"But what about you? And everyone else?"

"It is very kind of you but when I tell you to run, you *must* run. All I can care about at that moment is that you are safe."

Ben squeaked softly through his nostrils in the way hippogryph foals would. His dam halted beside his shoulder and groomed his withers. Flossie and Hamara slowed and stopped near them, both looking back to see that the komodo dragon had left.

"Thanks," breathed Flossie.

Hamara nodded, then took the lead again.

"You're bleeding," Obsidian told her as she passed her.

Hamara looked at her leg where the komodo dragon had attacked her and snorted. She sat on her hindquarters, pulling herbs from her pouch. Before applying them, she huffed a wave of flames onto the bite. Ben winced as he remembered doing the same for Obsidian. Hamara roughly pressed the plants to her wound, the undamaged scales naturally deflected the heat. They remained in the canyon for a little longer as Hamara tended to her injury, all of them keeping an eye out for more lizards.

"Let's get out of here, then rest," yawned Hamara.

Flossie sighed in relief. Hamara had a slight limp to her stride. They all headed down the path, so close yet so far from the palace.

CHAPTER 18

They had settled under an overhang and slept for a while after encountering the komodo dragon. Hamara was pressing another bundle of smashed plants against her bite. Obsidian and Flossie were perched on the edge of the cliff, staring into the shattered valley. Ben was the last to wake, stretching and yawning before coming over to the mares.

Before he could say anything, Flossie suddenly said, "I'm hungry."

Obsidian nodded. They noticed the young dragon at their side, his dam whickered to him.

"You're just in time, Ben, do you want to look around and hunt?" offered Flossie.

He nodded, and stretched his wings in preparation. He hadn't done much flying after leaving Setiir.

"Just don't go too far," Obsidian told them.

Ben whickered before following Flossie into the sky. He had missed the freedom of flight, no thorns or sharp terrain, just the wind under his wings as they soared over the peaks. He yearned to fly with Obsidian and his herdmates once more.

Flossie sighed, staring ahead at the towering palace. "We could've been there by now if we flew the whole way."

"I wish we could fly there too," said Ben.

"Yeah…"

"But it's not my dam's fault that we can't!"

"No, that's not what I'm saying at all! Sorry if it came off that way."

He cooled himself down quickly, but felt embarrassed that he jumped at her like that.

Flossie continued, "Fossil did that, right?"

Ben nodded, flexing his front claws

"Well, we're on our way to pay him back."

The thought of Fossil getting whatever punishment he had coming was one Ben had no problems with. After everything the dragon had done to his family, he felt no empathy toward him. He looked down at the rugged surface whipping past him, also keeping his eyes out for animals. He didn't spot anything, but perhaps Flossie's keener sight would.

"You haven't been speaking to Hamara much," Ben broke the silence.

Flossie glanced at him and sighed again. "I'm still so frustrated with how she was acting in Setiir. And she was ready to abandon our home just like that," she explained. "It doesn't seem like she really wants to talk either."

"You could try talking about it to her," he suggested. "My herdmates always talk to each other."

"Maybe. But it can be so hard to get through to her, she seems uninterested in *everything*. I'm not sure if she ever plans to go back to Setiir after this is all over. My whole world just changed so quickly."

"I know how it feels. I had to get away from my home suddenly to escape Fossil."

He wasn't sure how to help Flossie with Hamara, but he understood the detestation of change beyond their control. After a while, they went lower to the rocks but still remained above. Flossie clacked her beak twice to get Ben's attention. He looked over, her head was pointed at the ground. Ben flapped in place as he spotted it too, there was a small herd of markhor goats walking along a mountain ridge. Flossie glanced up at him then down to the herd, directing him to strike.

Ben gathered himself and soared out of the goats' sight, hovering for another moment as he prepared. He thought of the way Obsidian would tackle down prey, using her weight and speed to stun then kill. He didn't waste another heartbeat, tucking his legs close and folding his wings, he dived from the sky. It wasn't long before his claws were close enough to spear into the sides of one. He grappled the animal and pulled back up. The rest of the herd bounded away in panic while he swiftly killed the goat mid-air as he bit into its neck. A sense of pride rushed through him, his second successful hunt of large prey.

"Nice work!" chirped Flossie.

He flew back over to her, trilling softly.

"We should head back before they start to worry," she said, spinning around.

He followed behind as they returned to the overhang.

The next day, they continued into the mountains. The moment they began to climb the slopes, soreness seeped back into their muscles. But they weren't far now, they had chosen to sleep through yesterday's night since it began to grow dark by the time Ben and Flossie got back. Which would also decrease their chances of meeting snow leopards or cougars. Strangely, they had not seen any volcanic dragons as Obsidian had expected but if her memory served correctly, their route hadn't passed through any villages. They grew more impatient every time they reached the top of a peak and saw the volcano, it got closer and closer, yet it felt like they made little progress.

"Have you ever been to the palace?" Obsidian suddenly asked.

It took Hamara a little time to realize she was speaking to her, "Once, a long time ago. But that was before their current Queen took the throne."

"Who's their queen now?"

"Queen Gaar. Don't know much about her."

Obsidian was hoping for some insight on the palace, but she wasn't surprised by Hamara's answer. The group trotted along the trail of a mountain ridge. From here, everyone could get a decent look at the behemoth volcano. The land began to slope down, transitioning into smoother terrain, there was a cavern punctured into the side of a vertical cliff ahead, though it was not a natural tunnel.

"That's the pathway to the palace," Hamara informed.

Flossie sighed in relief. Hamara slowed her pace, causing everyone else to as well. As they neared the threshold, the ceiling was dug out high enough that Hamara did not have to duck. Low light entered the cave through both openings, revealing that the walls were covered with faded illustrations of beasts, predominantly volcanic dragons, and scenery. The trail was long, cutting through an entire mountain. The sunlight at the other end was blinding after crossing the dark center. As they stepped out from the tunnel, the volcano was just ahead of them, their path free of obstacles. They could fully see the mixture of intertwining black and blood-red stones that formed it, dwarfing every mountain surrounding it.

Colorful boulders, some natural and some painted, sat arranged on both sides, thick underbrush grew between. A pair of armored volcanic dragons were lying casually at the sides of the palace's entrance farther up. As the four were approaching the dragons, the salmon-colored one chuffed to them in greeting. Obsidian responded with a whicker, Hamara and Flossie bowed their heads. They stepped inside and ventured down one final tunnel, leading them into a massive cave system. Inside the first main room of the palace was a huge space leading to dozens of other halls throughout the volcano, large enough for a dragon to comfortably fly down. A web of ropes was strung above, holding stone bowls in nets, filled with embers that faintly illuminated the area. A statue of a crowned dragon sat in the center. The floor was unnaturally smooth with entangling, spiraling lines painted into the ground like rivers and winds.

There were more beasts here than Ben had ever seen in his life, mostly volcanic dragons, but with a few gryphons, wyverns, and forest dragons sprinkled within. The volcanic dragons were diverse colors of black, red, and orange. Some striped or dappled, some unmarked. A few dragons sat nestled atop ledges near the ceiling. A shallow stream ran through the cavern, creating a tiny waterfall as it flowed from the outdoors.

Hamara looked around, and after a moment, she began to walk farther in, her companions stuck close. The business of the palace was starting to overwhelm Ben, his eyes pointed nowhere but where Hamara was headed. He did like how mellowly lit the caves were though. Hamara stopped for a moment to read what was written into a wall, then led them down a tunnel. The asocial dragon had not said anything after getting inside their destination, silently guiding them somewhere in the tangle of halls. Obsidian tried to lift her head above the swarm of beasts but most of their shoulders were just as high as or taller than Hamara's.

"Are we supposed to speak to someone?" the mare asked. "What are we doing?"

Hamara groaned. "We will, but I'm too tired right now."

"And where are we going now?" Obsidian quickened her pace.

"The nesting caverns."

Deeper in, they could see a long room, the lighting was too sparse to make out any details from this distance. Once within it, stone lanterns posted atop skinny columns held gently burning fires. There was also an external source of light, tiny holes dug out on the thinnest wall which were also likely used for venting smoke. The tunnel system continued on the other end of the cavern, but they wouldn't be going there. At the sides were layers upon layers of dug out spaces, each was farther back into the wall than the one below, huge nests constructed in every one.

"We can sleep in here," whispered Hamara as she continued down the path.

They came across a pair of empty spots side by side. Hamara stopped for a moment, then stepped inside one. She sniffed around and padded it out before lying down, wrapping her tail around herself. She took up most of the one she had chosen, but Ben was small enough for both him and Obsidian to fit on the right. That left Flossie on her own. Obsidian lifted her head.

"You can come into our spot," invited Obsidian.

"Thanks," whickered Flossie.

Obsidian lay down at Ben's side. Flossie came into the cave and chose her spot, she got down close to Obsidian, but remained a few inches away. Exhaustion washed over Obsidian quickly. She welcomed the sleep. Flossie started to clean her talons before fully settling to rest. Ben closed his eyes and was also asleep shortly after.

When Obsidian awoke sometime later, it looked to be dawn through the air holes. She remained in her spot to not disturb Ben or Flossie. Well, she had *tried* to let them sleep, but hearing Hamara shuffling around in her bedding on the other side of the wall piqued her curiosity. She then heard her rising to her feet. Hamara took a few steps out and noticed Obsidian's eyes were open.

"We can start speaking to the dragons now," she said coolly.

"Why now?" questioned Obsidian. "Is anyone even awake?"

"Some of Queen Gaar's guards will be, and that's who we'll ask first."

Ben and Flossie started to wake from the dragon's voice, she made little attempt to lower it. Flossie's ears flattened out of irritation. Ben slowly opened his rosy eyes.

"Shouldn't you do something about your bite?" Obsidian gestured to Hamara's leg with her beak.

She brushed her claws over it, removing any debris. "Only my scales were broken. I can deal with it."

Flossie shook her thick coat as she stood up from her spot, white hair drifting off. "What are we doing?" she asked groggily.

"Going to try asking dragons if they know anything about Fossil," Obsidian told her.

Hamara spoke again, "What do *you* know about Fossil? I only know he is pursuing you because of a prophecy that probably isn't true or real."

Obsidian cleared her throat. "I know very little about where he came from or why he was in my territory. In an encounter or two I had with him, he mentioned something about the Queen needing to be punished and I assume he means Queen Gaar."

Flossie blinked. "So he dragged you into this mess because someone *else* was supposedly causing problems?"

Obsidian nodded.

"What a bastard!"

Hamara looked to be in thought. "I'll look into what Queen Gaar has done," she whispered as softly as possible.

"That seems dangerous," muttered Flossie.

Obsidian returned her focus to Hamara. "Why out of all beasts would you try to dig up something on a queen?"

"Why wouldn't I?" she responded.

Hamara took a few steps back and returned to the hall they had come in from. Ben and Flossie were both standing now, Obsidian was the last to get up.

"There are sure to be armored dragons in the main room," Hamara thought aloud.

Ben walked over. "Are we just going to go around talking to dragons?"

"Yes."

"That sounds…boring."

"I'm sorry, you can't go off on your own," Obsidian told him.

"I know," sighed Ben.

Flossie bounded to the rest of the group. "We could split up, Ben and I will go look around the palace in the meantime. I'm only two four-seasons old but still an adult, so…"

Obsidian looked hesitant for a moment. "Alright, just don't go so far that you lose your way."

"We won't," promised Flossie.

Hamara waited a moment before starting down the hallway. Obsidian took a few steps after her but stopped.

"I don't know how long we'll be speaking with anyone, but hopefully not long," she told the young beasts.

"Okay, we'll just have a look around," nickered Flossie.

Ben nodded and twisted around, padding off in the opposite direction of his dam. Hamara and Obsidian began heading back. They sought for any of the volcanic Queen's dragons, but there were none in these corridors; there were fewer beasts in the tunnels at this time of day. Trotting back into the main cave, Obsidian spotted a lone armored dragon who did not seem busy, an ash-colored dragon with black stripes. The pair slowed down into a walk and approached him. He seemed young and fidgety.

"Excuse me," said Obsidian.

The guard nodded in acknowledgment.

"Are you able to help me in any way? I have been trying to avoid a volcanic dragon who tried to burn my home and has been harassing me and my family."

His round ears raised slowly. "Go on."

"I come from the Redwood Mountains, this dragon wants to take my son because he believes in a prophecy that implies my son would have some kind of magical powers. I don't know anything beyond his name or vaguely what he wants to accomplish. Does the name 'Fossil' sound familiar?"

The dragon looked shocked, processing all that he had heard. He shook his head. "I admit that I'm not the most experienced of the guards, so if you're trying to find out *who* this dragon is, maybe an older one can help. Look for Raeliina."

"Where are they?" asked Hamara.

The young dragon pointed his snout down the hall behind him. "I last saw her up the spiral slope, to the room through the left tunnel."

"Thank you," Obsidian bowed her head.

She and Hamara trotted off again into the next cave. At the back of the passage, they could see the floor begin to gradually rise and turn. They followed the curve of the path up to the caverns above, the top of the sloped trail led them to converging halls.

The left tunnel, remembered Obsidian. They didn't stop to examine this new area of the palace. This path was a short one, soon opening into a circular room with a stone table in the center. There were pieces of volcanic dragon armor hanging on the walls. Four tunnels were dug into two sides of the cavern across from each other, completely unlit. One older, deep red dragon with maroon dapples along her spine sat at the table, her back to Hamara and Obsidian. She turned her head to look at them, revealing golden eyes. She chuffed the same way the dragons at the palace gateway had.

"Are you Raeliina?" Obsidian asked.

She nodded.

"We were told by another dragon that you maybe could identify someone for me."

"Who?" Raeliina stood up.

"A young volcanic dragon named Fossil, he's dark gray with black stripes, copper eyes, and his horns are golden."

Raeliina narrowed her eyes but kept her ears perked forward. Her sight trailed over to Hamara for a few heartbeats before she answered with another question. "What reason do you want to know?"

"He had been lurking around my territory for moon-cycles, burned part of my forest, wanted to take my son, and he tore my wing," Obsidian told her, drawing Raeliina's attention back.

"Did you speak to him?"

"I had spoken with him a few times and it all felt one-sided. He would only focus on his own desires. He had mentioned something about Queen Gaar needing to face 'consequences' but I don't know what that entails."

"A tracking mission, hmm? Fossil is not a dragon name so I cannot say I have ever heard of him, *but* I'm sure I can do something about this."

Raeliina padded over to the hanging armor and slipped on an iron helmet that differed from the previous guard's, it was toned with cyan paint.

"Stick around, we'll propose a solution for you within a day or two," she concluded before springing into one of the dark tunnels and disappearing.

Hamara and Obsidian stood side by side in silence, staring at where the dragon had jumped through.

"Barely even reacted to her Queen being in potential danger," Hamara muttered, turning back.

Obsidian followed, "Fossil is only one dragon, and Ben has no powers. What could he do to her?"

Hamara didn't reply. They headed back to the nesting cavern without another word.

CHAPTER 19

Ben trotted through the unoccupied halls with Flossie prancing floatily, flapping her wings beside him. He had been staring between his claws most of the time they spent at the palace, not because he was sad, but because he wanted to look at the line art on the floor. It wasn't until now that he came across an etching of a horned horse with a long tail. He stopped and stared down at it, blinking. He realized it was a unicorn, recalling a memory of Obsidian telling him about them and how they disappeared. Flossie paused to wait for him.

"What was it?" asked Flossie.

Ben trod over to rejoin her, "A drawing of a unicorn."

Flossie stretched her neck to see the artwork before turning to bound down the tunnel again. "I wonder what Veynekan would be like if the unicorns were still around…"

"What do you mean?"

"They were super smart, right? I heard once that they developed language to speak to horses and deer."

"Why would they want to speak to deer?"

"Your guess is as good as mine since we can't just go ask them."

They continued along the caverns for a few more strides, both of them still thinking about the lost equines.

"I wonder *what* could've even wiped them all out. There's no way to know without their magic," Flossie sighed.

"How could they figure that out?" Ben asked.

"They're the only reason we know what happened to the first dragon queens."

Ben tilted his head.

Flossie seemed surprised. "Oh boy, here we go. There was once a Guardian of Veynekan," she began, doing her best Hamara impression. "He protected the land and combined strengths with Queen Hoyhenet, the first and last ruler of her kingdom, to end the war. The beasts were at peace, all seemed right. Until the Guardian suddenly changed, he incinerated SearClaw and the first queens. We hope he is forever as lost as the destroyed city."

Ben had not expected that, "I didn't know any of that."

"Well, I guess it did impact the dragons and gryphons more than hippogryphs, after all."

The young dragon thought about the story a while longer as they proceeded down the halls. Walking around the palace had not been particularly interesting. It didn't help that neither of them could read it clearly. After a while, they came up to a fork in the path.

"Where should we go?" Flossie looked up at him.

He had expected her to make that choice. "Uh," he glanced at both entrances once more, then chose the left. "This way."

The corridor he chose took a sharp turn, then went up an incline. Flossie fluttered over it and landed up there just before Ben made it beside her.

"Let's look up here for a little bit then go back," said Flossie.

He nodded. It wasn't much different than anywhere else they'd seen already, but interspersed between the lanterns were the same holes in the walls that he saw in the main cave. It felt especially quiet here. They were coming up to an area where a couple of caverns collided. Ben suddenly stopped in his tracks as he noticed something new in the floor's patterns. Flossie did not hear him halt. Right in the center of the converging paths was the largest drawing he had seen on the ground, the lines were colored ivory and tinted with a ruby gradient inside. He stood right on top of the illustration and backed up to fully observe it.

What lay before him was a drawing of a massive bird with open wings and a long, elegantly curving neck, a long crest protruding upon its head. An extensive, swirling tail was beneath the bird's talons. All the designs he had seen on the floor had been real animals but this creature was unlike anything he had ever seen.

"Hey-" he looked up and couldn't see Flossie.

Ben squeaked in alarm, frantically looking around for her. He spun in a circle, calling out again, only his voice could be heard echoing off the walls. He thought to just go back the way they came but then caught a glimpse of something to his right. A tail tip slipped behind a corner. He tried to sniff out who was there, what little he could smell was familiar in the vaguest of ways, but also not at all. He cautiously crept closer, approaching the direction shift in the hall. He kept laying his ears flat then raising them again. He sprang out from behind the wall excitedly, expecting to see Flossie.

Both beasts were startled, Ben landed and froze. A volcanic dragon whipped around and met Ben's gaze with the same bewilderment, he shied away from the contact. In the low light, Ben could make out fire-red scales with dark stripes and maroon eyes staring at him widely.

Ben blinked. "Who are you?"

The dragon was silent, they seemed struck with fear.

"What are you doing?" asked Ben curiously.

"...Walking," he said quickly and looked around. "Don't tell anyone you saw me."

Ben tilted his head. "Why not?"

"I can't tell you," The beast seemed like he wanted to run away immediately. Then he suddenly noticed Ben's features. "What kind of dragon are you?"

"But you won't even tell me your name!"

The dragon snorted softly. He glanced down both directions again, and mumbled, "...Finiir."

"I'm Ben, I'm a hybrid."

Finiir seemed surprised. "Are you from here? I've never seen you before."

"No, I'm from the Redwood Mountains."

"Isn't that really far? Why are you down here?" Finiir's fright morphed into intrigue.

"I'm here with my dam, a volcanic dragon tried to burn our home and we're looking for help," Ben explained. "Have you met a dark gray dragon with stripes like yours?"

Finiir shook his head. "I've never been outside of the palace, my mom is the only dragon I'm supposed to talk to."

"What?"

"She wouldn't be happy to know I'm here alone and talking to you."

"But why are you doing it if she'd get mad?"

"I've probably told you too much."

Finiir started acting anxious again.

"Is your mom an important dragon?" Ben asked, wanting to keep talking without him running off yet.

"You could say that," whispered Finiir, glancing around uneasily.

"Does that make you important?"

"I guess."

Finiir stayed alert, staring down the depths of the tunnel ahead of and beside him.

"I probably shouldn't stick around much longer," he muttered.

Ben's ears drooped. "What are you looking around for? Is your mom here?"

"Oh, no, she'd never come alone. Especially not while everyone's in a meeting."

Ben didn't question further as he was losing Finiir's attention to a distant echo, the dragon's ears were twitching, trying to listen better.

"I think I should go," whispered Finiir.

Despite his large claws, he scurried away down the passage quietly. Ben peered around the corner and watched him jump into one of the smaller tunnels. The sound was getting closer, a stride of both hooves and talons. Ben turned himself around to see Flossie, she sped up once she saw him.

"I didn't realize you stopped!" she said apologetically.

"It's okay, something just looked interesting," he replied, shooting a glance where Finiir had gone, wondering if he was still there.

Flossie started to make her way back from the direction they both came from. "There was nothing fun where I went, a guard told me to go back. What did you find?"

"There was a big carving of a weird bird."

"I saw that while I was looking for you. Maybe we should go back and wait for Hamara and Obsidian."

Flossie took flight and they raced back through the tunnels they had come from. As they returned to the nesting room, which happened to be about the same time Hamara and Obsidian were coming down the hall. Everyone met in the center, Ben whickered to Obsidian once they reunited.

"Did you learn anything?" he asked his dam.

"We spoke to two dragons, neither knew who Fossil was. However, one told us to stay for a few days, they're going to work something out," she informed.

"Are we going home after that?"

"I believe so."

Ben bucked and let out a joyful roar, "Momma will be so happy to see us!"

"That she will," nickered Obsidian.

Flossie whickered softly, glad for them, then her expression faded as she faced Hamara.

"What do you plan to do after this is over?" she questioned.

Hamara stared at her for a moment. "I'll figure it out."

She did not continue. Dejection masked Flossie's face. Hamara flopped down into the same nest she had used before.

"What should we do while we wait?" asked Ben.

"Whatever you'd like to pass the time," Obsidian answered. "Personally, I am a little hungry."

Flossie lifted her head, "Do we have to go hunting ourselves or…?"

"I guess we'll find out. Do you want to come along?"

Flossie nodded. The three of them headed back out as Hamara stayed put.

On the next day, Ben wanted to explore the caverns again. Accompanied by Obsidian this time, they ventured down the hall on the left of the foyer. It didn't look much different than any other part they had gone to: filled with tunnels splitting apart, leading into rooms, signs they could not read. The Queen's dragons were more present than yesterday. Ben was secretly curious if he would find Finiir somewhere, he couldn't help but wonder about him. Though, Ben didn't have much luck. It was unlikely that Finiir would show himself with Obsidian around. He and his dam didn't explore far, not wanting to get lost.

They returned yet again to the nests for a break, still eagerly awaiting a response from the guards. Ben patted the ground with a front foot rhythmically as he lay beside her. He couldn't seem to keep still.

He pushed his head closer to Obsidian and sighed. "I'm bored."

"What do you want to do?" She looked down where he rested.

He answered after a few heartbeats, deciding in his head. "We haven't gone outside in a while."

Flossie raised an ear.

"Hmm," breathed Obsidian.

Flossie started to rise from her spot. "I can go with him if you aren't feeling it," she offered to Obsidian.

"The thing is, I'm worried that Fossil may find us again," Obsidian confessed. "He did it once, there is a chance he can again. I would rather not find out whether or not the guards would stop him from entering the palace or if they would see him as their own."

"Oh," Ben had not considered that.

He sighed and remained on his side, missing the forest and mountain air. Later in the evening, they managed to drag Hamara along with them and explore the farther caverns more confidently. Finding themselves upon a rather long path, a couple of minor tunnels split off from its sides but they ignored those, and headed towards the threshold they could see at the end. Hamara read the sign as they got closer.

"It's a library," she told them.

"What?" asked Ben.

"A place with a lot of writing and information."

Ben raised his ears, he couldn't understand anything written there but it wouldn't hurt to poke around. They entered the library, it was a wide room but the ceiling was much lower than most others. It looked like the floor abruptly dropped on the other side, but after looking over the ledge, they could see a walkway down into the rest of the cave. The walls had shelves chiseled into the sides from top to bottom, each looked packed with scrolls and tomes. Not nearly as many dragons were inside the library as compared to the rest of the cave system. Ben peeked over the edge of the crater before gingerly stepping down the path. He slowly strolled around the room, his gaze following the shelves. Nothing in particular caught Ben's eye, most were the color of plain paper with presumably a title written along the spine.

The four beasts split off into pairs, Flossie and Hamara were in another corner of the library poking around. Up ahead, Ben could see a sudden break in the shelves, quickening his pace to check it out. Obsidian followed him. There was an image engraved into the wall, an enigmatic shape with certain spots having more distinct details.

"It's Veynekan," said Obsidian. "We live up there," she pointed with her beak to a depiction of mountains far to the northwest.

Ben tried to imagine the paths they took crossing the plains, into the woods, and getting to the Volcanic Palace on the map. He continued to examine the illustration, and in the corner, he saw a compass, within the center was the same bird he saw painted onto the floor. Eventually, his attention was grasped by another drawing. The back wall had no shelves, only a mural of a volcanic dragon rearing up, wearing a crown and holding a small diamond-shaped object in their front claws. The space between one of their hind legs and tail was empty, but not plain, as if something had been meant to be there.

Obsidian decided to rejoin Flossie and Hamara, Ben following in tow. Hamara had a book opened, herbs and flowers were drawn on the cover, Flossie was stretching up to see the pages. A shape suddenly blocked one of the lanterns as a dragon appeared in the doorway. It was the same dappled dragon Hamara and Obsidian had spoken with.

"I have an update on your request," began Raeliina. "I and many guards discussed the details we were given, but we now have a plan. However, Queen Gaar herself wants to speak with you about it."

They all stared at her in surprise.

Obsidian blinked. "What would the Queen want with hippogryph problems?"

Raeliina shook her head, "She didn't tell me. But she wants to speak with you at dawn tomorrow, you're the first of that day to have an audience."

They continued to look at each other in disbelief. Anxious excitement rushed through Ben's chest. Everyone else looked a little uneasy and confused.

"Thank you," said Obsidian. "We'll be there."

Raeliina nodded. "A guard will come to escort you," then she turned and flew out as quickly as she had arrived.

CHAPTER 20

Obsidian's eyes flew open at the sound of claws, she lifted her head. A solid black volcanic dragon ambled closer, metal armor audibly shifting in their stride. Obsidian rose to her feet, the dragon stopped beside the nests the four occupied.

"The Queen is ready to speak with you," he said.

"Just a moment," Obsidian yawned softly.

She nudged Ben with her beak. He trilled quietly and sniffed. Flossie started to twitch awake before Obsidian even got to her. Ben jolted up suddenly, wide awake. His dam stepped over to get Hamara, but saw that her eyes were already open. She released a grumble before beginning to pick herself up.

"We're ready," Obsidian told the armored dragon.

He nodded. "Come along."

He started down the hall, leading them through the tunnel Ben and Flossie had briefly explored, then to a path on the right of a crossroads. A spiraling upward incline awaited them at the end with an incredibly high ceiling, supporting columns jutted out from the walls. As they climbed, they passed many openings of other passages, Obsidian glanced down at them as they proceeded but could only wonder where they may lead.

"We're heading to the highest cavern," said the guard, looking over his shoulder.

They continued up the long, circling trail. This indoor tower lacked any of the decorative stones suspended by roots and rope, allowing room for others to fly up. Their destination was in sight. Once they finally reached the highest threshold, the tunnel was lit brightly, flames burned more aggressively than the bowls of embers. Only a few other dragons were passing through, all of them armored. In-between the lights were stone volcanic dragons that sat regally, watching the beasts in silent judgment. The atmosphere made chills prickle under Obsidian's coat. Remembering Fossil's words, '*the Queen cannot stay in power, she will suffer the consequences for what she did,*' she was unsure of what to expect from the Queen. Did she even plan on helping her?

At the end of the cavern, the guard paused, focused on the slope ahead. He turned around.

"Go forward and you'll reach her throne," the dragon told them before walking back the way they came.

Obsidian took a breath and scaled the rising path. She could see light ahead, but not from a fire. It was daylight. The final tunnel was filled with shadows, the glow across from them was like a beacon. Four armored dragons were along the sides and acknowledged them, but were as still as the statues. Obsidian led Ben, Flossie, and Hamara farther in, maintaining her pace but felt the beating of her heart increase. She hesitantly entered the throne room, the back of the cave was heavily shaded and difficult to see behind the sunlight. She wasn't sure if Queen Gaar was even there. Gazing up at the opening above their heads, it was the peak of the volcano that opened to the pale sky, a large sheet of sandglass diffused the light.

Their attention was drawn to the black throne carved from a mighty stalagmite. Maroon eyes watched them from the darkness. The beasts instinctively bowed as the Queen made her presence known, she stood hunched and stared at them from her elevated seat. She wore a metal crown that held rubies and wove around her horns, it was difficult to make out the rest of her features. Another beast entered the room from a hidden passage. It was Raeliina, but she donned a full suit of armor this time. Queen Gaar padded out from the dark, her scales were an unmarked, desaturated red with a lighter underbelly. Everyone waited for her to speak.

"You are the beasts pursued by Fossil?" she asked, her voice naturally intimidating.

"Yes, Your Majesty, he has attacked my herd as well," answered Obsidian.

"I know all that already. I only need you here to carry out my plan," she rumbled as she stood beneath the skylight. "Tell me, what exactly does Fossil want from you?"

"My son."

"Precisely. Because he believes…"

"…That he has powers."

"Did you flee and he still found you?"

Obsidian nodded, shifting an ear back.

The Queen flicked her tail spines. "How fortunate that you will bring him right into my claws," an unnerving tone spilling out.

Ben, Flossie, and Hamara glanced at each other.

She continued, "I've been after that dragon for some time, you know."

"How did a single dragon evade your guards?" asked Obsidian.

"Quiet," she held her head high. "I-"

Another dragon crept in through a tunnel. Ben's ears perked up, he could see the stripes of Finiir. He wanted to greet him but was interrupted before he could even open his mouth.

"FINIIR!" the Queen roared, whipping around with her ears flattened against her head. "You should know better than to cut through here! Get out!"

She swatted at him, the prince bolted back out of the room. Obsidian and her group stood tense. Queen Gaar gathered herself and sat down as if nothing happened.

"I've summoned you to tell you my plan," she resumed. "Fossil will not come near my palace, but he would if it meant reaching his goal."

She got up again and took a few more steps forward, she was even bigger than Hamara.

"What are you going to do?" Obsidian questioned, being forced back a step sheerly by the Queen's stride.

"I will lure him into my mountains, but to do so I need bait," she rumbled, staring down at them. "This is where the albino comes in."

Raeliina rose off her haunches. Ben looked around, backing up.

Obsidian's ears shot back, her feathers raising. "No!" she hissed. "You can't do that!"

"Why not?"

"I will not let you."

Queen Gaar's ears slowly flattened, she began opening her wings and held them menacingly above her shoulders, the skylight illuminating her webbing. "You forget where you are. This is *my* mountain, I hold the power of my dragons. You have no right to defy me."

The four moved back. The armored dragons they had seen in the hall were marching up from behind them, blocking any exits. Raeliina came forward between Obsidian and the Queen and headed for Ben. She began to herd Ben away, her expression hidden behind the helmet. Ben struggled to find an escape around her, he glimpsed past the guard at his dam with terror.

"He will be taken to a chamber and will be accompanied by my dragons when I send them out," Queen Gaar's voice was like ice. "I advise against trying to escape. Doing so may assure that your herd will never see peace."

Obsidian's coat bristled, watching helplessly as they tore her son away. The Queen turned, and laid back down on her throne. The four guards remained behind them. She lifted her head and watched them from the darkness again.

"Do not think that Forest Kingdom news stays within its own boundaries," she eyed Hamara.

The old dragon tensed.

"Queen Reka requested that anyone who recognizes the thief is to inform her and keep them imprisoned until she can arrive to deal with you *herself.*"

The dragons surrounded Hamara. She scurried back, snarling with bared fangs and clutching the pouch around her neck. They forced Hamara along with them, taking her into the unknown out of Obsidian and Flossie's sight. The remaining two mares looked back at the Queen, unsure if she would do something to them as well. They dared not move until she spoke again.

"There is nothing left to discuss. You are dismissed," Queen Gaar told them, resting her head down.

Obsidian and Flossie hurried out of the throne room, the tunnel they had come from seemed deathly silent now. No sign of Ben nor Hamara. They ran all the way out of the entrance cavern as quickly as they could, their legs quaking. Then dashed into the outdoors, ducking behind foothills where no one would overhear them.

"What do we do?!" blurted Flossie.

Obsidian stared back at the palace, overwhelmed with emotion. "I don't know," she breathed.

"We can't let them do this! I don't know what they plan to do with Hamara!"

"I don't know what to do! But if she only wants to use Ben to get Fossil closer...waiting for that to be finished is all we can do now."

Flossie stared up at her, her expression despairing. "What about Hamara?"

Obsidian lowered her head, uncertain. "We'll figure something out."

They remained outside for a while longer, feeling too shaken to return to the palace for the moment. Going against the Queen was certain death, and they had no idea how much time they had until Queen Reka arrived. With no knowledge of where Ben or Hamara were being kept, the mares were filled with utter helplessness.

CHAPTER 21

3 days ago

Enraged and dazed, Fossil dizzily flew above the forest, branches whipping past his face. What had happened to him? The albino dragon was right there, then suddenly, faster than a blink, he woke up elsewhere. Having no idea how much time had passed, he was thrust into unknown surroundings. All of the canopy looked the same, his only point of reference was the gargantuan tree in the distance that held the palace. He knew that he was somewhere near the center of the Forest Kingdom. He flew north for a long while, the jagged line of mountains appeared on the horizon. He wanted to find that unicorn again, the stallion had gone somewhere else in the woods during the time Fossil chased down Ben.

His wings grew tired, he didn't know where to begin looking for Komeetta. He descended to perch on a branch, it bent and creaked under his weight. His head popped up just above the canopy, scanning the area, but it was still nothing more than a sea of leaves. Fossil was still panting, but he was able to relax on the limb. Though, he nearly tore off the branch when something unsuspectedly tugged on his tail. He spun around hissing, his tail was yanked away from the grasp of wispy claws. After he processed it, the hand slowly retracted back through the foliage. He watched the magical arm and followed, landing on the ground. Komeetta stood across from him.

"How did you end up here?" he asked immediately. "It's been a little under a quarter-moon-cycle since I saw you last."

"I don't know," grumbled Fossil, looking up at the treetops. "I nearly had him, then I was somewhere else."

The unicorn's eyes remained hooded but a hint of intrigue appeared.

"Well, I have news," began Komeetta. "During the time I was looking for you, I tracked the dragon in my mind."

"Where is he?!" Fossil demanded.

"Seems to be headed for the Volcanic Kingdom, right where I need to go."

Fossil tensed.

Komeetta started forward and walked past him. "Let's get moving."

The dragon was hesitant to speak out, but if he didn't he would likely run into more trouble than he was prepared for.

"What exactly is your plan? If they see me in the Volcanic Kingdom I will be hunted down," he told him.

"I am aware of that. I have an idea, but first, I would appreciate it if you told me where the stone I seek is within the palace."

Fossil turned his head skeptically, but kept his eyes on him. The ever-unreadable gaze of the stallion staring back.

"You of all dragons should know of its location," said Komeetta, taking a step toward him.

"Through the library, but I've never been past it."

"Then I shall carry on from there."

Komeetta resumed through the forest. Fossil had no sense of direction without the sky and needed to give his wings a rest, he would have to trust where Komeetta took him.

"What was your idea?" questioned Fossil.

"It's simple: I guard you with magic, get the dragon, I get the stone, then you are free to do whatever," he explained over his shoulder. "And after that is done, I will be parting. You must not try to find me again."

The inevitability of entering that mountain range put Fossil off, but Komeetta's last sentence gave him a little relief. He would not be upset to see this equine leave. He lagged behind at a comfortable distance from him.

Ben paced circles in his dark chamber, his mind and heart racing. The guards had placed him in the small confinement, with a boulder blocking the exit. There was at least a layer of bedding along the floor. Though they were not aggressive with him nor did they plan to keep him there long, he was terrified, panting silently. What if Queen Gaar's plan failed? He anxiously waited for someone to come by, unsure how much time had passed already. His mind was frazzled, he just wanted his dams back.

A while later, he heard the faint pad of footsteps from outside the room. Perking his ears, he listened closely. The beast came closer and seemed to stop right in front of the boulder. Ben scurried back as claws gently scraped against the stone. A few gentle taps, purposefully trying to be quiet.

"Ben," whispered the dragon.

"Finiir?" Ben peeped.

"I stuck around after seeing that you were talking to the Queen and saw them put you in here. What does she want with you?"

"She wants to use me as bait!"

"Shh!" Finiir hushed him, he waited before speaking again. "We'll both be in trouble if someone hears."

Another short silence fell upon them until Ben asked, "Why did she treat you like that?"

"...I don't know," Finiir's tone was laced with despondence.

The conversation halted once more.

"Are you able to let me go?" Ben hoped.

Finiir was hesitant. "I would, but I would be suspected before anyone else, even without knowing we spoke before."

Ben exhaled.

"I should go now, but maybe I'll see you again before you leave for home," said Finiir, his footsteps so stealthy that Ben was unsure if he had even left.

Ben responded anyway. "Goodbye."

He then jolted back up. "WAIT!" he shouted, hoping Finiir was the only one who heard him.

It sounded like no one outside of his chamber had heard him until Finiir's claws clinked on the boulder again. The prince did not speak, probably worried that someone else could've heard Ben.

"Can you find my dam and friend, and tell them where I am?" Ben requested.

"Yes," breathed Finiir.

"My dam is a black hippogryph. My friend, Flossie, is half hippogryph, she's white and gray."

After Ben finished, Finiir vanished. Ben wasn't sure how exactly he would find the mares and speak with them where he wouldn't get caught, but he wished him luck. If he reached them, Ben didn't know if they could do anything about his situation... or Hamara's. He had no clue where she might be.

After taking some time to process and calm down after everything that had happened, Obsidian and Flossie reentered the palace. Moving at a swift pace, they steered clear of any of the Queen's dragons but still hadn't come up with any ideas. Down in a quiet hallway with no guards in sight, the mares stopped close along the wall. "Where would they most likely have taken Ben and Hamara?" Flossie asked.

"Probably through those tunnels the Queen's dragons run down, but we shouldn't go in there," answered Obsidian.

"Are there any other ways to get to wherever cells would be?"

"Let's take a look. I can't imagine it'll be easy, though."

The two resumed down the cavern though they didn't exactly know where to start looking. Chambers for keeping beasts in would likely be in the deepest tunnels of the mountain but they already had a poor sense of direction within it.

The chances of avoiding guards within unknown paths were thin. It took them some time before they managed to find a hall that began to slope down and realized it was where Flossie had been told to turn back after she flew ahead of Ben. Strangely, there was no one blocking the way like before.

Obsidian was reluctant. "If we're caught, I'm not sure what will happen. The Queen warned us not to try to free Ben."

"But we have to do something," urged Flossie.

"I know. But if the Queen stays true to her word and nothing happens to him, then we can get this over with."

Flossie stared down the trail, ears tilted to the sides. "She didn't explicitly say we shouldn't free Hamara, did she?"

Obsidian let out a short sigh. Flossie slipped by, hoping nobody had noticed. The ground didn't continue down for long, they reached more flat-floored tunnels. However, the number of openings into the dragon warren immediately increased. Alarm flooding Obsidian, the pull to turn back was strong, and yet she persisted alongside Flossie. There was no one else walking through here, further cementing that it was off-limits. They slinked down the path, side by side in silence. There were a few narrower caverns that split off with writing above the openings, but they couldn't understand it.

As they went farther into the passage, the lights grew dim, dust collected at the bottom of the walls. They had still not crossed paths with anyone, which Obsidian found relieving. Did anyone still come here? Why was it so barren and unpolished? Obsidian stopped suddenly, Flossie noticed after she was a few steps ahead.

"I don't think anything's here," said Obsidian.

"But then why would it have been blocked by a guard before?" questioned Flossie.

Obsidian looked over her shoulder at where they came from. "I don't know. Maybe they were just dealing with something that day?"

"What about Hamara?"

"Trying to find her without any lead may put us in danger."

Flossie stared down the dark hall ahead of her.

Obsidian came forward, whickering, "We both know it's not smart to have come here in the first place. I'd like to go back while we can."

Flossie lowered her ears, exhaled, and turned herself around to backtrack.

"I understand how you feel," Obsidian stayed beside her. "The two of us, realistically, can't do much about this."

"I don't even know *what* Hamara did to be wanted by Queen Reka," mumbled Flossie. "I've known her all my life and thought I knew everything about her, but once Fossil came to the woods, she became so distant."

Obsidian brushed her withers empathetically. "Perhaps she was trying to protect you from something. Maybe if she stayed close you would be in danger too."

Flossie didn't respond, she kept her head low as they made their way back. It was still as unnervingly quiet as when they had come in. Obsidian just wanted to lie down and think. Surprise froze her body as a silhouette of a dragon jumped out from one of the tunnels ahead. She and Flossie stood like statues, the guard paused there for a moment and looked around, then turned their head toward the two. They stared back at the dragon. This beast wore a helmet, Obsidian could see the eerie glint of their pupils through the eyeholes. They began to approach them but not as threateningly as the lighting made them appear.

"What are you doing here?" he asked.

Obsidian thought of an excuse. "We saw that it was vacant and were curious."

The guard made a rumbly trill in his throat, he looked behind him. "If you leave now, you will not be reported."

"We were on our way," Obsidian dipped her head and hurried past him.

Flossie followed close behind. Obsidian could feel the guard's sight trailing the two of them as they exited. She and Flossie rushed along and made their way back to the nesting cavern. When they got there, they lay back to back in the bedding for a while. Exactly what Obsidian had feared had happened. She didn't believe that Ben would be safe luring Fossil out, not even with guards nearby, but there was nothing she could do. No one was going to help them. She couldn't bear to lose her family again or to return to Sunflower alone. She thought back to her battle with Fossil at the base of the mountains. Had he never gotten ahold of her wing… she would surely have killed him. On purpose.

Obsidian bristled with anger and defeat, all she could do was seethe. Flossie hadn't spoken since they left the tunnel. Every scrap of a plan that Obsidian could think of led to a dead-end. She lowered her head onto the nest, both remaining there for some time. Eventually, Obsidian could hear what sounded like claws tapping on the stone above her head. She slowly rose from her spot and peered atop the ledge. A dark shape emerged from it and was now making its way down the rocks. She kept her neck low, using the dim lighting to her advantage. Flossie poked her head out from the nest. The silhouette spotted the black mare and began to move toward her, Obsidian's tail flicked. Stepping into the embers' glow was a young volcanic dragon with flame-colored scales, and stripes. He looked at Obsidian and blinked a few times.

"Are you the right hippogryph?" he asked. "The one with Flossie?"

Obsidian stared back at the dragon. "Yes…?"

He immediately dashed into an unoccupied nest in the shade.

"Come out of sight first," he called in a whisper.

Obsidian flicked her ears, glancing back at Flossie who got up and came over to her side. They followed the beast under the overhang.

The dragon sat with his limbs tucked as close to himself as possible. "I spoke with Ben."

Obsidian's expression lit up.

"Wait, didn't I see you earlier for a moment?" Flossie asked. "Aren't you the prince?"

"…I am. But that's not important, Ben told me to come find you," he resumed. "My name's Finiir. Ben is being held in the hidden cells near the throne room."

"Then I've got to go there," said Obsidian, ready to move right away.

"Don't! You'd never get in and I'm not allowed to show you where it is,"

"Why would you tell me where my son is if I can't free him?"

"He wanted me to tell you."

"But you're the prince, shouldn't you be able to free a prisoner?" Flossie tilted her ears.

Finiir shook his head. "I don't really have much else to say. He didn't give me a message to bring," he mumbled.

Obsidian sighed softly. "Is Hamara in the same cells as Ben?" she asked.

Finiir's face turned to confusion.

"I guess not."

"If they got taken, they're probably in the dungeon that isn't secret," said Finiir.

"Where's that?"

"A little past the art of the Guardian on the floor and down a long tunnel, but it's usually guarded and purposely like a maze."

Obsidian twitched an ear. *The place we had just been.*

"Thank you, anyway," breathed Obsidian.

Finiir nodded. He then trotted past the mares, out of the small cave. "I should go."

And with that, he hurried out of the room and disappeared around a corner. Obsidian let out another sigh. Flossie's ears fell back.

"We shouldn't have turned back," she grumbled.

"I know now, but if we didn't, we still likely would've run into a guard sooner or later," replied Obsidian.

Flossie looked down at her talons for a few moments. "Now what's the plan?"

"I'm not sure. There still isn't much we can do."

They both returned to the nest. Sitting in silence, they kept trying to think of some way to save the two dragons. Obsidian would just have to trust that the guards protected Ben. But, Hamara on the other hand, would be much trickier to solve.

CHAPTER 22

Ben sat in the darkness, uncertain of how much time had passed. The guards had given him food, but he didn't feel like eating. He couldn't handle the loneliness for another moment, yet he felt unable to move. What could he even do? He wasn't strong enough to nudge the boulder, even if he threw his whole weight at it. A while later, he could hear noises from the other side of the wall, the muffled rhythm of multiple footsteps. He raised his head. The gaits of the guards came closer, he eagerly hoped they would let him out. But if he was allowed out, he knew what they would make him do. Neither staying in or luring Fossil was more favorable to him.

The footsteps outside had ceased. The massive stone lodged in the opening started to shift as it was pried away by hefty claws. Ben gingerly took a few steps forward, light spilled into the room past the shadow of a dragon. He saw four guards standing, they were all fully armored. Ben timidly waited for directions.

"By the Queen's order, you must come with us," said the rosy dragon who had removed the boulder.

Ben came out of the chamber and moved into the center of the group, the dragons' helms hid their faces. The one who had spoken began leading everyone down the hall. The armored dragons formed a snug diamond shape around him. He grew increasingly uncomfortable as he noticed the numerous cells they passed through this tunnel, wondering if anyone else was being held here. The passage narrowed and split apart, the dragons switched into a single file line and took the right. Ben couldn't see a thing past the guard in front of him, but he kept close through twists and turns, until finally, he could see light—daylight. He felt a nervous rush through his chest, his legs turning wobbly. No escape.

They emerged from the volcano and ended up somewhere outside the back. Ben's eyes felt like they were burning from the glare, he could barely keep them open. He found no comfort in the tense silence among the dragons. The leading beast gave a signal with their tail and flew into the air, the rest of them herded Ben into flight with them, resuming their formation surrounding him as they soared. Ben didn't know how they were going to track Fossil down but he was too intimidated to ask. But then, the front dragon started to explain. "If we see Fossil, you're going to go down there and lure him close to wherever we hide. No harm will come to you if you cooperate."

Ben could only manage a single mumble in return.

"We may not even find him today. If not, you will have to go back to your cell," the guard spoke again.

Ben took in a breath and continued flying, trying not to bump the wings of the others around him. Flying farther around the mountain range as they scanned the cliffs, Ben followed any orders silently. He felt too paralyzed by fear to do anything more. Eventually, they descended and landed in a ditch. Only the rose-scaled dragon climbed up to observe their surroundings, everyone else lingered where they first touched the ground. The dragon gazed upon the mountains for a long time but caught no sight of Fossil. They took to the skies again and traveled west, landing elsewhere to continue searching. The four volcanic dragons sat vigilantly, the sun had already noticeably crept a distance across the sky. Ben's face was becoming sore from squinting.

He let his mind dwell on what would happen if Fossil never came, if he had just given up, would they keep Ben locked up there forever? He knew Obsidian would try to free him but what chance did she stand against a whole palace? He almost wished he *did* have some sort of magic to get away.

They moved to yet another location, it was getting close to midday. Ben was getting hungry and felt miserable out here. Hopefully, the guards would decide to quit for the day soon. But, for now, the dragons watched the hills a while longer before the leader turned to Ben and approached him.

"We're going to make one last attempt today. Follow me," he spoke.

The group kept low to the ground, only leading Ben a small span from where they were standing before. Where they settled now was open land, a flat side of a mountain. From the corner of his eyes, the guards were slinking away anywhere they could hide. Ben dug his claws deep into the thin layer of dirt.

"You may wander freely *on foot*. Do not try to leave, we'll be hiding out of sight but we can still see you."

Ben didn't respond but blinked slowly in understanding while staring off into the mountains. He immediately felt vulnerable, standing like a petrified deer, a chill trailed beneath his scales. Feeling that the guards would get upset with him if he didn't start moving, he hesitantly took one step, looking around before taking another. Slowly making his way along the rough terrain. His terror was so loud in his mind that it silenced the mountain range. He expected something to leap out at any moment.

A while had already passed. Ben took the easiest paths to traverse, though he roamed aimlessly. If a beast were to approach him, he likely wouldn't see them coming with the sun hindering his view. A few rock formations made him flinch, his eyes tricked him into thinking they were silhouettes of a dragon crouched. Unease followed him with every pace. He decided to sit down.

Should I do something to get his attention? Ben began to wonder. He glanced around trying to get an idea of what he could do. There was a dry-looking tree not far from him, so he examined the trunk. It was thin and brittle on the surface. Igniting it came to mind. He didn't like that thought much. However, a billow of smoke would be hard to miss.

Ben took a moment before he built up fire, it had been long since he last tried. The uncomfortable sparking of flames rose behind his jaw, he narrowed his nostrils in distaste. With a huff, he scorched the bark. But it quickly dissipated and left only a meek little fire on the tree. He grumbled and tried again, this time exhaling a more steady stream. The wood started burning more lively, it wasn't as large as he had hoped, but the smoke began rising. He now waited in the area. As time passed, the tree became almost completely charred. The sun was hanging lower, he squinted at the horizon, trying to find the scent of a beast with the flames at his back. He couldn't smell or see anyone there, so he turned to look behind him.

He spotted someone immediately, an equine. For a moment, he thought it was his dam from the dark color, but noticed a spike protruding from its head. The animal saw him as well, and faster than he could blink, the creature vanished. Just as Fossil had in the woods. Ben immediately sprung to his feet, his eyes darting around. He looked back at where the strange horse had stood and saw something flying toward him. Fear gripped him tightly, he instantly recognized it as Fossil barreling his way. He let out a panicked roar and, thankfully, the dragons did not take long to respond. The four of them lunged into the sky, flames ready and trailing from their mouths. Fossil was darting toward Ben but was swiftly knocked out of the air by one of the Queen's dragons.

Ben scurried farther away from where the dragons began to battle, turning to watch as the dragon who tackled Fossil was flung off by a kick from his hind legs, the other three surrounded him. Their fangs bared, tail spikes rattling. With the guards distracted and Fossil outnumbered, Ben didn't hesitate to make his escape. His wings flung open and he frantically headed for the palace. The guards slowly circled Fossil, each one of them was ready to react at any moment.

The lead guard snarled. "Surrender and less harm will come to you."

Fossil said nothing. Something's foot knocked against a rock, the guards glanced in that direction but there was nothing there. Within a blink, Fossil pounced forward, slamming his weight against the dragon in his way, throwing them onto their side. He sprinted away and attempted to get into the air after Ben. The armored dragons bolted to catch up, gaining on him just behind his tail in flight. The one closest began to ignite their crop, Fossil suddenly spun around midair, the two dragons collided and spiraled down into the foothills. The guard scrambled up before Fossil could, pinning him down, smoke rising out from their jowls. The other three rushed over and snapped their jaws around Fossil's wings. Fossil roared and tried to kick and flail the beasts off. When he was about to blast flames, the dragon pressed his head down and away with a powerful front foot.

A flash of light snapped through the air, with a loud metallic clang the guard that stood atop Fossil was sent flying across the stone. The beast landed and tumbled, scraps of his armor littered the ground. The dragon's shoulder piece was nearly destroyed, a shallow gash on his scales appeared beneath it. Where the attack had come from was unseen. The other three gaped in shock, allowing Fossil to slip away. He rolled upright and leapt, swiping his claws against one of the dragon's helms. A stallion materialized from nothing, teal magic sparked from his purple forehorn, small jolts would shoot out like electricity.

All of the guards were in complete disbelief, they could barely bring themselves to move, the unicorn's mere presence froze them. Fossil had already soared a good distance away. Komeetta unleashed another magical bolt without warning. When the dust and blue wisps settled, the four dragons coughed and regrouped. Komeetta vanished again as he cantered away.

"I'm going after them, but only to beat them to the palace," said the rosy dragon farthest from the rest.

The others nodded at him and hurried to help their leader up. He jumped up and sped into the sky as fast as possible.

Hamara lurked in her dark cell, waiting for anything to happen. The guards had taken her satchel, she didn't care about losing her herbs but she luckily managed to conceal the important contents within her teeth when she was first captured. However, she hadn't found an opportunity to use it, her ability and knowledge of it was limited. The chances of being stopped were too high. Patience was her only option. Most of her time was spent trying to listen to what was going on beyond the walls, she had learned where the dragons were usually positioned. It wasn't until later that day when the guards sounded worked up, it began with muffled exchanges and claws trotting urgently across the stones. Shortly after, the thundering gallop of volcanic dragons passed through the tunnel.

Her future was uncertain, she didn't know how much longer she had until Queen Reka would come for her. The outside of the dungeon seemed to have settled now. Wherever those dragons were headed, they were long gone from the tunnel. This could be her only chance and she wasn't about to waste it. She crept over to what could loosely be described as a nest and pawed deep through the bedding, picking up a small object, but held nothing visible.

"Reveal," she whispered.

A stained-glass-like stone gained color as it appeared within her palm. She loped over to the boulder then she reared and pushed against it with her front legs and head. White light started glowing through the claws it was held in, the rock door began to slide. With one last heave, she was able to slip out of the cavern into the dim hall. As she had expected, it was not left completely alone, a lone guard stood in surprise but jumped into action. Without hesitation, Hamara tossed the object at the dragon as it shined brighter than before. It clanged off of the guard's chest plate. Fear stabbed Hamara, she was aiming for the beast's scales. She thought that her attempt had failed, but then the guard was quickly yanked away by their own armor, snarling in surprise as their claws scraped the ground and was dragged out of sight. Hamara froze for a moment, blinking. Not exactly what she had intended but that didn't matter, she grabbed the stone and hurried to the surface.

CHAPTER 23

Ben soared as fast as possible toward the volcano. He didn't dare look back, worried that he might freeze and plummet if he saw Fossil bolting after him. It already felt like he was being dragged down enough by his terror. His eyes were at their limit from being in the sun, he relied solely on the behemoth shape of the mountain to find his way. As he was nearly there, he drifted around to the front, looking out across one of his wings as he glided. Just as the angle of the volcano blocked the sun, Ben swore he saw a beast soaring after him distantly.

Once he found the opening, he wasted no time. Landing poorly, Ben's stumble startled the guards. They did not attack him, only seeming confused as to why he returned alone. Thankfully, they didn't stop him either as he dashed inside. Armored dragons streamed toward the main hall out from the dark caverns but they weren't interested in him. Ben flapped above the crowd to the end of the room. He galloped toward the nesting cavern, hoping to find Obsidian. Slowing to a trot, his exhausted eyes made out two silhouettes toward the center, they turned to face him with intrigued ears.

"Ben!" Obsidian called.

Under the faint lanterns, the contrasting coats of Obsidian and Flossie became clear.

"Mom!" yelped Ben, halting in front of them.

"What happened?! Did you escape?"

"They took me out to find Fossil," Ben panted. "As soon as he attacked, I ran away!"

"Do you think they caught him?" asked Flossie.

Obsidian's ear twitched back, listening to something out of sight. "Let's hope so. But the guards here seem riled up."

Just then, a pair of armored dragons sprinted through the room toward the entrance, ignoring Ben again.

"I want to get out of here," whimpered Ben.

"Not without Hamara!" Flossie protested louder than intended.

Obsidian's ears drooped. "I still don't know how to."

Flossie sighed quietly. Obsidian stretched her neck up to see past Ben, he and Flossie looked as well.

"There's obviously something going on though," said Obsidian. "Let's see what's happening first, we may have a slightly better chance at sneaking Hamara out while they're distracted."

The three followed the two guards at a distance. The halls were unusually barren, almost no other beasts padded through, and the few that did were all headed to the front. The voices multiplied as they neared the entrance. Just as they were approaching, the loud snap of metal breaking like a mere twig echoed into the cave, followed by roars from the guards in the threshold. The palace's residents backed away, the armored dragons began exhaling flames at whatever was outside. Ben's heart sank. A figure engulfed in fire prowled into the cavern, undeterred. A flash and an unseen force bashed several guards out of its way.

Fossil emerged from the inferno. Ben and Obsidian crouched down. The dragons attempted to attack him but their claws and fangs did nothing, he snarled at them and continued stalking forward. The whole crowd became petrified in fright. A roar echoed out from a tunnel, Queen Gaar shot out and perched atop the crowned volcanic dragon statue. Her subjects gasped at her appearance and that she would land somewhere so disrespectful. Fossil looked up, a surprising trace of fear crossed his face. The two stared at each other, their tail spines rattling. No one moved a muscle.

"Here you are, flying straight into my claws," the Queen's growl was low. "How dare you return without your wings bound, or have you come to turn yourself in?"

Her dragons stuck close, eager to strike if she gave the word.

"I will never bow to you," hissed Fossil.

"I would wonder what you could possibly want, but there is only *one* answer," she said coldly.

Fossil stiffened and flattened his ears further.

"You want to claim the throne that you still believe is yours? You threw that chance away long ago."

"No," answered Fossil. "If I did, I'd at least be an improvement."

"Then why not? I thought you wanted what was best for your kind."

"I do-"

"But you fled from responsibility to your kingdom and dragons. You don't mean what you say.."

Queen Gaar did not give him a moment to speak as she began to raise her wings.

"You wanted to be king so badly that you killed your own sister, Prince Ceer!" she uttered the dragon's true name with a snarl. "And you did it all for nothing!"

"That's not what happened!" he roared, stamping a foot down.

The youngest guards shifted around quietly, glancing at each other in disbelief, older dragons had unreadable or sorrowful expressions.

After a deep breath, Fossil spoke. "There was nothing that could be done for her," he muttered. Anger flared back into his eyes as he lifted his head. "That day was my biggest regret, if Melthrun were still here you'd already be out of my way."

The Queen's tail spines were twitching, guards began to inch closer. Fossil noticed but kept speaking.

"You make a big deal out of that as if we haven't committed the same crime," he growled. "Why don't you tell everyone what happened to the King?"

Queen Gaar blinked with her head held high. "Your father is history, he doesn't matter now."

"That's convenient. So why am I still guilty?"

The Queen did not respond beyond a snort. The guards around her started stirring uncomfortably.

"If you'd let your sister live," she began, "you would still be where you are now: alone, unwanted, and useless. Or dead. She would have removed all competition for my throne. There was never a happy outcome for you. You will always be worthless."

"Queen Gaar used her Catalyst to kill and hide the King's body!" Fossil snapped back with the same venom, staring into her eyes.

The Queen bellowed a roar to signal her guards, but most seemed hesitant to act. Barely a heartbeat after, a lightning-like crack sounded across the room followed by a scream of anguish from Queen Gaar. A cyan bolt vanished as quick as it appeared, particles swirled then disappeared around her, blood poured from a giant gash sliced across her throat. Beasts cried out in horror, life vanished from the Queen's eyes as she slid off of the statue and thumped against the stone floor, masking the paints in crimson. The room turned to chaos, dragons fled into the tunnels, conflicted guards darted around, too bewildered to charge at the ex-prince, who also stared in shock. But Fossil was the first to collect himself, he looked directly at where Ben was crouched and pounced toward him. Ben had no space to scramble back and flee, enclosed in the panic. He bumped into an equine with his tail, and when he turned to look, it was not his dam. It was the same stallion he had caught a glimpse of earlier.

Fossil knocked dragons out of his way, Obsidian was ready to fight but once Fossil got close enough, a blue veil covered him, Ben, and the unicorn. After it cleared, the three were gone.

"Ben!" Obsidian crowed.

She scanned the whole room but her son was nowhere among the stampede. Obsidian and Flossie backed away but weren't able to get far. From the other side of the room, a dragon sprang into the air out from a narrow hall, flapping over the blood-splattered statue. It glided toward the mares, fear jabbed Obsidian with no way to escape. No longer a silhouette, Hamara pushed her way to the ground and curled around Obsidian and Flossie, her wings fanned like shields. The two couldn't find words to say after the unexplained sight. Hamara whispered something to an item clutched in her palm, then they disappeared from the scene as well.

"What just happened?!" shouted Obsidian.

As she blinked, they were now all standing somewhere on a hill with the volcano in sight. Flossie stumbled at Obsidian's side, just as confused. Hamara stepped back and shook herself off, the usual satchel around her neck was missing.

Obsidian spun around. "And how did you escape?!" she questioned.

"It doesn't matter right now," Hamara answered tonelessly. "Where's your son?"

"I don't know!" hissed Obsidian. "Fossil ran toward us then they both vanished!"

"Then stop yelling and start looking!"

Obsidian clacked her beak. Flossie could feel Obsidian's patience wearing thin.

"Don't fight!" Flossie reared up in front of Obsidian. "You're right to be angry but don't take it out on Hamara! I know her attitude isn't great, but we need to work together."

Obsidian took in a breath. "How can we find Fossil? There won't be a scent trail."

Flossie glanced down at her talons in thought. Hamara lifted her shut palm and held it close to her snout, her ears flicked.

"Oh we'll find him," she started into a brisk trot.

Obsidian and Flossie stared for a moment before joining her through the foothills, neither sure how she intended to locate Fossil.

Before Ben could react, he had been cloaked in blue light and was now face to face with a wall of stone. For a moment it felt like his claws were bound to the ground, unable to lift them up. Once the glowing substance dissipated, he was freed of the weighing feeling. Immediately, he jerked away from whoever was near him, whipping around, his side collided with the rock confines. He raised what few spines he had, threatening to strike. Fossil and the unicorn were inside the shallow cave with him, their bodies shrouded in thick shadows. Fossil stood just as tense as Ben but paid no attention to him, staring at the stallion with aggravation. Komeetta looked back at the young dragon blankly.

"What?" he asked. "Was that not a part of your goal?"

Fossil frowned. "I didn't invite you to rummage around my thoughts and memories."

"The Queen is dead and out of your way."

Fossil snarled and turned to Ben.

"Don't get hissy just because you can't say *you* killed her, she'd cause more trouble trying to get back her Catalyst. Even if you somehow got out of that without me," he, too, now faced Ben, "This hatchling would do you no good."

"What?" Fossil looked at the equine, narrowing his eyes.

"You really believed that he had any sort of powers?" scoffed Komeetta. "I'm surprised you didn't give up on him when you met me, who has *real* magic."

Fossil's gaze grew angry. "But…the prophecy-"

"Will never be fulfilled," Komeetta growled. "It came from before I was born, why would you still have any hope in it?"

Fossil snapped his head back to Ben, rage transforming into dismay.

"What did you intend to do after you got what you wanted?" Komeetta questioned further, yet gave him no time to respond. "Did you ever have a plan afterwards? Now your brother has no choice but to be shoved onto the throne."

Fossil had no answers, just continuing to stare at Ben.

Komeetta's tone turned cold. "You have no one but yourself to blame, you chose to convince yourself that everything would go your way. Your worthless quest has led you in a circle, you're back to being lost and alone. Even in death, your mother has won."

Too many emotions were coursing through Fossil, unable to retort. Ben couldn't feel pity for him though. Fossil had threatened and harmed his family, he burned his home, he mangled his dam's wing. But he was too fear-stricken to speak, afraid Fossil would lash out against him. Komeetta cleared his throat.

"I have done what I promised. You have the hatchling, I have what I was after. I've already done you more than enough favors. However, I *did* plan ahead, I'll be on my way now." The unicorn took a few steps before speaking one final time, "Do not ever try to find me again. I will kill you."

And with that, he galloped off. Fossil watched as he disappeared behind a mountainside, his hooves fading from earshot. Moments passed while Ben stood still as stone. He just wanted to go home. He was tired of running from Fossil, silently begging him to accept defeat and let his herd be. He realized just how few times he had actually come close to the dragon. Ben took a single step, a few heartbeats passing before he took another. He kept a wide space between them as he slinked by, pausing when he was across from him.

"Leave me alone," were the first words he said to Fossil and he hoped they would be the last.

Fossil said nothing, his face hidden. Ben scampered away and didn't look back. He quickly found the volcano not far from where he was, towering as always. Heaving himself into the sky on stiff wings, he was still taking in what had happened. Only when he had a moment to clear his head did he fully think about how there had been a unicorn.

A crackling woosh erupted from behind Ben. Turning his head, he saw a plume of fire shoot out of the cave. He didn't waste a moment to speed away when he caught a glimpse of Fossil rising through the veil of smoke. The palace was close but not enough to make Ben confident that he could escape. He was vulnerable in the air, Ben quickly dived lower to the rock formations. Though shielded from flaming blasts, one wrong move would cause him to hit the ground, occasionally feeling the tips of his wings brush against the gravel below. Fossil knew better than to follow him down and looked for opportunities to spit flames into where the stones made an opening.

For a short span, Ben was unprotected, right as he flew back into the safety of another overhang, he heard the roar of Fossil's fire hit the rocks and felt the heat on his tail tip. The end of cover Ben had was coming up. He darted beneath it and as he reemerged, blazing stones smacked into him. Fossil had dived and obliterated the formation, both dragons tumbled down a rocky hillside with the scalding boulders. Now there was no other choice. Ben would have to fight or die.

CHAPTER 24

Fossil snarled and snapped his jaws as they crashed down the slope, swinging his claws wildly in blind fury. Ben batted away the dragon's heavy palms, trying to ignore the pain of each stone he slammed across. They hit flat ground with a thump. Both scrambled to their claws, hissing. Ben had to quickly recall any battle training he had been taught. Fossil's golden tail spines rattled threateningly. Circling each other with their necks low, Fossil had his fangs bared while Ben crouched like a frightened wildcat. He knew he could not fight Fossil and win, their strengths were not remotely an even match. He could flee again but not in this proximity, only if he evaded well enough.

Fossil's wings stretched up as he lunged with open claws. Ben dashed around him but fell onto his elbow, Fossil spun around to swipe at him again. Ben kicked against the volcanic dragon's jaw, pushing himself away. Fossil's claws caught the edge of Ben's wing membrane, tearing it. Blood dripped from the fresh nick, Ben could feel his shaking limbs as he rose to his feet. Fossil didn't hesitate to strike once he collected himself, but Ben sprinted away again. Fossil skidded on the stones and tore after him. Ben attempted to throw him off with quick turns but his pursuer sprang off of boulders and hillsides, still too close for Ben to try getting into the air.

Fossil gave himself a boost with his wings, pouncing on Ben, tumbling into the gravelly terrain once more. Fossil's claws latched onto Ben's scales, beginning to pierce them. Ben flailed his wings and tried to shake him off. He kept attempting to escape but to no avail. He didn't want to know what Fossil would do, he didn't want to die without seeing his dam one last time. Before Fossil could act further, Ben looked up as a wave of fire engulfed the dragon. Unlike before, Komeetta's magic did not shield him. Fossil roared and flinched back as the heat scorched his eyes, allowing Ben to scurry away.

Hooves beating hard on the stone drew near, through the embers leapt Obsidian, screeching like a vulture. She threw Fossil off with her entire weight. Fanning her wings out and raising her hackles gave her a wild look that was a rare and terrifying sight. Her eyes blazed with hatred that matched Hamara's flames as she stared down at the stumbling dragon. A loud snap pierced through the air as she clacked her beak. Ben bolted behind Hamara and Flossie who were farther back, their eyes all on Obsidian and Fossil.

"Do *not* touch my son," warned Obsidian.

Fossil only gazed back at her.

Obsidian did not break eye contact. "I should've killed you in the meadow. You don't deserve any mercy, you worthless ass. All you do is destroy everything around you and I won't let you continue any further."

She took slow steps forward, "I'm not running away anymore and neither are you," she hissed, standing the length of her own body away from his face.

"I don't care," he snarled.

Obsidian shot forward, her damaged wing had healed just enough to use as a boost. Fossil was ready to ignite his flames but she dived and sank her beak near his fire crop, blood gushing out. A heavy blow from his front legs knocked her back but her hooked beak ripped through his flesh, both of them snarling viciously. Fossil reared and lashed at her again, Obsidian dodged each attack, flapping out of his path. She spun around and kicked his face, throwing him off balance which she took advantage of, facing him again and raking her talons down the dragon's shoulder. Fossil swung his head into her side in retaliation but Obsidian would not allow herself to fall.

Though she prevented herself from being thrown, the blunt force of his skull knocked the wind out of her. As she gasped for breath, Fossil took the opportunity and charged. He slammed into Obsidian, she beat his face with her wings as she was taken down to the ground. Ben witnessed the battle from afar, rage began bristling beneath his scales and quickly overcame his terror. He galloped forward with his ears plastered flat.

"Ben!" exclaimed Flossie.

Within only a few strides he reached Fossil and pounced onto his back, claws hooking his scales. Fossil's focus immediately shifted to him which caused his fright to come rushing back. He fought the urge to run, he needed to give his dam this chance to recollect herself. While Fossil tried flinging the young dragon off his spine, Obsidian jumped to her feet, she saw Fossil bending his neck around to bite Ben with his fearsome tusks. As fast as a blink, she struck Fossil again, clawing his eyes once more. Ben flew away from Fossil and landed, ready to flee or help. Fossil let out an agonized roar, he stumbled back and unfurled his wings. He attempted to fly away but was quickly intercepted by the two beasts. Obsidian sprang as high as she could to bring him down, Ben soared up and bit one of his wings. Fossil fell back to the ground, landing on his side.

Ben retreated again, Obsidian kept slashing her talons along Fossil's body. He would kick, flap his wings or try to stand but she wouldn't let him up. She evaded him over and over as she relentlessly beat him, rearing and slamming down to stomp on his head. Eventually, Fossil's resisting ceased. The beasts standing to the side weren't sure if he was unconscious or dead but the mare refused to stop. Obsidian bit behind his horns and twisted with her head. He did not snarl or try to pull away anymore, the dragon was dragged limply in her beak. The stones around them were painted scarlet. The stripes on Fossil's face were masked with his own blood. Obsidian lifted her head, breathing hard, dragon blood dyeing her face. Fossil was dead. Ben approached his dam slowly, the scene made him feel queasy.

Obsidian turned to him. "We're done here," she breathed.

She began to walk off somewhere with a limp in her gait, leaving the fallen beast without glancing back. Ben followed closely, Flossie and Hamara were a ways behind them. Obsidian led them to a stream, she dipped her head in, streaks of blood being whisked away in the current.

Ben overheard Flossie speak. "What do we do now?"

Hamara exhaled slowly. "I'm not sure. We can't go back to the Forest Kingdom."

"Why not?"

"...Queen Reka will be looking for me."

"What does she even want with you?"

"I shouldn't talk about it."

"But why? I don't know what to do with you, ever since more of her dragons came to Setiir you've been acting weird," Flossie's ears fell back. "You won't tell me anything. I don't know why you're acting colder than usual, I don't even know how you escaped your cell!"

Hamara didn't answer.

She continued. "I always felt like we were family. I just don't understand. What did you *do* to upset a queen?"

"I don't want to talk about it," Hamara grumbled. "The reason why can't be undone now, it's not because of you."

Hamara turned her head away. Flossie stared at her, her pale eyes filled with dissatisfaction. Ben felt sympathy for Flossie but he shouldn't barge into this.

"I want to go home," Ben told his dam.

"Me too," replied Obsidian. Droplets flew from her head as she shook. "We can now."

Ben wanted to go back to the mountains more than anything, he wanted to see Sunflower, Komodo, Conifer, and the whole herd again. But possibly never seeing his friend Flossie again was leaving a hole in his heart. He nodded. Obsidian started to limp over to Hamara and Flossie for a final goodbye. Finally dealing with Fossil didn't feel as triumphant as she had hoped, coming down from the adrenaline only left her muscles aching. Ben felt the same, reasonably more excited to see their family once more. His mind dwelled on how he had fought too, he hadn't battled another beast before and was surprised he managed to do anything, really.

"Ben and I are going home," began Obsidian. "Thank you for taking us in and accompanying us." Her gaze became warmer when she trailed down to Flossie.

Hamara nodded.

Flossie sighed. "I'll miss you."

"What are you planning to do?" wondered Ben, coming up beside Obsidian.

"I don't know."

"We'll go wherever we can," Hamara answered.

Flossie remained visibly upset, staring down at her claws. Obsidian took a few steps back. She looked upon the horizon, searching for the northwest. When she found it, she pointed with her beak.

"So long," nickered Obsidian.

"Goodbye," Ben muttered to Flossie.

As they were about to set out, a beast appeared from behind the foothills, soaring low to the ground. They were approaching from the palace. Everyone paused to see what was coming. Ben recognized the striped red scales of Finiir, he seemed to be quite shaken. He must've been somewhere in that room when Queen Gaar was killed. He locked eyes with Ben for a moment, then descended toward them, stumbling as he landed. Ben trotted toward the quivering prince.

"Are you okay?" he asked.

"No!" wailed Finiir. "I can't handle what's happening! I'm not ready to take the throne!"

Ben nor Obsidian had the answer as to what the prince should do. Finiir looked down at his claws, his chest heaving after flying so wildly. Hamara seemed uneasy and ready to leave at the sight of him, perhaps thinking he would throw her back into the cell as the queen did. Obsidian stepped closer to the young dragon.

"I don't know what to do. I'm not ready and I have no one to turn to," cried Finiir.

He raised his head to meet Ben and Obsidian. "What happened to that dragon? The one who was supposedly my brother?"

Obsidian pointed her ears back. "I killed him."

"Oh…" Finiir stared at her, but no sadness crossed his face.

"He wouldn't have been any help to you though."

Obsidian started to turn away again, she looked back at Ben as she stopped a wing-length away. She wanted to leave but felt guilty about leaving Finiir here all alone. Ben hadn't gotten to know the prince very well but he wished there was something he could do. The five beasts stood quietly, shuffling in anticipation.

Hamara broke the silence. "I'm going to leave. I can't be here when Queen Reka arrives and I don't want to see how the aftermath of all this plays out."

Hamara started on foot, after a few strides she turned to glance at Flossie who had not removed. The mare looked at Ben and Obsidian, then to Hamara. It was plain to see that she didn't want to follow the dragon, but nonetheless, she slowly moved to join her.

"Goodbye, again," she mumbled.

Ben watched her trail after Hamara. He tried to think of something to say to Finiir.

"If the queen is gone, I think you'll be okay," he tried to sound reassuring.

Finiir turned his face away again. "But I don't know what to do."

"The dragons will help you. My herd always looks out for each other."

"Maybe. But we're not a herd."

Ben pulled himself away and headed toward his dam, still looking back at Finiir. They began to walk out into the rugged landscape, yet another long journey awaited them. Glancing back, Ben could see Finiir still sitting. But, the two of them didn't get far before they began to feel something, a low rumble began coursing through the stones. Ben and Obsidian stopped in their tracks. The vibration gradually increased, rippling in their lungs, pebbles and dust danced around their feet.

"What's happening?!" Ben yelped.

"An earthquake...?" Obsidian answered unsurely.

Wings suddenly flapped above them, Finiir rushed over and circled in the air. The trembling continued to the point where they felt unsteady on their claws. Once it finally and abruptly ended, everyone fell silent. Finiir glided down. After the silence, an explosion sounded in the far distance, an amber tower glowed and shifted shot into the sky and turned the whole horizon a blazing gold. It rose out of the plains not far from the Redwood Mountains, followed by the leftovers of the shockwave. Ben's pulse accelerated and his legs felt wobbly again. Obsidian was just as speechless. The spire vanished, a brisk wind blew over them. Immediately after, a voice none of them had ever heard before roared across the land like thunder.

"I HAVE RETURNED TO VEYNEKAN. LOCKED AWAY FOR A THOUSAND LIFETIMES, FORGOTTEN, AND LEFT TO ROT IN A BODY THAT IS NOT MY OWN. YOU HAVE TREATED YOUR GUARDIAN THIS WAY, EVEN AFTER I

PROTECTED, GUIDED ALL BEASTS, AND GAVE YOU PIECES OF MY
MAGIC. MY PATIENCE IS NO MORE. YOU WILL FACE MY WRATH AND I
WILL TAKE BACK WHAT'S MINE."

It sounded as if the whole world was muted after that, none of them could fathom what just happened. Nobody spoke, not even their shallow breaths could be heard. Only the caws of far-off crows dispersing into the sky reached their ears after a moment. The bellow of a forest dragon came from behind them. Obsidian turned her head to see Hamara and Flossie soaring back toward them.

"You're back?" Obsidian called.

The pair landed hastily, Hamara seemed unusually frantic.

"I don't know why, Hamara just pulled me back this way after we heard a voice!" panted Flossie.

"We heard it too," Obsidian told her.

Hamara's tail swayed anxiously, she didn't meet the eyes of the other beasts. She stared down at her claws, holding something tightly that they could not see. Her ears tilted back indecisively.

"I never wanted to tell anyone about this," she began. "But I don't think I have a choice anymore."

The four watched Hamara attentively, she slowly forced herself to open her palm, holding up for them to see the small crystalline stone resting on it. It was almost gem-like in shape, and its pale color came from the lazily swirling foggy substance beneath the surface.

"The voice mentioned having 'given pieces of magic.' I think this is what they were referring to," explained Hamara.

"Where did you get that?!" Flossie shrieked with her ears flat and eyes wide. "Don't those belong in the palaces?!"

A look of horror washed over Finiir's face and he backed away, shocked to see the item too.

"Let me finish!" barked Hamara. "I know very little about using it, but this is one of the Catalysts. Yes, it *was* from the Forest Palace. Supposedly, it's a slice of the Guardian's magic in a solid form that he had given to the four queens of Veynekan as a gift after the war ended."

Obsidian's eyes lit up in realization but she did not interrupt.

"I used it to escape from my cell, and obviously, teleported us out of there."

"So," Obsidian began, stepping forward. "How much can you do with it?"

"It seems to respond best to voice commands, and only works when it touches whatever you're trying to use its power on."

Obsidian remembered how Fossil had disappeared back in the woods, and how right after, Hamara was rummaging through the leaves where he was last seen.

"Wait, so you've had a piece of *magic* this entire time and you've barely done anything with it?" Flossie interjected. "Why didn't you use it to heal Obsidian? Why would you only transport Fossil somewhere else?"

"I don't know how!" Hamara shouted.

She breathed deeply to relax before speaking again, flipping the Catalyst over in her palm.

"Teleporting, getting things away, or finding things are all I can get it to do. They've been quite useful to me though," Hamara told her.

Flossie wasn't letting up. "But how did you get that?!"

"It's a long story that doesn't matter right now. There's no doubt after that message that the Guardian will attack beasts, but with this," Hamara held up the stone, "we might be able to stop him."

Everyone stared at her.

"You're expecting *us* to go against him…?" asked Obsidian, tilting her ears. "With merely a piece of his own magic?"

"What else do we do? This is the ONLY magic we have access to," Hamara rumbled.

"It just seems like using these should be left to the Queens."

Hamara snorted. "They haven't touched their Catalysts in generations, they think using them after the Guardian's disappearance would curse them. And there's more than just this one, I'm not waiting around to find out what happens if he destroys them."

"She's right," murmured Finiir, he had been so quiet his voice had taken them by surprise. "Another one is somewhere in the volcano but I've never seen it. There should be two more in the Cloud Kingdom and Gryphon Isles."

"I don't understand what's happening!" Ben blurted. He moved closer to Obsidian. "I thought we were going home, why did this happen?"

"We can't just yet, I'm sorry. None of us saw this coming," Obsidian told him, grooming his withers.

"That voice you heard before I came back was the Guardian of Veynekan. There was a place a long time ago called SearClaw, where he and a beast, who would become the Queen of that city, used magic to combine their bodies," Hamara began to explain. "It was meant to be temporary, but they continued like that for many four-seasons. Something in the Guardian snapped and he destroyed everything there. It's thought that he was only stopped by his exhaustion. The fused body of him and the Queen was still probably buried in the ruins. And now that he's awake, we can't just walk away and live as normal."

"But why did he wake up?" asked Ben.

Hamara just shook her head slowly, there was only so much she knew.

"So what are we supposed to do to him?" Flossie questioned. "I'm guessing we can't let exhaustion beat him again, 'cause if he got that far we'd all be dead."

Fear sprouted in Ben's chest again after Flossie's comment.

"Our best bet would be trying to reach the Catalysts before him, but that's going to be hard," responded Hamara. "But as long as I have this one, we can teleport closer to the others."

Obsidian raised her head. "I can't exactly go on adventures across the continent right now, even if we can teleport," she said dryly.

"T-there's a Catalyst in the volcanic palace," Finiir reminded them. "I don't know where it is, so if you want to try and help me..."

"I might as well."

"I'll look too," Ben told them, keeping close to his dam.

Hamada's eyes shifted to Flossie, she took notice and turned her head to the dragon.

"Will it be just us?" Hamara asked her.

"I guess so," there was hesitation in Flossie's voice.

"How much time do we have?" questioned Obsidian. "And where would he go first?"

"I'm not sure. But I feel like he'd head for the closest kingdom to where he awoke, which would be the Gryphon Isles," Hamara replied.

Obsidian nodded. "Be careful out there, and *try* to get in touch with any other queens. Maybe they'll know something about the Catalysts' powers."

The dragon stiffened at the suggestion. "I'll do what I can. Hopefully, we'll come back in one piece," she grumbled.

Hamara stepped away from the group and sat down, Catalyst in hand while she awaited Flossie.

"Goodbye and good luck," Flossie called to the three who would remain at the palace. "Even if we fail, at least we tried!"

She made an attempt to sound optimistic, but the weight of the situation was already setting in. Obsidian had little confidence in this. But as Flossie said, at least they would've tried. Flossie joined Hamara across the flat stones, she looked back at Ben and Obsidian one last time before she and the dragon were transported elsewhere by the Catalyst's power. In a flash of light that wrapped around the two beasts, they disappeared. Obsidian took in a breath.

"Let's not waste any time," she huffed, and began walking back towards the palace.

She waited for Ben to pad up alongside her before transitioning into a trot. Finiir hurried and took to the air, soaring ahead. Ben carried his head low as he moved. His dam whickered to him.

"Why do *we* have to do this?" asked Ben, anxiety riddled his whisper.

Obsidian exhaled. "Wrong place at the wrong time I suppose. I really don't know what could've woken the Guardian, nor do I know anything about magic."

"...I just wanted to go home."

"I know. I don't want to do this. But if Hamara is successful, this can be over faster."

They were fast approaching the palace, the sight of it was already soured by their experience there. But after this, they'd never have to look back. Watching over Ben, with the thought of her mate, family, and herd awaiting her in the mountains kept Obsidian going. Even with the twists and turns of their journey, she was grateful to have her son by her side. A feeling of helplessness and bleakness still latched onto her, but she wasn't about to stop. She had to be there for Ben, especially now. Yet she wondered, what chance did five ordinary beasts have against the Guardian of Veynekan? Once they stepped inside the mountain, their fates lied in the power of the Catalysts.

EPILOGUE

"You...can't do that. I can't let you."

Two beasts stood alone, high in the rugged mountains, hidden by stone formations. The eyes of the young volcanic dragons were locked onto each other, like cougars staring down their prey. The tension building between them grew thick, the dark striped dragon could feel it pressing against his chest like thorns. Fury was alight in his sister's gaze, they were merely a tail-length apart, and she was ready to strike.

"Are you on her side?" she growled. "You saw our father's body, she chased us, she would've attacked us! What do you mean we can't kill her?!"

"Melthrun," he tried to keep himself collected, he needed to choose his next words carefully. "I mean you can't fight her. We're not strong enough, you're not ready to be queen."

Melthrun's tail flicked, her spines clattering softly.

He continued, *"Right now is when we have to control ourselves. A lot. She's not being violent towards other kingdoms, we can wait a few four-seasons."*

"I don't give a damn how she's treating other kingdoms! What makes you think she wouldn't start harassing them? What about us? I'm not letting her treat me like dirt anymore."

"I'm saying that we can run away until we CAN fight her!"

"Don't you realize who she'll target when we're gone, Ceer? We'll be putting Finiir on the frontlines!"

Shivers ran through Ceer at the realization. She was right, the hatchling who couldn't even fly yet would be extremely vulnerable.

"I'm going to stop her, whether you want to or not," Melthrun said coldly *with her head raised.*

Her face was shrouded in shadow as the sun fell behind her, naturally forcing Ceer to step back. His sister's posture, words, and burgundy scales seemed all too identical to their mother's.

"I'm trying to help you. We can try to sneak Finiir away," Ceer breathed.

"You're too optimistic, there's no way we'll make it out of that volcano without being caught. She'll have already made up a story for her guards to attack us on sight."

Melthrun turned away from her brother, looking out at the towering mountain. She raised her wings for flight.

"You can't stop me!" she snarled as she heaved herself into the air.

Before she could flap again, Ceer lunged forward and clamped his jaws around the end of her tail, getting yanked up before she was pulled down. His heart immediately began to race, impulse had gotten the best of him. He knew

Melthrun would not react positively to that. She sprung to her feet and faced him again.

"Are you with me or against me?!" she spat.

Ceer reeled back. "I... I don't know."

Melthrun approached her brother with her wings flared up, her thick claws purposefully scraping against the rocks, the two nearly face to face.

"We don't get along the best but I'm trying to help you. You know how we act is also our mother's fault," Ceer tried to reason with her. "The choices we have to make are hard because right now we can't beat her."

"Maybe for you," she scoffed.

"What?"

"You can run off, but I'm still going. If you're not coming with me now, I don't want to see you step foot in this kingdom ever again."

Ceer stamped his foot and lashed his tail. "Stop being so difficult! We can't win!"

Melthrun took another step forward, leering at him.

"I'll prove that I can win," she hissed. "By crushing you."

Within a moment, Ceer was bashed across the face and knocked onto his side. There was no more trying to get through to her, the intent in Melthrun's dark eyes was clear. He had no chance to rise before she sprung at him again. He was quick to brace his hind legs between them, Melthrun's jaws snapped as he forced her head away from his throat. He kicked her off and flipped himself upright. They both reared up, swiping at each other with their claws, trying to take the other back down.

She reached up and grasped one of his horns. Ceer twisted and bit her foreleg in retaliation, beating his broad wings in an attempt to fly. He managed to get into the air as her claws slipped away, and thanks to the wind. But he couldn't make an escape, she knew these mountains just as well. Melthrun launched herself up, ascending higher as they circled and rode the drafts. Luckily, she was more hesitant to attack in flight, both knowing how dangerous aerial combat was for beasts their size. One wrong move and they could both plummet to their deaths. But she knew exactly what she was doing, there would be a point where Ceer could no longer look above him while flying. He perked his ears, hoping to hear her approach over the wind rushing past him before it was too late.

He couldn't catch a glimpse of her anymore, but he didn't dare to rise, she was still going to dart at him either way. He soared in anticipation, searching for a change in the whirlwind of noise surrounding him. From directly above, he found the whooshing of Melthrun diving, he turned himself over just in time with his claws outstretched. She was caught off guard as they collided midair, both of them unable to regain stability, the air slipping out from beneath their wings. They broke away from each other but not before Ceer could spin her around and spit a small plume of fire at her, not realizing how close they were to a ridge of stone below them. Their pained roars rang out for no one to hear as they fell between the walls of a ravine, the rocks cracked and crumbled, breaking from impact. Huge chunks toppled into the crevice after them.

The dust began to settle. Ceer coughed, spitting blood. He opened his eyes, shafts of light still managed to seep in.

"Melthrun…?" he whispered.

It was a moment before he got a response. All he heard was a low grumble and shifting pebbles. He tried to stand slowly, just barely managing to stay on his feet. He stayed in a crouch, quickly feeling a rock above him touch his back. He crawled toward the sound cautiously. He couldn't see her through the shadows. As he got closer, he realized Melthrun was right across from him, her wings and back half pinned beneath a stone. Blood trickled around her ribs, her breaths were uneven.

"I don't want to die," she rasped.

He didn't know how to respond. There was nothing he could do, and if there was, would he even want to?

"I...can't help you anymore," he said with emptiness.

He could barely see her narrowed eyes but knew that she was staring at him. She couldn't be saved.

"I won't let you suffer here," he told her. His voice shifted into a growl, "And I won't let our mother get away with this. Not for your sake, but for the kingdom and Finiir."

She continued staring at him silently. Ceer looked beside him, spotting a large and jagged rock, he began to feel light-headed as his pulse raced. He reached his stiff claws out to take it, pulling it closer to him. He lifted it, pain surging through his muscles. He looked down at Melthrun. Her eyes remained nearly shut, all she could say were meek roars of protest. Ceer remained seated on his haunches with the stone held up. Then, he finally threw himself down toward her head, the sharp end of the rock pointing down.

It was over, silently. Melthrun's ribs stopped rising with her breath. Ceer got back on his feet and moved backward. He didn't want to linger here any longer, he spotted an opening to the surface wide enough to escape through. He leaped and flapped his wings, nearly falling as his claws dragged against the cliff. Once he pulled himself up, he gazed at the palace once more, bitterness boiling within him. Twilight fell upon the sky, he took to the air despite his weakened state and did not look back.

Komeetta replayed the memory he had pulled from Fossil's mind once more, he found him to be somewhat interesting, but simultaneously glad to travel on his own again. After leaving him behind, he had teleported to the site of ruins, ones even older than his birthplace. It barely resembled a city after all this time, what remained of the structures had turned to ash and charcoal after the fire and countless four-seasons. The vague remnants of a castle sat towards the center. Komeetta traversed the terrain effortlessly, bounding across ancient piles of rubble. The tattered valley was soundless except for the beat of his hooves echoing off boulders. Magic glowed around his horn, turning his head to survey the area. It didn't take long before something caught his attention, exactly what he was looking for. The land sloped down and was filled with pieces of stone, a fallen tower lay atop it, the building still surprisingly recognizable.

The stallion headed toward it and his footsteps became more careful. He approached with his neck low, anticipating *something*. Once reaching a distance that he deemed close enough, he stopped and raised his head high, light enveloping his horn again, then tossing it down, pointing his horn at the ruins. A magical bolt crackling like lightning and fire as one entity shot something into the tower, burrowing beneath it. A shattering sound and deafening roar ripped through the air, followed swiftly by the ground shaking, blue light began shining from beneath the pit of rubble. Komeetta turned and fled, flames soon hot on his trail yet his face showed no fear at all. A cyclone of fire arose into the air. The vengeful Guardian of Veynekan returned to consciousness.

KOMODO

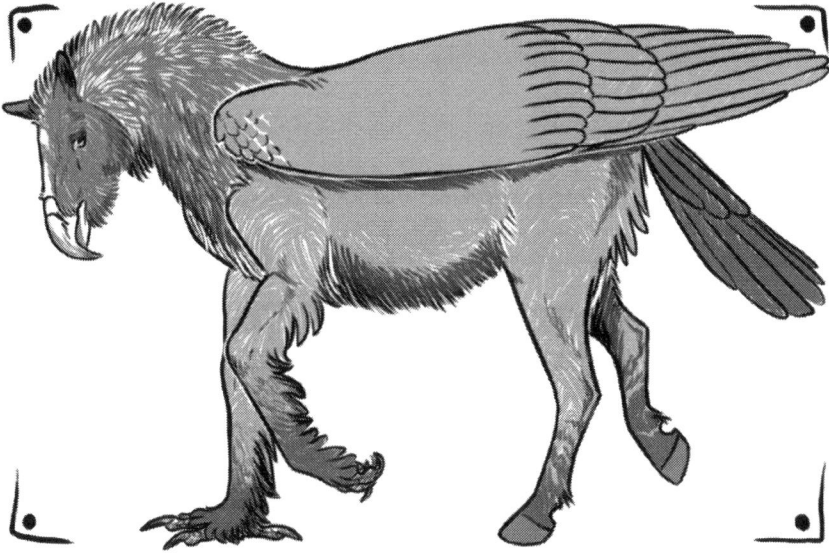

During the events of Chapter 10 and onwards…

As Komodo followed his herd away from the valley, it felt that a piece of himself was left behind. Having to leave his birthplace, even if only temporarily, and being separated from Ben. His memory didn't go back far enough to remember a time before Ben had hatched. He felt…out of place. He still had the rest of his family, but wasn't as close to other foals his age like he was with Ben. He wouldn't know what happened to Ben and Obsidian until they returned. If they ever did, that is. Feeling this shaken and uncertain was foreign to him, and on top of it all, he questioned his own hopes of growing into the Herd Stallion. Perhaps it was no more than a childish dream.

The herd reached the top of a hill, all of them turning their heads to look back. The woods grew dark while the amber glow of Fossil's flames still lined the horizon but it did not spread as fiercely, leading them to assume that Obsidian led him away. Everyone could only wait and watch it burn until the fire put itself out. They continued farther into the forest, eventually stopping in a clearing far enough away. Sunflower turned around to face the hippogryphs.

"We'll clear snow to make space to lie down tonight. After that, anyone willing can join me to try to hunt again," she instructed, kneeling and brushing away the thin layer of snow with her wings.

Komodo and several others assisted. He remained quiet, unable to take his mind off today's events. After the task was finished, he laid down beside Conifer and waited. When prey was brought back late in the night, he didn't feel like eating very much. Once the herd finally settled down, he remained next to his dam in anxiety-filled sleep.

Sunflower stood atop the tallest point on the hill in the pale dawn. She no longer saw the smoke rising from beyond. Shortly after, she trod down to the group of exhausted hippogryphs. Komodo was already awake and opened his eyes as he heard her steps approaching, other herdmates' heads rose to meet her.

"It looks like the fire's gone out, which means we *might* be able to return to the valley," whickered Sunflower.

Hippogryphs who had been laying down began to stand, but not Komodo. Conifer lowered her beak near him.

"Are you alright?" she asked.

Komodo flicked his ears "...I don't know."

Sunflower continued as she moved through the group. "We need to be careful, any burned, but still-standing, trees could crumble."

As the herd followed her back home, Conifer stayed by Komodo, waiting for him to rise. With a shallow nicker, he rose to his feet. They caught up to the back of the herd. Komodo's worry for Ben and Obsidian and the dread of going home to see it scorched and barren alternated in his mind, causing an unpleasant fluttering that persisted in his chest.

They neared the valley, and being at the back, Komodo couldn't see ahead and at the same time, almost couldn't bear to see whatever had become of their land. The hippogryphs slowed their pace as they broke through the forest's edge. At the far end across from where they stood, there were blackened, needleless pines lining the perimeter, but thankfully, it didn't spread much farther into the valley than that. However, clusters of burnt trees gathered behind it, as if a parallel to the herd. Silence fell upon them, Sunflower inhaled before continuing forward. As they pushed on, coming home had never felt so…desolate to Komodo before. Like something had left with their Lead Mare.

"Well, It could've been worse," sighed Sunflower. She turned around to face the hippogryphs. "We should inspect our surroundings before trying to clear anything. Avalanche, I'll lead one and will you lead another?"

The gray mare nodded, both immediately picking out some herdmates.

Komodo lowered his neck, staring down while others shifted around him. He couldn't think of anything to do now except sulk. Then his sister's voice broke through his thoughts.

"Komodo," she was joined by Spruce and Monarch. "Come along."

His ears slanted back, she had only ever invited him on one *small* scouting flight before. He plodded over nonetheless. He wasn't very familiar with Monarch but her chestnut coat was as vivid as the butterfly species.

"We're going to check around our river and make sure nothing's blocked. Sunflower's checking the hunting grounds," explained Avalanche.

"And if something is, we get help to move it later, right?" asked Spruce.

Avalanche nodded again, then unfurled her wings, giving her party a signal to follow with her tail. The four beasts soared upstream, landing at the top of the riverbank shortly after. They took in the sight of what had become of their territory, the farther in they went, the more charred trees had been taken to the ground. What was left of the snow in the area had melted away, replaced by a blanket of ashes. Avalanche snorted and began forward.

"I just hope Ben and Obsidian are okay," exhaled Spruce.

"They will be," Monarch assured her.

Komodo hoped she was right but still couldn't tear himself from his thoughts. He lingered at the back of the group.

"Well," Spruce shook her neck. "We need to focus for now. How far should we follow the river, Avalanche?"

"As far as the fire spread," she replied.

Komodo gazed along the water's edge, at least it stayed the same after the flames and the trees across it were unharmed. Spruce kept talking but he had tuned her out for the most part. His attention was snatched back when they came across a pair of toppled trees resting half-submerged in the river. They inspected it for a moment, flicking their ears and tails.

"The limbs'll collect branches and leaves swept away and potentially block the waters if we don't deal with that," grumbled Avalanche. "We're going to need most of the herd."

Spruce sighed and looked at the horizon. "It sucks. So many of these trees were so old, it'll take forever for new ones to take their place."

"It's a shame but forest fires aren't all bad. We've lost a lot of trees but it also discarded dead foliage, finally allowing our woods some room to change and grow new trees with the season," Monarch added.

"I suppose so…"

Avalanche pressed onward. They got a good distance from the two trunks in the river and hadn't yet come across many more like that. The four went quiet for a while and Spruce looked like she couldn't keep her beak shut much longer. She had noticed Komodo staying behind the entire time, so she slowed to move near him.

"What's wrong?" she asked.

"Everything," he pinned his ears. "Everything that's happened is just so much…"

"Well, it's all Fossil's fault. So why don't you yell at him?"

Komodo tipped his head.

"When I'm mad or upset with something, I just yell for a while. It makes me feel at least somewhat better," she raised her hackles as if readying a screech.

"I dunno if I have the energy for that."

"You could just call him names instead, not like he's gonna know."

Komodo took a breath and a moment before speaking. "Bastard."

"Yeah, let it out," nickered Monarch.

Spruce tossed her head. "Imagine trying to destroy someone's home because you got told 'no.' What a loser."

"Creep!" Komodo spoke louder.

"Shithead," Avalanche added.

Spruce continued, "FREAK!" she crowed so loud it bounced off the mountains and she immediately laughed about it after.

Komodo gave an amused whicker. They were beginning to reach the point where the fire had not reached and everything aside from the one area looked clear.

"We can check the rest of the river in the air, then head back," directed Avalanche.

All of them sprung into the sky and inspected the charred woods edges, and when they turned back, Komodo raced alongside the mares. The wind whipping around him was nice, that and being around the three hippogryphs helped his mind begin to relax. It felt a little more like it had before the fire.

Komodo chose to remain in the valley with Conifer and rest while a portion of the herd went to dislodge the fallen trees. The next few days were busy with clearing away the ash, he tried to be in the same parties as his sister, Spruce, and Monarch when he could. Cleaning was keeping him too occupied to worry, but that wasn't the case when he tried to sleep. However, it wasn't just Ben and Obsidian that filled his head, there was something new. Something he didn't quite understand. He was enjoying the newfound company of his sister and her friends, they had even given him a few small fighting lessons, and when he was with them, that feeling disappeared.

Or did it? What if it only faded into the background and formed a harmony with the rest of him in those moments? He wasn't sure. He paced through the valley, hoping to piece something together, but was soon interrupted by Avalanche approaching him.

"Do you want to clear more branches with me?" she offered.

He gave her a nod and followed her into the twilight sky. They soared over the peak that bordered their home, and away into the woods, landing in a pass where thick sticks gathered.

"Floodwater collects here in the spring, it'll need room," she told him.

They quickly got to work stamping down fragile charcoals and removing branches. The night was fast upon them, they had only cleaned part of it so far. With the serene darkness, Komodo still had room to ponder. Avalanche's body language suddenly became tense and she halted. Her ears shifted around. Komodo watched her and listened. She kept very still until a noise came from the forest.

"Cougar!" she whinnied, whipping around as the cat lunged from the shadows.

She let out a vicious hiss as she raised her wings and plumage. Komodo felt frozen in place, but he had to do something. He stiffly moved his legs before managing to recall what he had been taught and pounced forward. Avalanche and the cougar bounded from side to side in the narrow space, both evading the other's attack. Komodo swiped while it was focused on Avalanche, then it turned to him and slashed at his chest, only managing to rip out a few feathers. He swiftly spun around and kicked it in the jaw while sister came from behind the cougar and stomped it with both front legs. While pinned, the feline craned its neck back to bite her leg. She released it while raking her beak into its back.

The animal yowled and rushed back, lashing its tail. Komodo took a step away but Avalanche pinned her ears and charged. Flapping her wings and cantering forwards scared it off back into the darkness. Komodo took a few heavy breaths. Avalanche bucked a few times as she spun around as if kicking the last of the adrenaline out. Blood trickled from her leg.

"Isn't the feeling of battle so wild?" she huffed with her ruff feathers all messed.

"No! We could've died!" whinnied Komodo.

"Well, it's what I do."

"Dying?"

"What? No- fighting."

Komodo started to head back, he had enough for tonight. "I don't think I like it very much."

His sister smoothed her coat out before catching up. "Then I'd not bother with being Herd Stallion, 'cause it's a lot of that," she snorted. "But you aren't bad at fighting either."

"I've…already been thinking about that. When Fossil attacked, I imagined myself in a situation like Mom was. I don't think I could've handled it, especially not if I were at the front as a Herd Stallion."

Avalanche walked beside Komodo, listening, but stayed silent.

He continued, "After I've heard and seen the real thing, I don't *want* to fight. I don't think I'm cut out for that role. But I love the herd and I want to contribute, but if I'm not working towards that I'm not sure what to do."

Avalanche shook her neck. "It doesn't matter."

Komodo's ears fell back.

"Like, we're just- …It's not a big deal if you change your mind," she continued. "It's very easy to avoid battles how we live. You're the only one who's pushing any 'role' onto you and you don't need to follow it. You could spend your whole life only hunting and scouting and the herd won't think that you've failed anything. We're just all living."

He perked back up, pondering Avalanche's words. Though blunt, perhaps it was just what he needed to hear. They continued through the pass a while longer with no further words. But Komodo wasn't quite finished. A single sentence perched on the tip of his tongue that only managed to escape as a mumble.

"Maybe I'm not a stallion at all."

Avalanche paused and looked back where her sibling had lagged behind.

"I've been feeling strange ever since Ben and Obsidian had left, but when I'm around you and the other mares these last quarter-cycles, I felt like myself again. But in a different, more at ease way, somehow," Komodo admitted.

Avalanche stared for a moment before simply asking, "Do you want me to call you a mare?"

"I'll try it," Komodo nodded slowly.

Her sister nodded in return, then they resumed their walk home. A weight felt like it had been lifted from Komodo but at the same time left an anxious feeling under her skin.

Komodo came trotting into the valley beside her dam, just returning from assessing new trees beginning to sprout in burned areas. Avalanche, Spruce, and Monarch were up on their usual hill in the distance. Komodo whickered and exchanged wither grooming with Conifer before soaring over to the three. She was greeted with the familiar whickering and playful hoofing at the ground by the other mares. She kneeled and laid down into the grass, the wind ruffling her feathers under the sun. It was a lovely beginning to the season. She was content with the way things were now, maturing into a hunter and finding comfort in her identity, changing and growing beside the forest itself. But still, she waited. One day Ben and Obsidian would come home. Daily life would fully return to the way it was and she would share her new experiences with the rest of her family.

To Be Continued in

THE TALES FROM VEYNEKAN

Book #2 - *Catalysts*

Astiriuh - *"Aster-rye-uh"*

Ceer - *"Sear"*

Finiir - *"Fin-near"*

Gaar - *"Gar"*

Geshiya - *"Gesh-shy-uh"*

Hamara - *"Ha-mar-uh"*

Hoyhenet - *"Hoi-hen-et"*

Iiku - *"Ee-coo"*

Komeetta - *"Koh-may-tah"*

Melthrun - *"Mel-thrun"*

Pivikeli - *"Pih-vee-kell-ee"*

Raeliina - *"Ray-lee-nah"*

Setiir - *"Set-teer"*

Veynekan - *"Veyh-neck-ann"*

ABOUT THE AUTHOR

F. J. Thornburg is a beast woman(?) with a lifelong passion for animals, particularly ungulates and fowl, and the natural world. He has been a self-taught artist for over a decade, and the world of Veynekan and its characters are deeply loved and personal to her.

"Don't actually interpret me as this shadow figure, please."

Learn more about the novel series, art, and himself at

artof-fjt.weebly.com

Made in the USA
Monee, IL
05 December 2021